SHALLOW LIVES

Lucy Swan

For my girls.

CONTENTS

Title Page   1

Copyright   2

Dedication   3

The Prologue   9

 PART ONE   13

AF   15

Wrestling   22

The Run   25

Bondage   29

The Folly   34

That Night at The Folly   38

The Morning of the Non-Halloween Disco   45

The Morning After the Non-Halloween Disco   51

The Night of the Non-Halloween Disco   54

The Night of the Non-Halloween Disco   57

The Morning After the Non-Halloween Disco   64

 PART TWO   66

Five Minutes Later...   68

What a Girl Wants.   71

Aphrodite's Island   79

 Torn   87

Forgiven 90

Paradise Lost 95

PART THREE 99

The Backpacker 100

I Do 116

Return of the Prodigal 118

In the Wings 126

But How Did I Get Here? 130

The Night before: Meet the Out-Laws 135

Apparently, I Do 139

PART FOUR 141

Isolation 142

Lost 149

The Visitors 153

Hiroshima 163

The Second Visitor's Confession 173

Nagasaki 176

PART FIVE 180

After the Happily Ever After... 181

And then... 188

Sister Suffrage 192

And the Winner is... 198

Alexis and Crystal 201

The Drugs Don't Work... 211

In the Morning, I Know You Won't Remember a Thing... 214

PART SIX 217

The Reckoning 218

The Aftermath 222

Pregnant Pause	227
Limbo	234
Opening the Tomb	237
The Stand Off	242
Let's Hear it For the Girls	245
And?	249
Deja Vu	254
Only Fools Fall in Love.	258
But?	261
What is Worse?	265
Rose Tinted Spectacles	267
Heading into the Light	270
Absolution?	277
PART SEVEN	279
In Sickness and in Health	280
His Role	284
Her Role	287
A New Dawn	289
Dearly Departed	293
Dear John…	295
Finding her Feet	302
Freedom	305
THE EPILOGUE	313
About The Author	317
Acknowledgement	319

THE PROLOGUE

Now
Patrick
London
New Year's Eve 2016

When I was younger, before I became the man I am today, but after the Christmas of 1991, I made a vow that I'd be different to the man who was part of my making. I made an agreement with my teenage self that I would be a better man. I decided there and then that I'd never do to someone I loved what he was doing to my family by 'doing' (what we coined) the 'side piece' - the latest 'classy bird' to be employed in one of his many businesses. Our dad: businessman of the year four times over; pride of Yorkshire; millionaire, family man and all-round Lothario.

Unfortunately, now when I look at myself through my naïve fourteen-year-old eyes, I realise it's not that easy. Children see the world in black and white, good versus evil. What we only realise, when we grow up, look back, that there are a million shades of grey (the irony). Therefore, as much as I realise that I am despised by many, I feel I have some grounds of defence. As much as a serial adulterer can be allowed...

It wasn't easy getting to this point. It wasn't any fault of my own that brought me here. In fact, if I was put in front of a court of law, I think the jury would feel sympathy for me. You see, any fool can see, and those in the know, well err...know, there's not only me who is solely to blame for my short comings -there's my wife of fifteen years: Jessica.

Jessica, my other half. Some would say 'better half' but I

think that could stretch the truth (even with my misdemeanours), if you knew how cold and callous, she can be. 'The Glacial Goddess', as I sometimes call her, swanning about all plucked and preened like she is staring in 'The Real Housewives of Yorkshire' Tanned and fake: these days you'd be hard pressed to find what is real. I recently joked, during a particularly lively slanging match, that we could play spot the difference between her wedding picture and one of our fifteen-year anniversary picture.

I no longer recognise the woman I married.

Sometimes, I like her looking like that on my arm. Other men staring with their green eyes. I get a kick out of it. Having something else to flash: my car, my house, my watch, my fake wife…but it's not me she does it for. Like me, I know she's only in it for the money and status now; that and our two-best works – our children.

On occasion, I try to conjure up the memories of when we first met. The intensity of our relationship. Was it ever love? Sifting through the memories, I am blinded by the bitterness that had seeped into our relationship. We seem to have erected barbed wire around our souls, making it torturous to try and get close to each other again. Our foreplay is this cat and mouse game of sadism where we see how far we can push each other's buttons before one of us cracks and goes to lick our wounds in a solitary corner. That is when we look at our children and realise; we need to play clean for a while. And I've often used money to paper the cracks. I used to think money solved everything…

You think I'm an arrogant, selfish and superficial person, don't you? A few lines in and you'd be right. You think this and I've not even told you the worst of it. You feel sorry for Jessica already and I've not even told my side of the story yet - the one that got me to the age of 39 and being no better than The Heff (very apt teenage coinage for the father). But, as I've begun to find out, there's two sides to every story and I think mines worth hearing.

But, before I take you through the car crash of my personal life, I think it's worth setting the scene of where I am now. Before I do though, please understand I need you to see who I have become so I can restart my life at 40. They say life begins, don't they? Well mine needs to change drastically or I'll never be the man I promised myself I'd be at 14 years old.

So here I am in my superficial surroundings. I'm comfortably sinking into a queen size bed. 1000 thread count Egyptian cotton sheets and a mattress and pillows so incredibly soft that I can only imagine it would be like this sleeping on a cloud in heaven (the closest I shall ever get). If I look to my left a huge picture window frames the world outside. Twelve storeys up, a ridiculously expensive view of London negates the need of the equally expensive artwork of the Manhattan skyline, on the opposite wall. A whole world of city lights winking wickedly like diamonds enticing a jewel thief. Temptation beckons. A façade of London life advertising its greatest assets like in the bling in Tiffany's window. Tiny lights pricking the dark underbelly of harsh realities and lost souls of our capital. Nothing is ever as it truly seems is it?

Take this hotel. Exclusive and luxurious and nestled on the South Bank in London. A cool calm exterior and a rich interior of opulence, which smells of money. A mirrored epitaph for power and wealth, this place juxtaposes appearance versus reality on a cerebral level. Behind each gilded door, another reality laden tawdry story unfolds. This room represents the high life: its vaulted ceiling releases suppressed inhibitions, glimmering marble surfaces dulled by lingering faint traces of white powder, and, a once fully stocked, champagne mini-bar.

As a smoky dawn breaks, just like my soul's understanding, the bold and iconic skyline casts its shadows onto this vulgar tableau. Power mimicking power.

And I think, up until a few weeks ago, I felt like the prize cock (how ironic that simile is) strutting arrogantly - untouchable.

To my right; her soft contours sleep softly. Resting, after a night of surprises and lost love. I marvel at the magnificence of her. I devour the memory of her in the pink dress which she appeared to have been poured into, which I can't believe was only ten hours ago, it feels like a lifetime has passed since that first moment.

Lust stirs and I smile. I promise myself not to wake her; after all, when she opens her eyes, a lifetime of regrets will flicker between us. Too many times, and memories to remind me...I want to drink this feeling of what once was in. The bitter sweet feeling of this will be the last time releasing from my soul. As history goes, I've never been good at keeping promises. But I want more than anything, for this new beginning to work.

Check out isn't until 12pm – it feels like we have all the time in the world before the new chapter dawns. Then, my promise is, I'm going to change.

Why do I want to change from being a person I despise? Stupid question, but then again, to change is harder than you think. After all, I have lived with him – this persona - so long, that he is deep within me; like a drug I can't live without. I am an addict. However, all addicts get to that point where they must make a choice. You can see what path you're on and you must be strong to make the right choice. Well, I'm at that crossroads. All the wealth and trappings...well guess what? I am far from happy. Don't get me wrong, like all addicts, I have tried before. I have made knowingly empty promises to myself and others. Shallow and hollow lies, which I have subconsciously built my, what should be, my most important relationships on. All a façade like the view from my expensive suite. Deep down I wasn't ready, but something new has brought us here: me and her.

As I reflect back to my teenage self, I decide that it is not too late to be the man I vowed to be all those years ago. I will find the inner strength to change. I know I've said it before, but this time I mean it.

PART ONE

DEARLY BELOVED

Then
Aimee

*When you've already had your Happily Ever After, and had it
stolen from you after a very short time, what's next? To exist?
No, you do more than that. You grow another layer;
build yourself up again and find different reasons
to live. My children, my friends, my art.
And of course: my dog. What else could I possibly need?*

AF

Saltness
Early September 2016

It was a relief to be honest. I know every parent says it, but after six weeks of being all singing and all dancing mother, chief cook, event organiser, bread winner, entertainments manager...I was glad Phoebe and Harry were going back to school. Being a single parent can be exhausting at the best of times, but the holidays are the worst. You see, there's no one to rely on. There's no one to take them (*please take them*) for an hour whilst I shop (*anyone?*) or if I want a quiet coffee with the best one: Jenna, in town (Not that Frank was that good at taking the reins anyway but having an option would be nice). Instead it had been a constant juggle between work and child minding. Don't get me wrong, I adore my children. I'd kill for them and protect them with every fibre of my body. They are my everything and more. But sometimes I could cheerfully strangle them.

Phoebe, oh beautiful phoebe. With her crown of golden hair and delicate balletic posture, gives her an ethereal quality... until she opens her very opinionated and caustic (some might say that's harsh to describe a ten-year-old but hey, I'm her mother) mouth. Always on the money and close to the bone, that's our Phoebe! She can make me proud, cry with laughter and want to crawl into a hole; all in equal measure. She's mine though and I cannot express the awe I feel for her toughness and beauty. She has Frank's Celtic spirit and for that I am grateful. She's a survivor and take it from a fellow survivor - it helps.

For all Phoeb's outspokenness, Harry is the Kofi Annan of our world. Placid, calm and courteous. My beautiful Pear's Soap poster boy could charm even the most curmudgeonly of people. Hazza, the eight-year-old wonder boy, smooths every feather Phoeb's inadvertently ruffles. Thus, providing me with a daily living reminder of his much-missed father. How Harry could possibly have taken on Frank's best bits is something I equate to genetics. How could he ever, at the age of three, picked up and been moulded into the affable character of his daddy?

So, that was me. I was a widow of five years and mother to two opposing personalities. It was an interesting, rewarding and somewhat difficult position I had found myself in at the age of 39. It was also not something I was relishing. But what choice did I have?

As in all public/social occasions, at this stage, I feel the need to get it out of the way: The elephant in every room I walked into - over the past five years. The topic of every knowing look and whisper in the playground: The loss of Frank. Our lives fall into two categories: BF and AF. The BF were the days of wonder, laughter and uncertainly (Frank wasn't what you'd call stable or reliable. Fun yes, but he just preferred to wing it). AF signifies the tough, five long years since he was taken from us. Five hard years. My God, yes, I still miss Frank, (every day to be honest) but I don't want to bog down the narrative with 'The Dark Days'. Instead, I will tell you where I was then: better than I was.

I went through shock, horror, anger, frustration and (I'm in no way trivialising things) but eventually, we gained a stability. And as guilty as I felt, and in reality, I understand now that I was going through a process. For quite a long time, I became fed up. For as much as I loved him and for as much as I adored our time together, it was not a perfect marriage (show me one that is - no you can't can you?). All his faults (he had quite a few) seemed to have been forgotten, forgiven and buried (unlike him who was scattered off the end of the cliffs where he used to walk the children and Sandra Dee Dog), with a commemorative bench to match. And my husband; father to our children; and to those who knew him, had taken on a rose-tinted glow. A reinvention with a sainthood firmly in place.

And what about me? Where did all this leave me? Fed up because I was the one left, still dealing with the (chaotic) legacy which he left us with. Being fed up with the excuses they made for him. Being fed up of having to keep my mouth shut. Being the boring one.

Recently though, I'd decided to take Phoeb's lead and get tough. Although I'd allowed the sainthood to continue for the children, I had begun to make changes. Routines, which Frank balked at, had been embedded. As was a healthier lifestyle. I felt I'd found an inner peace and calm in my work and discovered that I was as good as I remembered. So good in fact that people had started to pay me quite well for what I do (well enough to pay the bills). And it was for these kinds of 'adult life' I realised I'd been longing for; six weeks of 'mummee...' had begun to wear a bit thin. I felt ready for the solitude that came with my work.

"Mummee..." broke my reverie, and as if on cue, Harry was calling me from the depths of his 'Dinoroom' (as it was currently called).

"I can't find my football boots and Toby's taking his because apparently we can wear them at lunchtime to play football in year four at lunchtime and if everyone it is taking them I don't want to be the only one in year four who hasn't got them and I really want to join in"

"And breathe Hazza" I muttered under my breath. Then, "Don't panic!" I shouted, "they're still outside after Sunday's match"

Anxiously, I glanced at the clock and thinking that the fresh start of our agreed goal of *being on time every day* was getting off to a bad start.

One look in Phoebe's direction proved she was thinking the

same as she impatiently tapped her foot at the front door.

"Haz, come on! chuck em in your bag and les' go". *Before your sister kills you...* As he whizzed past, SDD the chocolate lab ran at his heels with the anticipation of a walk fuelling his ageing body. A move which threatened to whisk Phoeb off her feet and potentially cause fisticuffs pre 9am (my boy might have the makings of a UN peacekeeper, but his chaotic, boisterous energy can inadvertently cause his sister distress in her perfectly ordered world)

See what you're missing Frankie Boy?

Eventually, with children ready and Sandra Dee Dog in tow, we took the ten-minute walk to School. Although the mornings had taken a distinct nosedive in warmth, it was always a pleasant walk down hill to the local primary.

We live in a large Victorian folly, precariously perched upon the cliffs of the town of Saltness. Built in the seaside town's heyday, it was almost certainly put there to be wondered at and admired - in a weird Victorian kind of spectacular way. You see, it has a distinct gothic frontage complete with turrets and gargoyles, but someone forgot to tell the builders it needed a door; hence a less grand side entrance allows access. Its uniqueness was what attracted us both to it, those 11 years previously. Frank, ever the romantic, and me his easily-led naïve (then pregnant) wife, thought it symbolised us; our special and idealistic relationship. We were different to all those other couples – we were like the folly, something to admire for its idiosyncratic beauty and quirkiness.

We met and had quickly wed, in Thailand. After a brief courtship (as my old nan coined it) - what might be called a whirlwind romance. Two impetuous youths, we roamed Asia, then Europe like nomads on the Inca trail. Frank toured (he was a fledgling musician) and I was his number one groupie. Me trying to be an artist, picking work up along the way – commissions from people who saw me sketching on paradisiacal beaches, busy piazzas, outside iconic buildings such as: the Sagrada Familia Basilica; the Parthenon, or the Rialto…It was an exciting time of new experiences and adventures. We had just enough money to survive on and the band relied on me to do some of their publicity. We were brilliant.

All a lifetime ago - so distant and so far away now. I save these memories for when I am feeling particularly generous and sentimental:

I was painting on a beach. He liked 'what he saw', admired me from afar. Later, he made himself known, and very soon the feelings were reciprocated. Frank: the incurable romantic bowled me over by his exuberant Irish impishness. His enthusiasm for my art was encouraging and the next thing I knew, it was two weeks later, and I was agreeing to start the new millennium with him.

My parents were mortified when they heard. They'd been waiting for me to come home. Waiting for me to, well, to have got 'the silly artist stuff out of my system'. They thought I might get a job at the local gallery or museum; finding myself a nice husband in the process. They liked box ticking. Nice easy lists…

And then, when (and it took us a very long time) I did go home, I had a wild Irish husband and a bump in tow. They were overwhelmed by everything we represented: the heathenness, the uncertainty of our lives…so, upon the homecoming of their little girl and her burgeoning family, they decided to retire and spend the '*Aimee wedding fund*' on various long-haul trips and cruises. So much so, that the children and I barely saw them.

Anyway, I digress. The house was part of our frivolity of falling in love, hastily marrying, and paid for by a (small) inheritance left to Frank by his dear departed godfather (thank the lord as Frank never had much earning power as he spent it as quickly as he earned it). With such romantic visions came reality…a leaky roof, noisy plumbing and draughty turrets (I know, what a complaint!). Luckily, he had some song rights that came from some hits in Australia, which paid for some of the immediate problems, and it didn't feel so bad suddenly. However, our kitchen was heated by an ancient aga and our sea view garden (complete with orchard) meant that my grumbles were most definitely, 'first world problems'. That and the fact Frank left us mortgage free, afforded me some comfort in the middle of the night. I knew that if I was careful and worked hard that I could just about manage to hold it all together. My children being fed, clothed and warm was what was important now. Our distant travels a mere dream.

So...that morning, leaving our folly, we trod the back to school September path, we didn't realise that there were more new horizons, than new teachers and classrooms. That day was when all the carefully constructed calm life I'd managed to build, all began to unravel.

Then
Patrick

Being unmasked, as I was that autumn, was like experiencing a mid-life crisis in reverse: everything that happened was all forced upon me. I had to change or there would be serious consequences. Maybe it was because I already had the trappings of 'what a man wants'. In reality, I needed something new. That something new needed to be real. I needed to be my authentic self – whoever that was. One minute I was strutting around like an emperor in his finest clothes and then, well, then someone told me I was actually naked.

WRESTLING

The Best Place to Start is in the middle.

The school run. What can I say? Since Jessica had decided she was going to 'take time out for myself' (her words not mine.) and reclaim her life, I'd been made to take the children to school. That was why, plus the fact the doctor had given me a talking to, that I had become 'the Dad who walks to school with his children'. Also, I felt (I'm writing this whole narrative with honesty so if I look a knob by what I say so be it - I was), it was good for my image. I was all about image you see. That's one of the reasons I married Jessica - well not the only reason but more about that later...so letting Jessica think she had got one over on me by letting her think she'd 'forced me to take our children to school' (over heard on the phone to my mother) I felt I was winning a moral victory.

Imagine...

'Ooh look at Patrick Green. He's such a good father.'

'Hands on Dad he is!'

'Where does he find the time?'

'I wish my husband was more like him'

All things I imagined the school run mums cowing about whilst they herded their broods into school. And yes, I can remember thinking, that I must be their dream man: perfect father, good looking, money, lifestyle, and although the effects of a lavish lifestyle had started to show, the physique of a rather sturdy rugby player. I arrogantly (I'm not stupid just full of myself) thought they loved it…watching me! I'd seen the way some of them looked at me. I sensed I had options if necessary. However, in times past I had crossed into the dangerous territory of a brief encounter or two with…but (for want of a better analogy) I had learnt not to shit on my own doorstep. No, instead I chose to cast my net far and wide. This meant I was not only a bastard but a calculated one too.

During the summer term, the school run had become a time for me to bond, reflect, people watch and the trek up and downhill. Therefore, it was keeping my aforementioned wife and doctor happy (albeit for different reasons). But then we moved, my route changed, and the September term came about. And it was on these School runs that my (what I thought was) perfectly engineered world was revealed to be the ugly and selfish thing that it was.

First day back at school - she was determined to set the tone. Apparently, it was payback time. And there I was: trackies, trainers and messed up designer hair, with two boisterous boys in tow. She'd left me to do the breakfast, pack-up and kit, whilst she spent 'me time' on an online ashtanga yoga class and a twenty-minute meditation class beforehand. So, whilst Lady J was channelling her inner bitch, I was on the frontline with the boys; fighting like two champion wrestlers.

"Oi, you!" shouted Oli as he launched himself at Toby as he ate his dippy eggs. "Gimme some toast or I'll piledrive you if you don't let me have some of your soldiers"

"Soldiers, ha-ha! Like you're in command. You couldn't run a …"

"Oli! No! For Christ's sake – ", I didn't know where they got this stuff from.

"He won't help you Dad. That's what Mrs Pearson at school says"

"Don't swear Oli mate" I challenged.

Oli looked at me innocently, "I wasn't going to. I was going to say: you couldn't clothesline a girl"

"Sexist and aggressive, aren't you doing well this morning?" The sarcastic tone was coming from the hallway. Like a ghost from the ether.

"Bloody woman" I grumbled. Shouting "I thought you were down-dogging?"

The boys sniggered. I wondered where they even had got that term from. No innocence these days.

"I'm going now. Have a good day boys. Love you" She air kissed.

"And just like that she is off in a cloud of Chanel" lamented Toby.

"With the boys fending for themselves" countered Oli.

Two pairs of expectant eyes fixed upon me – Freddie, our energetic pup too. *It's like that is it?* I thought. All boys together. Was this really my time to start with all that camping and combat malarkey? It was Jessica's intention this. All of it. She said she'd had enough. She said that they needed me for a change because they 'were becoming too much of a handful'. I needed to 'show them how to be boys' and not be holed up in their rooms on 'screens'. I had no idea why she couldn't do it. After all, I had businesses to run. She just had a diary of beauty appointments to meet, a week in Marbs (to get over the summer holiday exhaustion of two boys) and her 'inner self to find' because apparently, I had so badly neglected it. I don't know what she expected from me anyway – who did she think pays...?

"Dad. Time!" I shot a look at the clock and realised we had to be on our way. At that, Fred's ears popped up and he rushed to the door.

'*Game on.*' I thought

THE RUN

THEN
Patrick
Saltness
Early September 2016

'*Oh god, please* don't'

I couldn't help such negative thoughts but seriously, my kids...Oli and Toby were running shouting one of his mates from footy. Now I was all good with that, but it was the fall-out I'm wasn't so keen on. It was the mother you see, she was one of those arty and bohemian types. A widow to boot. Not my type and someone who I'd normally avoid: *I'd rather cut my right arm off than talk to her.*

I'd not realised this was her route to school. You see we'd only just moved over the summer. Jessica wanted to immerse herself in a project (all part of finding herself) so we bought a small cottage on a large patch of land, at the top of the cliffs, which she's spent five years twisting into some sort of glacier iced mint style box. The 'Ice Palace' (as I'd learnt the locals had begun calling it) was a bit marmite for some tastes. The views were amazing, but it was quite a project, which I had begun to regret agreeing to; Jessica's plans and designs started to look like a bad photo shoot in the playboy mansion - all tack and no style (sort of summed her up really).

However, with the new house, new school year, the new school run was the first from our new house. And bastard that I was, I remember thinking: *if the current situation continued, I was going to have to rethink my route.*

Fred, the feisty Jack Russell, was pulling. Dragging me towards the two boys excitedly discussing footy boots. In doing so, Fred pulled me into line with the mother (Annie I thought), a chocolate lab, and her rather striking daughter. The women flashed me a warm smile, which kind of took me aback. I'm used to disdain, flirting and blanking. Warmth is something out of my comfort zone. The girl however gave me a quick up and down and hastened her pace to catch up with the boys.

'The daughter is the canny one in that household' I thought.

"It's all he talks about"

The children continued to chatter about their summers. Words overlapping and giggling as Freddie tried to keep up.

"Are Oli and Toby trying out for the new team this week?"

'Bloody Jessica,' I thought to myself. And there was no way out of this for the next few weeks as she was booked into a retreat to heal her broken soul (who was going to heal mine?). And then I looked at my boys and thought about my mum reminding me about my loud declaration of *'I'll be the Dad that I never had'* that...

"Excuse me, are you being rude for a reason?"

Was she talking to me?

I looked over at her. Her gaze told me I might have had something to do with Bambi's demise...

Am I being rude for a reason? Now, this was a very good question from the arty widow. Firstly, because I'd like to argue I'm not rude, but I have a filter which stops all bullshit getting through. Banal small talk rarely entered or registered on my radar. Secondly, because I'd not heard her and had no idea what she was asking (white noise to me) I couldn't be accused of being rude.

And then I did what my therapist advised me to do when being challenged: assess the situation with a clear head. I glanced at all our children chattering rapidly, realised I had to feign some kind of 'give a shit' and... (rather weakly in hindsight) replied,

"Err, not intentionally. Were you talking to me?"

Arty widow waved her arms "err, who else?"

Just me and her then. oh god, this can't happen every school run. I'm going to have to set off really early to avoid her or really late and the kids will be in trouble. Smooth the waters it is then.

"Sorry Annie isn't it? I'm in a world of my own. I'm not used to talking to people"

Widow Annie just looked at me puzzled.

Did I really just say the out loud? God I can be a tosser.

"Erm, in other thoughts, I'm thinking that why on earth should I ask you about Oli, Toby and football, when I can get a more eloquent and smarter response from either of the dogs"

Bloody hell, and she accused ME of being rude! In fact, I'm not sure I remembered a time a woman spoke to me in such a way before. I'm used to my ego being stroked. People being pleased I'm giving them the time of day. Grateful...is this what my therapist called 'a reality check'?

"And not that I care but it's Aimee, not Annie! Do I look like a little red headed orphan?"

I looked at her, she had a point. Although petite (like the orphan) at five foot something, she appeared to have a glorious, healthy, translucent glow to her sun kissed skin. The crazy mass of golden corkscrew curls framed clear blue - almost Icelandic fjord eyes - which at that moment were boring into me, ready to laser me to death.

How could such a quick tongue come from such a fairy like creature? It must be the Scandinavian in her. Was she Scandinavian?

And then I thought about all those Scandinavian murder things I'd been filling my time with since Jessica had begun to turn around global warming with her glacial feel.

"Are you from Scandinavia?" I blurted out.

She looked puzzled. "What?"

And then I began to laugh. Really laugh. I'd been put straight by a viperous Swedish water nymph. And as I laughed, I continued to look outside in (therapy again) and reminded myself, (yet again) that I was the arrogant knob I swore I'd never be.

Too much to say and explain. Instead I turned on the Patrick Green super-charm and reverted to using the manners which were drilled into me by my mother from a very young age.

"I'm sorry, bad form of me. I've been warned about speaking out loud"

"Really?" she laughed, whilst raising her eyebrows.

She appraised me. I arranged my features into my best reticent face and awaited her reply. I was good at awkward but didn't like it.

She frowned. I could tell she was far from one of my adoring fans. What did I care?

"Ok. Fair enough"

And it seemed I did. Somehow her response didn't seem enough.

This Scandi woman had something about her. I looked at her chaotic/arty look, her fresh face and glow and she made me feel healthy. Like one of those 'eat our healthy yogurt' adverts that the Swiss make. She looked clean, wholesome, but with an edge – the complete polar-opposite of Jessica. Maybe that was why I cared (that and the fact she hadn't been wowed by me). It felt like she was holding me responsible for the ending of 'Marley and Me' (I still can't watch that film…I've always loved animals more than people) This said, I've no idea to this day why I cared so much about a near stranger's opinion of me…

"No, truly I am. I can be a knob" Maybe that was why I did something else totally out of character and offered my hand to her "Aimee, I'm sorry I was rude. Let's start this again"

And with that she cracked that warm smile again and we shook hands.

BONDAGE

Then
Patrick
The Eco Park
Late September 2016

"Great idea this Annie. They're loving it!"

"Don't thank me, thank the kids" she grinned.

"Seriously, it has taken the edge of a long weekend. With Jess away in Marbs, this single parent shite is…oh, sorry" Even I knew I was being insensitive.

Aimee rolled her eyes. "Are you? Don't be, it is shite! And very tough to keep them entertained. However, it does have some upsides - like not having to share all my guilty pleasures"

"Shite! Yeah, let's drink to that" I decided, holding my take-out coffee aloft.

We pushed our polystyrene coffees together and laughed. *How had this happened?* I thought to myself. *Me and the merry widow on a platonic playdate. Actually enjoying myself with a woman, without trying to talk her into bed.*

Who'd have thought that first meeting would have become a regular thing? The walk, the children, the dogs. They all got on. It was so easy.

Although, not initially…

She asked me the second morning, as she bounced up in stripy socks peeking over her wellies, and an arty fedora (which I couldn't make my mind up about as I don't do quirky) cocked on her head, if I was "saying good morning any time soon?"

With me quickly replying "Hey Annie" and "Nice hat and socks".

"Liar" she grinned.

Again, that refreshing honesty.

Then on the Friday when I called her the 'Merry Widow', I thought she was going to swing for me, but her face quickly recovered when she said, "I'm putting a good front up then".

I smiled, but we were mere acquaintances, I was not going there.

And so, it continued...

And then Jessica went on the holiday. And I was responsible twenty-four-seven. School, the house, the cooking...I was a businessman, not a house-husband. The boys were driving me up the wall. Then, as they usually do, all four children arranged to go den building at the eco-park. *Why not?* I thought. It might tire them out (please, please, please) so I could get some work done at home.

"What are you doing for the castle project? Phoebe wanted to start making it tonight, but I really can't face a night of paint and cardboard. I just want to watch Strictly, a bottle of wine and eat pizza. I'm knackered already and we've only been back at school for what? Two and a half weeks!"

"Castle? A project?" I was frantically searching my mind for mentions, letters: *had I actually been in their bags since Monday?*

"Yes, a castle. A model is required for them to show the key features. Moat, a drawbridge, battlements, that sort of thing. There was a..."

"Letter." I finished for her "There usually is, but I'm not great with those" *A shitting castle.* "When for?"

"Monday. So, I'm going to get on with it as soon as we get in. If I help her make the model, she can get painting on Sunday. That way I still get Strictly" she smiled.

"Shite. I've not a clue" How *the fuck was I going to build a flaming castle, when I had a shit-load of invoices to go through and interviews for a new sales manager on Monday? Jessica has seriously dropped me in it.*

"Dadddddeeeeee, Toby's being salty" wailed Oli.

What *does that even mean?*

"Shut up or I'll kneecap you" Toby threatened.

Aimee raised her eyes at me

"Walked in on me watching Peaky Blinders. I was in bed. He was having a bad dream. Maybe I should have turned it off" I admitted.

"Get off you..." Oli had hold of Toby's head between his legs. He was ready to piledrive him to the grass. I opened my mouth to shout but before the words could come out...

"Boys stop!" immediately they both stopped. Dead quiet. "Drop him" which he did, straight onto the ground.

"Ouch" Toby moaned.

'Numpty' Bit Oli.

"I told you two when we were building the den, that if you didn't get on, I wouldn't even consider either of you to be my deputy. And you know what the deputy gets to do don't you?" admonished the blonde-haired Phoebe – a force to be reckoned with. I wondered if she was too old for the management position.

"Tell people what to do if you get sick Phoeb." Answered Oli.

"Gets to hold the marshmallows and chocolate" drooled Toby.

"That's right and Alison, the eco-lady leader, said that if there was any trouble, we wouldn't be allowed the bonfire."

My feisty boys nodded their heads, retreating back into the woods with Phoebe. *Fair play to the girl, she has balls.*

"Where's Hazza?" Aimee called after her daughter.

"In the den mum. He's fine don't worry, I have it all under control"

"That's the worry" laughed Aimee to me.

"I don't know," I admired "she seems to have it sewn up for me. I could do with her around this weekend. Never seen my boys so meek"

"Bossy, that's her. She had Frank wrapped around her little finger. Daddy's golden girl. She had the rule of the roost even back then!"

"Frank. You don't talk about him much" She looked like she was retreating into herself. *Why did I ask her?* (It made me sound human and that was very unlike me). The warmth we'd shared at her daughter's spirit seemed to begin to evaporate. I'd never mentioned him before. It wasn't my place. "I'm sorry. Have I offended you?"

She looked sad and stared out towards the woods. "No, not at all. It's sad that I don't talk about him much. That was what I was thinking. No one really wants to talk about dead people; especially him. After all, they all think it makes me too upset."

"Does it?" *Did I really want to know?*

"No, it's nice to remember him. He was very much alive when he was here. He was usually the life that ran through everything."

"You must miss him?" (stupid question) I watched her face become still. It was like her sunny smile moved under a black rain cloud. Holding out my hand, I briefly touched the top of hers (I'm not a total bastard). "I'm sorry, bringing the mood down". *What to say now?* It was all getting a bit serious for me.

"Yes, every day and for many reasons. He was exhausting for many reasons...You haven't upset me and let's not spoil this by becoming friends you arrogant sexist fool!" she brightened.

"Fair play Annie!" I conceded with a laugh.

Watching her recover made me realise that I quite liked her by this point. She was a survivor and I liked that in a person. Strength.

"Yes. Stop pretending to be nice, or you'll ruin your twattish reputation" She ordered in mock seriousness.

"And there she is Annie the ballbuster. Now we know where Phoebe gets it from!"

"You're joking, aren't you?" She laughed, "I get it from her'

With that, a piercing scream shattered our conversation. Something was wrong. All lightness evaporated, as Aimee and I immediately jumped up and ran towards the pathway into the woods. Heart racing: that scream was feral, it said pain.

Following the noise of the incessant wailing we neared a clearing with a half-built shelter. The children and Alison were clustered around a body on the ground. Quickly skimming the faces, I saw that Toby was missing.

I felt sick. The screams shattered my thudding heart. 'Toby!' I screeched with fear and pain.

THE FOLLY

Then

Aimee

Saltness
Late September 2016

"Just keep gluing Oli. Phoebe, you hold it for him...that's right, a bit of team work and you will have finished in no time"

For once I was pleased that we had some ridiculous school project to keep us occupied. I say ridiculous, what I mean is, a 'project for too busy parents to complete as it is too difficult for a child to do on their own'. *Poor Toby.* He looked so white and sick when Patrick drove off in his Range Rover. The children were all quite subdued and had a strange white pallor, so I had to quickly think of things to distract them. Oli was trying to be tough, but I could see the worry etched on his face. He was to stay with me though as we had no idea how bad Toby's injury was. A break, sprain, or badly bruised? There were mutterings about football, and I had to shut it down with statements like *'we don't know anything yet'* and *'let's think positively'.*

We swung by Patrick's 'Ice Mansion' as Phoebe called it 'Ice Palace' Oli corrected. We picked Freddie up *'Thanks Aimee, I just don't know how long we will be, and he needs to go out'*, Patrick had hurriedly thanked me as he was strapping Toby in. Then we picked up Sandra and all traipsed down to the sand for an ice-cream. The children, fuelled by ice cream, nerves and a slight terror, chased each other and the doggies, around on the sand. I sat with yet another polystyrene coffee (God, the environment) and willed them to burn all their energy off for the afternoon.

Eventually, after a game of catch (the dogs fielding), we all hiked back up the hill to our folly, for well, *'We might as well do the project hadn't, we?'*

"Are you sure that it won't matter it's joint?" worried Oli.

"No, it'll be fine! Besides, we've upped the scale and you are putting so much detail in, that anyone can see how much work has gone in" I admired. I noticed that Oli grew another foot with my compliment.

"This is great Aimee. Dad would never have managed to help with anything like this. Do you think he got Toby to fall out of that tree on purpose?" he joked.

"Ha, maybe, seeing as you weren't meant to be climbing those trees any way!" I smiled.

All the children looked down sheepishly at this. The initial recriminations and worry fuelled anger, was not quite yet a distant memory. Patrick had been shaking - rightly so. I went numb - as in all times of crisis. I managed to get the children away from Toby and after the *'what were you all thinking'* (It wasn't all of them, just Harry and Toby), their worried and guilty faces had tears falling them. That scream coming from Toby: scaring us all. Patrick looked ready to kill.

"Recriminations later" I looked at his worried brow creasing. "I'll look after Oli, you take Toby"

Patrick looked angry "Sorry, I'm taking over..."

"Don't be and I'm glad"

That was hours ago now. The beach, playing ball, the dogs, the project...I was making pizzas (they'd be no Strictly at this rate) and still waiting for a text. Patrick had text earlier to say he was calmer and that they were waiting for an x-ray.

"These are lovely Aimee. Thank you so much for looking after me."

"You're welcome and what lovely manners!" I was impressed and ashamed by how surprised I was.

Oli grinned up at me from the ruins of a castle "Mum says they cost nothing"

His mother. I bet she's feeling awful for not being here. "Your mum, I bet she's so worried. I bet she feels terrible at not being here?"

Oli looked a bit unsure "Maybe, she's not around much at the minute"

Oh Christ, "That's because she's gone on a holiday with your granny and auntie isn't it? She'll be back soon and spoiling you, I bet. I bet she feels awful about not being here with you"

To be honest I wasn't sure. I'd not sensed much maternal warmth coming from the boys, but she was their mother, and living with Patrick couldn't be easy. You could see he wasn't t t exactly low maintenance; *the man actually loves himself!* However, I liked to think we'd reached an understanding back on that first day - when he was so rude to me.

Although, I hadn't always stuck up for myself. I think I had just learnt to out of necessity. It's not easy bringing the children up and Frank was such a whirlwind. Well, if I had let him, we would have potentially been living on some remote island in Scotland, rearing our own cattle and growing our own food (with no experience or understanding how to do it). *And if that have happened, where would we be now?* He was a dreamer my husband. I had learnt to stand up to him.

Then AF, fighting the grief made my embarrassment of asking for help into telling people what's what. I had no choice in toughening up. So, when I was met by rudeness that first day back at school, I didn't stand for it. However, his honesty, warmth and blatant rudeness, was refreshing. Too many people tip-toed around me and that, I couldn't stand. Being called the 'Merry Widow' both appalled and humoured me.

"I wish you'd go away mummy and leave us for a few days" chimed in Phoebe; her words piercing my tender heart. "I mean, we love you and all that, but I've been thinking about this and it's called 'time out'. You need to be thinking about yourself more". Her face was so serious and earnest. An old head on young shoulders.

I raised my eyebrows at her "You been sneaking watching Dr Phil again?" I guessed "It is not really age appropriate is it?"

"He talks a lot of sense *'mommmm'*" she drawled in a fake American accent.

If only things were that simple. "And who would look after you?"

"You could send us to Galway on the Ryan Air to Nanny and Pa's"

"Nice thought." *Only we have only seen them twice since the funeral* (always tense and Nanny so sad and almost hostile...)

Like she could read my mind - Phoebe looked down and went silent for a minute. I felt for them, I really did. My parents always half-way around the world and Frank's lot piled into the giant farmhouse near Galway. Well, they only had me really. Although love is sent from these corners of the world, it was as much use as us looking through the baby albums or watching CDs from memories past: a comfort but no real help. However, this was not a point to be addressed until, well... never.

"Anyway, don't worry about me *'I'm grand'* as Nanny would say!"

This was chorused by Phoeb's and Hazza, then very quickly Oli was joining in the Irish chorus too. And as I watched them lighting up a dusky autumn evening, with their chatter and laughter, I knew I was.

THAT NIGHT AT
THE FOLLY

Then
Aimee

Saltness
Late September 2016

The doorbell finally rang as we'd all settled down to watch the Saturday night telly. Homemade pizzas were in the oven and snacks had been loaded onto the side. Oli was loving it! They'd been upstairs and got all the blankets and duvets, making a massive '*bed-den*' as Harry was calling it.

"That'll be Toby!" Oli squealed excitedly. He'd been so good but there'd be a couple of occasions when he'd gone quiet and I could tell he'd been worried.

I pulled myself up off the comfy sofa and answered the door. Freddie and SDD at my heels, excitedly battling to get to Toby.

"A cast – can I sign it first?" shouted Harry and Oli at the same time.

The children and dogs crowded around him, jostling to get to him first. "Calm down, give him some space."

"But this is important Mum! I am his best friend"

Phoebe rolled her eyes "Like that's a reason! Oli is his brother. Blood's thicker than water. That's why I've got no choice but to hang around with you. And play with those sniffy cousins of ours in Galway. Not Auntie Siobhan's but Ciara's, they're just…"

"Stop Phoebe. Stop!" *Why does she do that?*

"But you said Auntie Ciara was…"

"Never mind what I said. Give the boy some space" Does *my girl have to remember everything?*

Patrick raised his eyebrows at me and grinned. He seemed to like watching Phoebe drop me in it. The children ran off and ensconced Toby in the den. Lots of giggling and some bickering as to who go to help him followed. Phoebe won of course, she *'is oldest and the most mature to nurse the patient'*

The oven timer rang out and Patrick followed me through to the kitchen.

He looked tired, almost haggard, like he'd started to prematurely age in the middle of A and E. "Have you eaten? Pizza?"

"Yes please, if it's not too much trouble?"

"Nah, we've made loads. Although I warn you, the children made them!"

He watched me take out the misshapen shapes, the haggard look easing as he grinned at the country shaped pizzas "Is that Australia, or New Zealand?" He laughed.

It was good to see him laugh. His face looked so grave and serious when we last saw him, I was worried. I wasn't used to a serious Patrick. A rude one, or a funny one, but not serious. It didn't suit him.

"Drink? There's a bottle in the fridge, feel free to open it"

"What about your merry widow evening with Strictly? Am I stepping on Bruno's toes?"

I was glad we were back on familiar ground. Joking, that was better.

"In other thoughts, that one looks like China and that one could be Sardinia – it is very long!" he motioned to the pizzas.

"Well yes they do, but I'll forgive you for missing Strictly, you've had a shite day"

So we ate *'not too bad, although maybe a bit chewy'* and drank *'I'll have to go and buy something decent from the shop Annie, this is like paint stripper'* (It was a perfectly good Pinot Grigio, but how do you please someone with gold-plated taste?) and we drank Patrick's Sancerre: *'seems like we've run out of the good stuff, we'll have to go and drink that lovely paint stripper'* (not so fussy now) and we talked about what united us in our bizarre new friendship: our children.

Toby's arm was broken. He needed to go back next week, and have it reset. There would be no football for at least eight weeks. He was gutted. So was Harry.

"Don't worry mate, I'll stick by you!" promised Hazza as they all nestled down to watch Minions. Phoebe was tucking him into the den, and they all had snacks arranged around them. SDD and Freddie in the middle, ears cocked for sounds of packets rustling.

Strictly was now an ancient memory.

"Thanks Aimee. You have been very kind. Kinder than I deserve, calling you names and being rude all the time" His stupid smile meant that I didn't believe him. That and all the wine.

The man was tearing up. *'Shit'* I thought, maybe he does *'I can't do men tears'*

I went a bit blokey, "You're alright. You'd have done the same"

"Would I? I doubt it. I'm not a good person like you. I can be rude, arrogant and irresponsible with my family's feelings- "as Madame J keeps reminding me. Being solely in charge – well it makes me think…"

I didn't want to talk about his marriage. None of my business.

"Look Patrick. Stop." *Him and Jess was something not up for discussion.* "You're not all of those things" I laughed.

"I am. Nice try, but you know it as well as I do. Don't be kind Aimee – look I'm even calling you your own name, but I'm a bastard"

He was on his second bottle.

I don't do self-pity. He needs to give it a rest, or things will get messy. His children are next door.

I looked towards the living room door and at the mass

of quilts and pillows surrounding the children. He quickly pulled himself together.

"That's good" Patrick nodded towards the large canvas on the wall "One of yours?"

"Yeah, what makes you say that?"

"Well, the fact that those children look very much like a younger Phoebe and Harry. Also, Sandra Dee Dog hasn't altered much!" He was smiling again. I was glad.

"A bit greyer around her ageing muzzle"

The canvas was one I'd painted before Frank died. Phoebe was four and Harry was two. It was sketched on a day at the beach. It was during a particularly good patch. Frank had been his usual exuberant self and I had sat back and soaked it up. A perfect day caught on canvas.

"It was one of the last times we had together on the beach. It took me a while to finish it too. It was one of the first pieces I'd done in a while"

"Since you lost him?"

"No. I finished just before funnily enough. And then the grieving came, and I lost myself in my art once more. I have since managed to make a business out of it"

"So, you're earning from your misery now?" he was winding me up again.

Laughing at my expense. *This man!* Most people I would want to kill for a comment like that. He just made me laugh! "Ha-ha...Yeah, if you say so!"

"Bloody good though. I didn't realise you were so talented. Why did you stop?"

Praise indeed from a man who was notoriously hard to impress. I'd heard the rumours and learnt enough about him during our brief 'friendship' (if you could call it that). "Sorry? Stop?"

"Yeah, you said it was one of the first-"

"Well, when I had the children I struggled to cope. Baby blues and Frank was busy...it took me a while to find myself again" I didn't want to go into all the details. He didn't need to

41

know. The edited version was better.

"I know that feeling. I'm out of my depth here. I've not been the best dad" *oh God, the self-pity again.*

"Stop being maudlin. You've had a shit day and Jessica isn't here. You've had to take all the strain. I bet you haven't had to do that before?"

"I do the business. She does the kids. That's been the recent issue – she's had enough; that's why I'm having to do all this. That and the fact that I haven't always been the best husband. She needed some space – "

I had to stop him, I didn't want to know all this

"Look, Patrick, should you really be telling me all this?" I had to stop him. Other people's affairs aren't my problem or business. I am a clam Jenna tells me, but it means that no one gets upset. I might be strong, but I don't get involved, even in Jenna's relationship problems (not that she has many 'long term' relationships).

"No, but like you say, it's been shite, I need to exhale it all out, like when I was told to breathe out all the negative air, at couple's yoga." He laughed to himself "Now that was an experience! Me with my arse in the air and my head between my legs"

I couldn't help but laugh at the image. "Was there a leotard involved?"

"Could you imagine?" and we fell into fits of laughter. *That was better, back on firmer ground.*

"I'll tell you what though Annie, I don't know how you do it."

"Yeah well. Annie my arse" I trilled in my Irish accent "If I'm an Annie you're a Paddy" I laughed to myself.

"No way!" he argued.

"Oh yes. No double standards here! You should know that by now. We are all the same"

"Bloody hell! Whatever, but just don't shout it down the street, will you? People will think I've gone soft"

"Gone soft? Your reputation you mean? What are you

afraid of?"

"I'm Patrick Green, people expect me to look a certain way. Behave a certain way. My family has a social standing. Things are expected of us. Since dad left and mum took over the hotel, it's on my shoulders"

That's a well-rehearsed speech.

"Don't you have a brother?" I had vague memories of something from a time of the boys' and girls' school dances.

"Ha, I forget you grew up around here."

Yes, I did, and I know your family had a reputation. Admission time: "Yeah, but I went to the girls' school in the next town. My parents were preparing me for a rather different life than the one I chose"

"Ha-ha, really? Like they wanted you to be a lady?"

If only he knew. "Something like that. Educated but submissive"

"I can't ever imagine you as being submissive" He raised his eyebrows in a comical way.

"Piss off. You know what I mean"

He was trying to stifle his laughter "well yes I do have a brother. Charles. He's the educated and submissive one. He was allowed to go to uni and is now a heart surgeon in London. *'The one that got away'* I call him. I've had no choice: the lifestyle, reputation, the family business...so many people rely upon me" his laughter had dried up. He looked solemn.

From his tone, I felt some sympathy for him. Why else would he be trying to open up to me of all people? I felt I needed to say something. "I'm sorry Paddy. It must be exhausting"

"Yes, it is, and lonely." He looked through the open door to the children engrossed in the film "Mind if we watch this before we go?"

I looked at all the contented children snuggled under the blankets and dogs and thought how contented they all looked together. And then I turned to Patrick and saw he was looking at me, but his face was blank; he was miles away. He looked so lost.

Lonely?

"Of course! I think we all need a bit of down time after today" I smiled. "Top up?" I offered.

"Thank you" He replied warmly. And something told me it was not just for the drink.

THE MORNING
OF THE NON-
HALLOWEEN DISCO

THEN
Aimee

Saltness
Late October 2016

It had been four weeks since 'Arm-gate'. We'd fallen into an easy pattern of school runs and dog walks. Paddy was still on his own. No sooner had Jessica returned from her holiday, she went to a retreat in Thailand to learn how to teach yoga and meditation. It was for a month and seemed completely bizarre to me that she'd leave her child with a broken arm, but it wasn't my business. I wasn't really one to judge. It's like I told Paddy – none of my business. However, what was even more bizarre was that we were becoming firm friends. Although it wasn't necessarily through choice and we never meant it to happen, but we found out that we quite liked each other.

It started out that our children seemed to just love the bones of each other. Similar interests, same sense of humour and a shared love of football and wrestling (not Phoeb but cool Phoeb brought her own energy to the 'school run' party) had built the foundation for firm friendships. Frankly, I was glad. They needed some kids close to them. Having no cousins (well the Irish lot we never saw). Oli and Toby - such beautiful boys with their infectious energy. Plus, however strange I found the whole Patrick/Jessica set up, one thing was for sure: they were well brought up children.

"There she is! The elusive bestie"

A tall race-horse of a woman bounded over towards me through the busy coffee shop. Her thick, long, shiny brown fetlocks of hair were pulled up into a high ponytail. A light sheen on her bronzed cheekbones and a wide smile, all made the customers stop and stare and this Amazonian goddess; even if she was dressed in her gym gear.

"How do you do that?" I wondered warmly "Straight from the gym, effortlessly chic – like you've not even broken into a sweat, and you still smell of Jo Malone. Not that I'm jealous. Maybe a little – "

"Pah Aims. Don't do yourself down. Look at you! You've wrestled my godchildren to school, handled the horse of a SD Dog, and probably managed to clean and redecorate before I'd even thought about going to Pilates – that's why I look like this – no sweat just stretch. Ha!"

"Decorate? Fuck off, who do you think I am, Kirstie Allsop?"

"No, you're fitter than her and have more sass. She's lovely but very *Cath Kidston Home Counties*; if you know what I mean?" she grinned wickedly. Always one to try and get a rise. You see, she thought I was drying up. This seemed to be her number one priority at the moment – to get me 'out there' again. The fitter comment was to build confidence, but I knew this, so didn't really believe her.

"Fitter? Do you know the last time a man – "

"Oh, I do, only you have no radar for it any more. You aren't interested and so don't understand the signals. You know there's plenty that would Aims" This is something she always referred to at this point. She liked to remind me of the men who started hovering about after Frank died.

"Oh, this again! I was a grieving widow for God's sake!"

"They were lined up Aimee. And remember Connor?"

Back to this. After Frank died various men started trying to help me. Some just wanted to help me with the house 'men's stuff' that they thought I'd miss Frank doing. They weren't to know he was bloody useless around the house, were they? Then there was the son of my parents' best friends – the accountant. He wanted to help with my finances, as it turned out, he thought I must be loaded owning the big folly house! He soon scarpered when he realised, I was not wealthy, and I was not going to sell my childrens' own home to some sodding developer who wanted to turn it into luxury holiday apartments. But the worst one, the one we couldn't believe was Connor.

"Who asks a widow out for a drink at her husband's funeral? Seriously! What on earth was he thinking?"

"Claimed it's what Frank would have wanted" I laughed at the memory. We can laugh now. After Connor, there were others too who thought they could rescue me.

"Anyway" I giggled "You make up for the two of us with your exploits. We wouldn't cope if we were both dating – they'd not be enough hours in the day for us to discuss two love lives!"

The waitress came over and put my order on our table "Two lattes and two fruit custard tarts" The coffee smelt great and the tarts fattening but delicious.

"I ordered for you. Thought we deserved the tarts – it's Friday. Plus, my treat as I've just got a new commission". It still didn't feel right, but I knew I couldn't afford to be proud. Patrick wanted me to paint the boys with Freddie. He wanted them in the woods at the bottom of their garden. Just through the trees you could see the sea. He wanted me to capture their childhood before it became tainted by growing up and well, life. At first, I didn't want to do it. However, Patrick said he loved my painting of Phoebe and Harry '*Your style shows energy and joy. You capture their spirits Aimee*'. I knew he was being serious because he called me Aimee. '*If I asked someone else, they wouldn't get that. You know the boys and they would respond to you. Plus, you're very talented you know'.* I had no idea if he did know if I was talented or not. So far, all id seen of his style was the 'Ice Palace' mansion and apparently that was all 'Jessica'.

"A commission. Excellent news. I won't ask, I know you don't like to discuss these things until they're finished. Latte and tarts don't seem to quite cut it though – not if we're celebrating!"

Jenna was right. We didn't discuss my commissions. When I'm creating a piece, I like to concentrate on it and that means no discussion. I find painting a very personal and moving experience and discussing the project seems to diminish its magic. After is fine, but before and during, I like to quietly create.

Knowing this was the case, she ploughed on "Anyway, what are you doing tonight? I'm free and wondered if you wanted me to come and entertain my two-favourite people? Plus, you, with fun and games. It feels like an age since I spent any time with them"

Today was to be the day of the Halloween disco. The intolerably noisy event which sends my children into loud, ear piercing raptures every year. However, (praise be) a leaky pipe has meant it has had to be cancelled! But Paddy had other ideas.

'You see A, we can't let them down. They've been looking forward to dressing up so much, so I think I'll hold a party at mine!'

Now this was hilarious to me.

'What about Jessica? How would she feel about children messing up her white/glass/shiny home?'

Paddy paused. Didn't think he'd thought about that. He'd become very carefree recently. *'The Ice Palace?'* Oh, fuck he knows. I must have started to colour up as *'Well that's what you O'Donnell's call it isn't it?'* He asked cracking a grin *'I happen to agree. It needs softening up, just like my lady wife'*

To this I stayed silent. What the past six weeks had taught me was that our new friendship was built on 'fun'. I tended to steer him away from the heart to heart stage and we'd certainly not reached the stage where I want to discuss the state of his weird marriage.

I considered my answer to Jenna carefully, "Well we could, but I have plans"

Jenna raised her perfectly tattooed eyebrows. "Plans? Since when did you have plans without me? With the children I presume otherwise I'd have been drafted in" she mused. "and we've already established there's not a sniff of a man"

"Yes, plans. We are going to a party at the Green's"

"The Green's?" She was searching her brain

"Yes, the Green's"

"The only Green's I know are…you mean Jessica and Patrick Green's?" She laughed.

I nodded.

She looked shocked. I wasn't surprised. "Bloody hell Aims, what are you doing making friends with the Hollywood set? I'm surprised she's even allowing anyone to mess up her glass cube. Wouldn't the children put paw prints on those walls?"

Everybody knew about their house as it has heavily featured in '*House and Homes Yorkshire*' when she'd had it built. It was an 'outside-in-house' and was built to blend into its natural landscape. Whether it did or not remained to be seen. However, what could be seen, is on pages 7-11 in the June 2016 issue.

"Hang on, isn't she at that yoga retreat in Thailand? Polly was saying something this morning at Pilates. Something about her thinking about opening one up here" Jenna's brain was ticking over. I could sense it. She was like a dog with a bone and although she worked as the chief tourism officer for the area, I always joked she could have had her own private detective agency. She was like a sniffer dog for a story. "So, he's having a party on his own? Brave man, he'll have to get the bloody cleaners in after he's had a load of primary school children round to the glass cube" she laughed.

"The Halloween disco was cancelled so we've relocated" I

replied. I didn't know why, but I just didn't want her to know it would be just us. She gets ideas does Jenna.

"Well good on him. Although highly unusual. He can be a right one you know Aims. You must have heard the rumours?"

Thing is I knew the rumours. His philandering and rudeness. The arrogant rich kid all grown up stuff – the old town folklore...I might have met that Patrick Green, but I'd got to know someone completely different. Only, something stopped me revealing my recent new friendship to her. It didn't feel right. Plus, I wasn't sure how I felt about these other versions of Patrick Green.

THE MORNING AFTER THE NON-HALLOWEEN DISCO

THEN
Patrick

October half term 2016

Ever seen Spectre? The bit where Bond is strapped in the chair and Blofeld is about to perform cranial surgery on him? Well that, or the pain of a drill boring into my brain would be preferable to how I felt that morning, if you really don't want to know how bad by head felt, then look away now.

It felt like a tiny bird was scratching around inside my cranium and pecking away at my stupid brain. Scratching away like the way chalk sounds when it is pulled down the blackboard. Screeching like my 'darling wife.'

'Stupid brain'. Stupid is not really the word I want to use. I really think a more adequate term would be 'bastard'. And there's no better reminder of how you should/shouldn't behave when you are awoken at 6.30am on a Saturday morning, by two incredibly loud sons bouncing and shouting on top of me. Toby (as is custom) was trying to prise open my gritty eyes with his podgy little fingers, on his good hand, "Dad-deeee, get up. It's time!"

Time! Guilt was pulsing, as well as all the alcohol through my ravaged body. Time: something I wish could be moved, controlled and manipulated. *Patrick, you have seriously fucked up.*

Last night! I had no idea why it happened. Why I allowed it to happen. My therapist however, would say different. He would tell me it's because of the constant state of denial I lived in and the fact that I needed to control. He'd tell me to be honest with myself - my dishonesty being the thing which had put me in this position – I was one hungover bastard who had gone too far.

Today: ground zero.

I knew I had undone all my hard work. But, not only that, for the first time in my adult life, I felt like I'd let down someone really important to me.

How did it all go so wrong? The day before, the boys and I had been throwing cobwebs, spiders and skeletons around all morning. They'd made me go out and buy huge pumpkins, which they carved into ghastly silhouettes of doom. I had never seen them so excited. I watched them smearing ketchup all over their white shirts and couldn't help but think how Jessica would shriek. She'd hate all this: the mess, the destruction, the unruliness of it all...she'd have ordered costumes and had a theme for the house. Tasteful pumpkins would have been carved in an orderly way and there would never have been seeds and shite all over the kitchen floor.

They'd also made me get lots of party food in. We weren't allowed to buy a takeaway as they said that *Aimee makes everything herself.*

She bloody would, I thought.

However, I knew this was unfair of me as I secretly liked the fact that she could make stuff; it's the artist in her. That painting of the children on the beach, well it was something else. I'd commissioned one of the boys for Jessica; a Christmas present. Something thoughtful (for once she'd say).

Mr Thoughtful - that was then, the beginnings of a new me – I had been mulling over our future. I didn't actually know if we had one. But I did know that she had given us two wonderful boys and for that she deserved more than I had been giving her. Her absence had made me think. *Was it worth saving?* Had kept me awake many a night.

Half drunk, guilt-ridden and full of self-loathing for the mess I was making of my life...The bottle of JD mocking me on my bedside table. The previous night I'd obliterated all rationale. And why? It seemed my therapist had to add another item for discussion to the list: jealousy.

THE NIGHT OF THE NON-HALLOWEEN DISCO

Then
Aimee

Saltness
Late October 2016

"Ready children?" My two gorgeous creatures of perfection – my best work, bounded towards me in their homemade costumes. Phoebe had a bandage (old ripped up sheet) wound expertly around her body. Just her face, hands and feet, stuck out from the mesh of 'bloodied' (tomato ketchup) bandages. Her face powdered white with flour and my 'best' red Chanel lippy on. Hazza slid alongside in his 'suit' (school trousers and a white shirt), with a black cape tied around his neck. His dark hair was slicked back and horrified, I noticed he'd more (expensive) red lippy smeared around his mouth. *What on earth will my lovely lippy look like now?* He had on an old bowtie from the dressing up box and plastic fangs from the pound shop, sticking out of his goofy grin. They both looked fabulous! I felt the tears brimming. *Times like this...*

"Mum, you can't go like that!" they complained, eyeing up my jeans and top combo. "You need to be on theme".

"I've got a pair of cat ears" I argued whilst placing them on my head.

"Where's the rest of your costume?" demanded Harry. "You can't let us down. You need to go all out! Tell her Phoebe" pleaded Harry.

Phoebe looked me up and down, her thinking face firmly on. "I know Mummy, why don't you do your face with whiskers and a nose? And I bet you've got something cat-like to wear"

"Cat-like?" I laughed, "Not last time I looked!"

"Well I bet we can find something. You can't let us down. Patrick's gone to so much trouble and the boys are so excited" Mother Phoebe's telling off meant I was whisked into action.

Fifteen minutes later, she had found me some black skinny jeans and a cute black fluffy jumper. Phoebe had painted my face with expert precision (she had been inspired by someone called Jeffree Star, so I gained winged eyeliner and some sort of glitter effect on my lids – *'I'm not sure cats have glitter'* I argued).

"Come on then guys, it looks like we are all ready to – "

Then the doorbell rang. *Early trick or treaters maybe?*

I hastily grabbed some sweets out of the cupboard and got ready to thrust them out at the children. However, it was Jenna dressed in some sort of black combo with, what looked like, her ancient Chanel cape. She had a pair of bat ears perched on top of her head.

"Auntie Jen why are you dressed like Harry's bat" asked Phoebe as she opened the door.

"Hi poppet! You're a mummy! I'm Harry's date to the party, didn't he tell you?" she laughed.

Phoebe and I eyed each other. This was news to us.

"You're here! You're here! You're here!" Hazza cheered.

"Yes, I am, and all ready for the 'Ice Mansion' party. Ooh, I can't wait to see inside!" Jenna giddily exclaimed.

'Shit', I thought, *'this could get complicated.'* What I didn't mention to Jenna earlier was that no one else was invited to the party. A bit weird maybe (in hindsight) but it seemed like a good idea last night when we discussed it as we walked home enthusiastically. We just decided to have a laugh with

the children. Toby was still fed up over his arm and the disco being cancelled and all that. Patrick offered to do it at his as I had everyone round the other week after the 'arm-gate' thing. He said it was to repay a kindness. And I thought nothing of us just hanging out – after all that's what we'd been doing, just hanging out, whilst the children did their various activities.

"Hazza FaceTimed me and asked me to be here for half six specifically – didn't you Haz?" Jenna said sheepishly.

There was something fishy about the way they looked at each other. I had no idea who'd instigated what, but I doubted Harry had invited her using his own free will and initiative. My best friend had always been a nosy cow.

At times like these I just had to suck it up and see. "Well here she is! Harry, your date and 'bat-friend' Auntie Jen!" I couldn't help but laugh. She might find it a bit odd that it's just us, and Paddy might wonder why my best friend is dressed as a bat, but what could I say?

THE NIGHT OF THE NON-HALLOWEEN DISCO

THEN
Patrick

Saltness
Late October 2016

I've no idea why, but when Aimee turned up with her best friend, I admit it, I was really annoyed. Maybe it was because it was meant to be 'our' party. She was just an interloper. A gate crasher.

The evening started well. They all looked fantastic as I opened the door to them.

"Hi Paddy" Aimee smiled at me, handing me a bottle of wine. The children were bounding past me – one mummy and one Dracula "Great costumes guys, the boys are – "

"Boo!" they chorused, as they both jumped out from cupboard under the stairs. A mass of cobwebs and spiders were thrown into the air. Phoebe and Harry fell to the floor in stiches – holding their sides in some sort of silent comedy dramatics.

I looked at Aimee, or should I say, I was taken aback by Aimee. Second acknowledgment: she looked good. Not just good: hot. She was all glammed up like a cat. Big surprise: Pretty? *Yes, I knew*. Hot? *Who knew!*

"Looking good Aims!" I admitted "You scrub up well dressed like a feline". I glanced at the wine "and this is an improvement from the last lot we drank!"

My third secret... *I do have a slight crush on the girl. And it started before tonight. Why not? She is very attractive – inside and out. I am a man. I have a pulse. I am a man of discerning taste. But we are friends and that is a novelty for me. Therefore. the crush stays a crush.*

"Yes Paddy, I'm 'feline' just fine. Although Phoeb's is responsible for the look! Just as Aimee was coming into the door, I noticed another figure in a black cloak, looming behind her like the Grim Reaper.

"Hi, I'm Jenna" said the dark apparition thrusting another bottle of wine at me. "Aimee said we had to bring good wine as you won't drink that paint stripper stuff we buy from the Spar."

Aimee looked nervous and quickly explained that Jenna was 'Auntie Jenna', 'The God-Mother' and 'Best Friend'.

"Call me whichever title you like" she quipped flirtatiously, "but tonight I'm Hazza's date"

As we moved through to the large kitchen diner, I could sense their eyes scanning the vastness of the open-plan space. Jessica had insisted that most of the walls were removed and this meant the ground floor was mostly like a very glamorous aircraft hangar. Glass, chrome and marble shimmered from every surface (well until the children started playing with the fake blood and throwing sweets everywhere). The children were running around shrieking, scaring and spooking each other out. The noise was ridiculous; echoing off the surfaces; they were so excited. My two especially so, as they would never normally be allowed such boisterous fun in The Ice Palace.

Aimee caught my eye and laughed "I hope you've got your cleaner coming in the morning!"

Guided by my mother's good upbringing, I pushed the negative feelings towards my guests away (yes, I was annoyed with

Aimee – *what was she thinking just bringing her friend without asking?).* I generously poured us all a drink, which Aimee took and sipped, and Jenna and I downed very quickly. Too quickly.

What I need to remember here is that whilst I was trying to curb my annoyance and to find a way to make my peace with these women, Aimee was being a bloody saint *How could I ever get mad with her?* She was getting the children into some kind of order. She was organising some sort of game and getting them to quietly listen to the rules.

I should be ashamed with myself.

"Is there anyone else coming?" the bat-face asked. She was a very attractive bat. Tall, leggy and she had an amazing mane of chestnut-brown hair. She reminded me of a thoroughbred straining at the traps. I sensed an energy about her, and I guessed that she would usually be the type to stray (total opposite to Aims). However, there was nothing stirring. I would have to be a monk not to have noticed her assets, but I wasn't interested in the slightest. For some reason, I kept looking over at the cat-woman in my lair.

"Top up Jenna" It wasn't even a question. I knew she'd be up for it. I could spot them a mile off. Aimee must have a particular taste in friends.

Blind man's bluff, pinning the tail on the witch's cat, and apple bobbing later, and Jenna and I had polished off about two bottles of wine. Aimee had barely drank. I was on bad form again. I blamed the bat. I also felt very confused.

"I think we should eat" motioned Aimee to the buffet table. The children had already been sneaking stuff. I sensed that she thought we were drinking too much. Aimee was getting them to put a bit of everything on – even the fruit. The boys were like little lambs, lapping it up. *Bloody Saint Aimee,* I thought. *Here she was playing the hostess, yet where was my wife? And why am I entertaining her shitting friend 'Jen'?* Who seemed to like to tell me about where she's been, what she has done, what she hasn't done, what she is about...I didn't bloody care. On and on…self-interested.

"Paddy, you eating?" shouted Aims over the Monster Mash.

"Yes Annie, I will have a plate of crap party food please"

She asked Jenna, whose eyes were passing between us both. She had an odd look on her face. "Yes please. Lots of sausage rolls please!"

She eyed us both like naughty children, "Well I'm not your bloody waitress. Come and get it before the children eat it all"

We both eased ourselves out of our chairs and begun to wobble across the room.

"Crap? This is great Paddy. So nice not to have to bother for a change! You see, you aren't the bastard you like us to believe" she whispered with a wink.

We both laughed.

Fourth admission: Her laughter sounded like pure joy. *'Too much time without my wife or anyone else's'* I thought.

The evening just rolled, and all time fell away from itself. There were more games, dancing, drinking…the children eventually collapsed in front of 'Corpse Bride' around half eight. I helped Aimee to wrap them all in the quilts and blankets. Finally, we retreated to the sofas looking out of the glass wall, into the forest and out onto the black North Sea.

"Such a lovely night, thanks Patrick. I still can't believe that all that was just for us" purred Jenna. I sensed she was on predatory territory. And, if I wasn't on my best behaviour, I would have told her that it wasn't for her and that it was actually for Aimee and the children. Auntie Fucking Jenna had not been invited at all!

"Yes, thanks Paddy" Grinned Aims. "It is just what they all needed. After all the stress of Toby's arm and the longest school term ever. It has been so full on hasn't it? And we've still got the football in the morning"

She'd stretched out on the long sofa. Her glass of wine in one hand and her gaze reaching far out to sea. She was visibly relaxing. My God, I'd been an utter bastard tonight. She had done loads and I had just got drunk and pissed off with her friend Jenna – who, as it happened, was quite sharp and good looking. She was no Aimee though. Guilt edged its way in.

"Well Annie, are you okay?" I sang in a Michael Jackson way. "are you okay Annie?" I laughed.

"Are you drunk Patrick Green?" Aimee joked. She knew I was really; in hindsight I think she was trying to calm the waters.

I decided to face it out though. "No drunker than I was around yours the other night"

I noticed Jenna's eyebrows reaching her hairline. *Oh, so she knows nothing about Aimee's other best friend then?* A secret thrill flashed through me.

"The other night? Have you two been secretly drinking?" laughed Jenna, as she nervously looked between the two of us. "I didn't realise that this was an actual regular thing. How often do you do this, have parties and not invite anyone?"

"Never" interjected Aimee quickly. "This is the first time. Last time Paddy was drunk was because Toby had fallen out of a tree and I was looking after them all. They came to mine to pick Oli up from the hospital. He was in shock"

Aimee's quick-fire reply meant she was struggling with something: me, or her? I quickly backed her up, "Yeah, the kids hang out though. Aimee is my walking buddy and sometimes we go to the beach on a Saturday" I admit it, I was bragging. Ever the competitive one, it felt good that I had one over on A's other best friend. For some reason I felt jealous – of another woman. Now that was a first.

"And *Annie*? Since when has your name been *Annie*?"

"Well that's a funny story..."

"Yes, Paddy, tell it" urged Jenna. "I'd love to know why you're a Paddy too" Ha, she was jealous of me! There was an edge to her tone.

Aimee shifted in her seat. I should have stopped, I sensed her tension. However, I was too busy enjoying the fact that I was winning. Jenna seemed to be getting a bit louder and sharper with her questions. Plus, I could sense that maybe I wasn't being my 'best self anymore', only I couldn't stop it. *'What's it to her anyway?'* I thought, *it's not as if she's Aimee's keeper.*

"It was just a misunderstanding Jen. Nothing special" said Aimee as she jumped up. Phoebe was shouting her "Coming hun!"

"Yeah, and she calls me Paddy because she thinks she's funny. Well you know what A's like?"

"Well if you'd have asked me two hours ago…" she commented stiffly.

"What is that meant to mean?" I argued. Her tone was getting sharper.

She shifted towards me and quietly hissed, "What have you been doing with MY best friend Patrick Green? I know your reputation." She spat.

"It's not MY fault that MY best friend has kept things from you is it?" I spat back like a four-year-old fighting in the playground.

"Well, I don't trust you" I pulled a ridiculous mock-horror face at her "I've seen the way you look at her"

She knew nothing. She'd seen nothing. "What way. We are purely friends. I am a married man you know." I stood up indignantly.

"Well it has never stopped you before – "Jenna stood up and faced me off.

"Look, I never invited you here" my voice was rising.

She grabbed her coat "Clearly, I can see what YOU had in mind" she accused loudly.

"They just all want a drink – oh, what is going on here?" She was standing, hands on hips. It was like our mother had just come in to stop some sibling spat. Only this mother was dressed like a cat and looked gorgeous when she was angry. *What the hell was I thinking?*

"Nothing, I'm just going" hissed Jenna.

"Jen?" enquired Aimee with her eyebrows raised.

"What the fuck is it with girls' names that begin with J?" I slurred. *Shit, I was slurring.*

"Oh, for fuck's sake Patrick. What is going on?" Aimee did not look pleased. "Jenna, where are you going? What has he said?" shouted Aimee after the retreating bat lady.

Aimee flew out of the room after her and I refilled my glass.

Five minutes later she was back. I refilled my glass again.

"She's mad with me because she thinks I have been hiding stuff from her. You, she's mad with you, because you've acted like an absolute knob. Why Patrick? Why would you upset my best friend?"

The words were washing over me. I was focused on her lovely lips and glittering eyes. They were full of fire and rage. "Well, for one I never invited her"

Aimee snatched her bag from the side and thrust her phone at me "I text to warn you. Harry had invited her, and I couldn't stop her. She's their god-mother and they love her. What could I say? I'm sorry, it's not that type of party? Well, I've a good idea what impression she's got now"

"Text? Huh" I pulled my phone out of my pocket and it fell onto the marble floor. There was a noise that sounded like a crack. I stumbled. Aimee picked it up as I fell to the floor.

"Shit Paddy, how much have you drunk? And more importantly, why?" she was on her hands and knees next to me. "I'm mad with you Patrick Green, but I will help you up anyway. And then it's to bed"

I smiled "Really? I thought you'd never ask. You're so beautiful – you don't even know do you?"

Her voice faltered, "Shut up. Come on, you're drunk, hold on"

And I couldn't help it. My mind was fixated, her body was holding onto mine and I went in for the kiss. Only she pushed me away and I threw up on the floor.

THE MORNING AFTER THE NON-HALLOWEEN DISCO

THEN
Patrick

Saltness
October half term 2016

"Dad!!!!! Aren't you getting ready?"

"Daddy, Daddy, Daddy!!!" Shouted Toby, whilst bouncing up and down on my bed. "Bounce, bounce, bounce...I'll keep bouncing until you get up Daddy!"

You would, you sadistic shit, I thought unpaternally in my head. I opened one eye and looked at the time on my bedside clock 6.55am. Shit, I'd fallen back to sleep. My head, still being pecked at from the inside by Woody Woodpecker, the empty, shit empty bottle of Jack Daniels sitting next to the clock.

I attempted to move my head and yet another pain sprang through it with the doorbell. The boys ran hell for leather out of the room and clamoured down the stairs. And there was a momentary peace. And I closed my eyes.

The softest voice was worming its way into my head. Lulled into a false sense of security, I thought the angels had taken pity on me. I'd gone to Heaven after all. I prised open one eye again: 7.05am.

I could smell her before I saw her. There was a fresh and pure air in the room. She was opening the windows. *It must smell bad in here.* The angel was her and it was like – sharp and straight to the point. No honeyed edges for me. "Patrick. I've got the boys. I'll take them all to the football match. It looks like you need to sleep it off"

There she was: Aimee O'Donnell, like a vision at the end of my bed. Only, her face said, 'I'm really not happy with you at all'. The smile which had begun to escape as I had sensed her being there, was quickly extinguished by a frosty glare Jessica would have been proud of. "I'll drop them off later. I doubt you'll be going anywhere very fast" she added icily.

Next thing I knew there was a loud bang and my eyes shot open. 7.15am. In strode a woman with an icy look which kicked Aimee's to the curb. This was now Hell.

"Why the fuck is there and empty bottle of Jack Daniels on your bedside table? What the shit has happened to our house? And why the hell has that bitch just driven off with MY children in her car?"

I'd seriously fucked up – Lady J never swore.

PART TWO

THE GARDEN OF EDEN

BEFORE THEN
Jessie

When you're young you think you have it all in hand...
whatever the hand you were dealt at birth.
Your teens give you foundations; your twenties provide the
drive, and your thirties mean you should have made it.
I had such a plan. It was fool proof, but then
again, it didn't involve emotion.

FIVE MINUTES LATER...

BEFORE THEN
Jessie

Corfu 1996
The Morning After

"Breathe Jessie" I had my head between my legs, and I was taking deep breaths. Spiros was standing with a glass of water and Maria was holding my hand. Last night's ouzo was bubbling away in my empty stomach – we never did get that gyros to line it. I was petrified that I was going to decorate the taverna's floors with it.

I couldn't get my head around what Spiros was saying he was talking about flights and money and my head was just whirling round and around. *My Mam! God love her. It couldn't be true.* She'd always been so strong. If there was a nuclear bomb, she'd be the last one standing.

"So, I have been making calls to my friend Effie. She does bookings and we can get you on the twelve thirty flight. One of us can take you to the airport. Have you the money? If not, we will help." I stared at him blankly. My mouth was full of ashes.

"Family is everything, no?"

When Greek say 'no' they usually mean yes. And to a point, he was right. His family was everything. Any fool could see that. For the past few months I'd felt like an honorary member. Maria and I were treated similarly – Maria was right, if we'd have messed up last night, we'd have both been in trouble, not just her. I'd loved that about being here. I'd loved being wrapped in their overprotective blanket. In fact, Corfu had brought me so many different types of love, I felt like I had been given the opportunity to start my life again.

And then I thought about my family in Leeds. And in the nineteen years of us being together, I'd never felt the same warmth. But then I thought about *our mam*. Quietly loving and non-complaining. Always there in the background being as supportive as she could be.

I'd left her.

Another pang of guilt washed over me.

What was I doing here with another family when my mother needed me?

I'd abandoned her and this had happened. Of course, I was going home. I had to. She had always put me first. She had encouraged every dream and sacrificed so much for me to succeed. And now she needed me. The boys and Stace would do fuck all. I knew that. And dad would be useless. I had no faith in any of them.

I rallied my thoughts. I needed to be stronger. Falling to pieces with self-pity was not going to help her. "I have some money saved. I wonder if I can change my flight home?" Maria hugged me with tears in her eyes and Spiros patted me lovingly on my back. Such kindness. Tears threatened. I could not fall apart.

Within minutes Spiros had hustled Maria into action and they had my ticket and passport and were onto the airline. Within half an hour, I was booked onto the twelve-thirty flight to Manchester and Spiros was pressing my week's wages into my hand – with a summer bonus included.

"No, I can't I'm leaving too soon..." and I was. The tears caught in the back of my throat. The bitter sweet feeling of leaving one family for another. Love and duty.

I was forever torn, even then.

Spiros insisted I took the money.

For the next few hours I was numb. Maria was in full bossy Greek mama mode. She pushed me into the shower. I was fed (although I struggled to get it down). She helped me pack and organise and come ten, I was ready for Spiros to drive me to the airport.

Tearfully, I hugged Maria tight. The fight to stem them was becoming futile; tears were spilling down my face. I could have blamed the tiredness and shock but that was *skata* and we all knew it. I didn't want to leave, and I was going out of love and duty to the one person who had always put me first. My mother had suffered a serious stroke and I was needed. It was my duty. My duty of love.

Then there was my other problem.

"I have a letter. It tells him everything and has my address and number on it" I handed it to Maria. "I tried ringing him at his apartment but there was no answer. I know there never usually is. He will be worried when he realises I've gone and I've no idea where he is to say goodbye!"

Spiros gasped and ran into the bar.

"This is not goodbye Jessie. Your mama will get better, and you will come back. This is home now no?"

Spiros came back with a piece of paper. "I am sorry, with all that happened this morning, I forgot to give you this."

It was a note. It was folded in two and it said:

My Beautiful Jessie,

Sorry. I know I promised, but you will never guess what happened to me! We are going to have the best life. I hope you enjoyed the party. I will see you tomorrow night. 8pm, I promise I will be there and on time.

I love you forever,

Frank.

WHAT A GIRL WANTS.

Corfu
Summer 1996

It was another day in paradise. Waking up day after day, with a smile on my face; I'd never known anything like it. I felt like I was permanently bathing in sunshine. As I came too, the heady air soothed me; a womb-like feeling washed over me – the warmth, the peace and the sense of new beginnings. Life was good. Life was in my hands – for the first time ever. I was free, alive and full of optimism.

Contentedly, I stretched and unfurled my arms and legs like a starfish. Touching the right side of the bed, it was cold and empty. Anxiously, as I opened my eyes, I could see his indentation was still on the pillow.

It wasn't a dream then.

I smiled to myself.

The early morning sun was streaming through the opened shutters, bathing the room in golden light. I felt rich and blessed. This was all so new to me and the reality was not lost on me – even now. I felt lucky. I was living on a beautiful island, with a job and a roof over my head. I had friends; the coolest best friend. I had no responsibilities. Life was one big party! And then there was Him. The man who was casting a shadow at the foot of my bed. '*Oh, there he is!*', I smiled to myself. '*My Adonis: My own naked, bronzed warrior.*'

Now, this was something new. Although I had been 'involved' with a handful of boys in the past, he, this man, was on another scale. And when you had led a life like me, you'd understand that I needed to commit every detail to memory. Good things did not usually happen to me.

Thoughtfully, maybe shyly? I had no idea, but I hugged my knees into my chest and savoured him. Experience told me I had to preserve this moment – I knew what it was like to lose things: all too badly. Therefore, my photographic brain was on sensory overdrive. After all, it wasn't every day you met your future husband (Technically, we actually met three weeks previously, at an all-nighter) but it wasn't until last night he'd become my fiancé.

There he was. My naked chef was standing proudly, holding a tray filled with coffee and baklava. Plus, what looked like, a collection of bougainvillea stolen from the terrace. I laughed at the absurdity. If I even flashed my mind back to three months ago, I would never have predicted this scenario.

"Breakfast for my bride-to-be" he grinned mischievously. "Like what you see Jessie?"

My stomach did some flips, and not for the food either. I had to pinch myself that I was actually bloody there.

'Heaven: did he have wings?' I thought 'Eros was certainly present'

A secret romantic, that was me. A level English lit had been my downfall and had secretly stripped me of my hard-faced feminist independence. I had spent the summer two years previously willing my GCSE results to be as good as I thought they should be, so I could take it and devour the classics. I spent the time in between working at the local 7/11 (aka Ram-raiders Central), pre-reading Jane Austin, and lusting after Mr Darcy in his dripping breeches. I developed a new (very controversial and anti-feminist) love of 19th century women who required rescuing. Maybe it was because my life had been full of pigs so far? Or maybe it was because I yearned for a way out of what had come before? I couldn't go back to that. Anyway, the naked angel, grinning at the end of my bed, was sent by Eros and he had rescued me from what might come after.

"Like what I see? You know I do!" I grinned wickedly at him.

But it wasn't just that. The early morning was knocking softly at my window; sparkling, catching the corner of my right eye, like the diamonds would soon be, on the ring I had been promised.

Many whispered promises.

And somewhere beyond, somewhere way beyond the shutters, the shimmering blue waters glistened gloriously in the morning sun.

Was this real?

When I'd first arrived there had been an emptiness to the room, a trace of cockroach behaviour preceding my stay (there was a spray under the sink). The winter rains were still lingering, and for those first April days, I felt lost and alone.

Had I done the right thing?

But then Easter hit, and I was enveloped by my boss and his family, into a religious world of fasting, painted eggs and roasting of the sacrificial lamb. In Greece, Easter is bigger than Christmas and they were horrified I was alone at such an important time. As soon as I met Spiros and his daughter Maria, I felt I'd come home. Their friendship, help and kindness had shaped my life from thereon in. As my landlord and boss, Spiros had very quickly helped me sort out the 'roach' problem (it had been empty all winter and needed a good clean). Plus, Maria became my sidekick and she introduced me to the opening parties on the beaches of the island. And we were wild.

Three weeks previously - Dassia Midsummer Beach Party, June 1996...

We had danced like it was the promised land. Hands in the air and with a hedonistic abandonment that was thrilling and new to me. It barely got dark that night. We chanted and sweated and at some point (I say at some point like I can't remember) I met the Adonis in my room, who was now organising my breakfast and making my pulse race.

My god, and they said I was wasting my life coming here.

Them. My god-awful shameless family. They really had no idea. Since I'd arrived fresh from the estate in Leeds, I'd buried them, along with the miserable grey skies of Yorkshire. This place had been my remaking. And between him and here, they made me feel like I'd grown into some Amazonian beauty. Love does that to you doesn't it? My body was bronzed. I felt more cultured and with this new confidence, I felt interesting. Gone was the pasty white pallor which had haunted me for all my teens. Summers of Boots 17 fake tan were a distant memory. Spending wet weather days (most) reading in the library, to escape from estate politics. I had spent summers past, faking it. Whilst my wealthy friends got real tans in a host of Mediterranean destinations, I had been living a harsh reality. My feet had been itching for this for years...and it wasn't because I was ungrateful, but a £10 Sun holiday in a caravan in Scarborough, just didn't cut it then and certainly didn't now – after all this, I was different.

You see, we never had much. My dad was still recovering from a Thatcher induced redundancy from the pits. He spent his days simmering away in his own pit of depression, which left him unable and disinclined to find work. My poor mother tried to feed all six of us (two brothers and one waste of space sister) by juggling three cleaning jobs and weekend bar shifts at the local pub (with the latter only serving to pay for our dad's bar tab). My saint of a mother, I loved deeply. She was my reason for leaving (not that she understood). I vowed that I was not going to go down that path - being trapped into a harsh life with little reward. An existence: a half-life. I wanted to make something of myself. My grammar school education had taught me two things: I am clever and can achieve anything the rich girls can. Plus, travel broadens a cultured mind. Therefore, I knew I needed to go away after acing my A-levels. I couldn't afford a gap year or university, but I could work abroad for a summer and I could get an apprenticeship at one of the big companies back home. I was on a path to not only be successful for me but to help my mother too. I needed to repay her for her years of drudgery to give me the best she could.

My two brothers were pretty much of the same opinion but had made different choices from me and each other. The twins: James and Mark (older by two years) had always been competitive, creating tension in an already highly charged household. James (oldest by ten minutes) liked to think he was in charge. This, in itself, was a blessing and a curse for *our mam.* A blessing because it propelled him out of the door at the age of twelve to bring money into our poor household. However, job opportunities were very few and far between, meaning his way of earning money was both illegal and dangerous. Petty theft and dealing in stolen goods had kept us warm and clothed (and paid for my school trip to France) in my adolescent years. Whilst our dad languished on the sofa and our mam scrubbed floors, James had built up his own criminal network by the age of sixteen.

Mark abhorred him. He was jealous of the adoration his brother gained for being a criminal and in an act of gaining pious glory, he signed up for the army. I say 'pious glory' he did a bunk. Pissed off. Daren't tell us…There one day, gone the next. A note left on the kitchen table. I found it. I was the one who had to tell our mam. *I didn't think cowards could go in the army?* Was what I thought as I broke the news. Then our poor mam lost the only amount of sleep she used to get, worrying about my selfish brothers both being shot.

Whatever their crimes against *our mam's* sleepless nights, the sister was far worse. Our Stacey, or Stoner Stace, as she was known at school, had fucked up majorly. A year younger than me, she already has one kid, a shitty flat and boyfriend to match. Baby number two was cooking and god only knew what else…I very much doubted she would be allowed to keep the new one (if rumours were true) but her life was no longer my problem. They didn't know it, but I'd decided I wasn't going back there. Ever. Except for one promise I'd made: one day I'd be able to help *our mam.* I dreamt of rescuing her…

The plan was in motion. The first step was my new life.

Corfu had been an education. It had opened my eyes to a different world. A world I wanted to be part of. Yes, the Greek history and culture were interesting, I also had grown to feel a great deal of respect for the poor families living in the mountains, who struggled with basic modernity. The way they lived, worked, but opened their arms with such generosity shamed me. Where my dad was sprawled on the sofa moaning about his lot, I saw men just getting on with life; any age, working tirelessly, embracing their lot. They were fighters and worked valiantly through historical and modern adversities. The Greeks were resilient and that was a quality that I admired and one that gave me hope. I'd got this far through sheer determination. I'd excelled at school (against the odds), got myself abroad: work and a roof, and then I'd found someone to grow with...I thought about my family and felt ashamed. What had made one half choose to live such destructive lives?

However, my materialistic side learnt what money bought – power: I wasn't stupid, I knew from my posh school friends, what having a big bank account did for someone. But here, well, it was another level...not just the nice designer clothes and jewellery, but the big stuff like property and goods: villas, pools, yachts...the high life of the privileged. A life I had felt ignorant of: I was an outsider to this other world. When I thought about how hard my mother worked and looked at how the rich lounged around all summer...the sheer audacity of their quiet wealth made me angry. It made me question if power and wealth was nothing to do with how hard you grafted, but rather a birth-right dependant on your postcode and your lineage.

This feeling of outsider was nothing new, I had muddled through the English summers, whilst, my friends would have been taking for granted this birth-right of theirs. They were children of businessmen, doctors and lawyers. They walked carelessly in gangs to school from their detached suburban homes. I had to get the service bus to school on my own - pretending I didn't mind that I was alone. I spent the time cramming. I made friends as I was clever, and they weren't necessarily. Tutored within an inch, to get into the best school; they simply didn't have the hunger or aptitude I had. Cosseted in their luxury lives they didn't have to be. So, they befriended me as I could help them get the grades. The parental rewards which came with it were often shared. I'd glimpsed the power and money but never seen it in such technicolour before.

But then again, what's to say I couldn't end up on top?

And then my education continued on the glorious island of Corfu, and I met the gorgeous man. A man who promised me a life beyond September. A home away from our street. But not just that, he was offering me a love I'd never experienced in my life. For the first time I felt I was worthy and special.

The romantic in me had always longed for the grand passion. That said, my overriding realist side didn't believe it would ever exist. So, imagine my surprise when, in true Patrick Swayze style, he rocked my core and swept me off my feet. In only three weeks he had awoken my deepest and darkest desires. He'd chipped away at my hard veneer, which had taken many fake and lonely years to create. How else do you think I survived? I was a foundling. A child who had grown up in the wrong shoes. I was the only intelligent one in our family. Living a half-life had made me tough.

Corfu 1996 - The here and now is amazing...

I watched him unload the tray. Making me a Greek coffee from the briki. Humming a carefree tune. I grinned and hugged this memory into myself.

He held out my coffee to me, "For my fiancé"

Fiancé! If only he knew what doors he'd opened with that proposal.

As Browning wrote 'How do I love thee? Let me count the ways.'

Well, there were many. The first thing was he could dance. He could actually dance! That night which we first laid eyes on each other, we danced before we talked. The energy between us had sizzled and jolted something deep within me. As the sun rose, we began to relax and find each other for the first time. Breathless we broke and introductions were made: Me, living a new life on my gap year. He was in a band, spoilt baby of the family. I instantly saw why. He had a warmth and instant lovability about him. He was someone you wanted to be caught up with. His emerald green eyes sparkled with flecks of gold, as he chatted animatedly about his adventures of touring with his band over the summer. You wanted to be the one held by those eyes. Lengthy dark locks framed his open face, welcoming me. When he finally kissed me (under the early morning sun), it was like coming home.

And he knew how to play the game. He'd taken me home, held my hand, we'd kissed with such passion and depth, (he had not even tried to grab my boob). The man was a saint. All the boys round our way were full of it and wanted to stick their tongue down your throat and hand down your top, the minute you agreed to hold their hand. He was like something I'd never thought really existed. His chivalry didn't stop there though. He'd played the long game with flowers, love notes, day trips to heavenly places and finally, unadulterated nights of passion built from a mutual feeling of wonderment.

Sickening maybe, and when I think about it, it's like the Mills and Boon shite *our mam* read to escape the life she'd existed within. Looking at him, into those eyes, I knew it would never get any better. This was it.

APHRODITE'S ISLAND

BEFORE THEN
Jessie

Corfu 1996
Three Weeks Later

The sun was melting like liquid gold, pooling into the azure Ionian waters. The oppression of the day was making way for the sultry night. It was the height of Summer – July. The mercury was maxing out on the thermometer and Leeds was but just a distant memory away. The taverna was busy and by day we were either sweating it out in the restaurant or cooling off in the clear blue sea. A free evening was sacred. Few and far between, they were magical when they arrived. Just as were the hours of sleep I got that summer. However, I still felt invincible and that I was living the eternal dream. Corfu had given me a cloak of possibility.

Tonight, we had plans to make. It had been another three weeks since the proposal and the summer was rolling along. We had been working so hard and although we made every effort, it was very hard to spend time together.

Days off were spent watching life move by. Not that we weren't loving life - the opposite! We'd spend all our spare time exploring: just living for the moment. After all, our new world endless in its possibilities. Corfu was just the start, and it was paradise. We felt like gods feasting on the riches of our Kingdom. I knew we both felt the same. Something magical and mystical was happening; it made the heady air fizz with energy and excitement.

After a power nap and a long shower, I felt ready for such a time. High up on my balcony, I watched the sun roll into the sea, like a comet firing down onto Earth. The image made me think about the trip we'd been meaning to take. There was a place called Kaiser's Throne, in an old hippy camp called Pelekas. It was said that you could see all the island from this vantage point – even across the water to Albania. And, if you went at sunset, the sun would roll like a fireball down the mountain, until it was extinguished by nightfall. And I reflected, soothed by the beauty and calm of the evening – a rare window in the crazy life I was building for myself, that this was what living was all about. I gazed as my own fireball submerged itself into the sea, leaving a pink and purple backdrop to the twinkling life left. And I felt a small shadow cross my contentment as I realised that time was ticking by.

He was late. Normally, this wouldn't have bothered me, but they'd been a recent shift. Everything had been really good. Too good. But perfection had been bubbling away for days. The realist in me knew it would reach its peak. I'd felt it the moment he'd opened the letter.

It was waiting for him in his post-box at his apartment block. I spotted it on my way to work earlier. A bright white envelope with his name written on the front. He picked it up silently - no comment as to its existence. I wondered why he wouldn't say. Was it secret? It struck me that I didn't really know him. The letter could have been from anyone – although, the lack of stamp and address told me it could have been hand delivered.

Then, as I was chatting about a trip we were planning, he opened it. That's when I knew he was not the open book I thought he was. Only for a second, a flicker, a flash of something I didn't recognise ran over his face. Then it was gone. He smiled that brilliant smile, quickly extinguishing the unease I'd felt. His eyes warmed to my smile and we arranged to meet after my shift. I packed the feelings away and got on with the day. Maybe it was only me who had secrets?

It was the height of season and we had been ridiculously busy. I'd felt the sleep deprivation of too much work and play catching up on me. Happily, Maria had been on form and I'd agreed to her getting us some tickets for the full moon beach party. Since the night that I'd met my knight in shining armour, I'd neglected my sidekick. It was something I felt bad about as she'd been my rock since when I first came to the island. Agreeing to the party was part of my way of making my neglectful behaviour up to her. Plus, at nineteen, it wasn't lost on me that I was starting to act like some sort of needy girlfriend. Always agreeing to his plans. Always following his lead. When had I become so submissive? I felt annoyed with myself for letting it happen.

Hadn't I learnt anything from my mother?

Earlier, Spiros sat us down to our post-lunch-rush meal. He poured the wine, and I reminded myself how lucky I felt since arriving on the island. To those who have the good fortune to possess family and love in their lives, I felt sometimes, could take such things for granted. However, I knew Maria and Spiros did not. Anna, Maria's mother had died when she was young, and I knew they felt the loss keenly. They never took their time together for granted and I had often taken part in big family dinners with them: Maria's siblings and her grandparents, at which their love for each other was passionately evident. I had thought about my own family and realised that right then I had made good friends, and a table full of love, food and wine – why should I ever feel anything other than happiness from now on?

This was my life after all!

Therefore, sitting on the terrace, high after a busy shift and family lunch, I knew I should feel blessed. I thought about all the mystique attached to Greek life. How they were ruled by the gods. It wasn't difficult to understand how the ancient Greeks had created order in their world; it was beautiful and an odyssey. I took in the night sky: the late sun had melted into the sea: Helios's gift to Poseidon. Then it was as if his sister Selene was taking her lunar ride across the inky sky. Tiny sparks of brilliance pierced the indigo blanket. Corfu was enchanting. It was like I'd just opened my eyes and I'd been gifted with the secret of life. *Had I been stumbling around in the dark for all these years?* It was like I was just awaking from a dark and troubling dream.

I'd never been good at waiting. I had always been impatient. Time passed and the earlier shadows had started to encroach on the edges of my bubble. And as the minutes ticked by, I thought about the way I was changing. How he'd changed me.

I'd never been possessive (I'd never felt that bothered about most boys before) but when I was with him, ever since I'd met him, something deep within me had changed. His energy was infectious and whenever we walked into a bar, café... he would instantly be accosted by his hordes of acquaintances.

At first, I felt flattered that he'd seen me from within the crowds and picked me out. After all, who was I? I was some young girl from Leeds waitressing for the summer at a taverna on the west coast of Corfu. And there was him: rock god! Lead singer and guitarist of 'The Helios Kings'. The flattery, the romance, the sex: it was pure hedonism. The security of the proposal was what sealed us, and with it brought a jealousy. His popularity had begun to jar. His 'fans' were beginning to annoy me. I didn't want to share him. But being the man he was, I had to be careful.

As time had gone on, I began to feel slight stirrings of resentment to these 'hangers on'. My feelings were all consuming and try as I might, I couldn't see beyond our time together. They encroached on our precious love story. *Why couldn't they see that we needed space?* When we were sharing a bottle of retsina over a table at the local bar, why did other people want to come and say hello? Join us? I can admit it now, and I know it sounds a bit 'full on', I lived and breathed him. So, as the minutes ticked off and built up to half an hour to an hour, the unease I'd previously felt built into an inner sense of doom. I could feel a deep destructive side, which I knew would not serve me well in life.

Where was he?

****

A shout came from the stairs "Jessie!"

He was here.

I didn't speak, I wanted him to do the talking. I was sulking and I knew it didn't suit me, but I felt slighted, so there. He came to the top of the stairs and gave me that smile. The one that had knocked me off my feet all six weeks before. For a minute I was ready to back down, but I held firm. I kept thinking about the way I had been neglecting Maria and the way I had become so submissive. He walked over and kissed me on the cheek – a sign that he knew I must be mad. He would have ordinarily been much more passionate. He smelt fresh, of citrus and sandalwood. A smell I could easily bathe in for the rest of my life.

"Sorry I am later than we planned. Something came up and I had to take care of it."

I raised my eyebrows. I might have been mad, but I was not prepared to start grilling him. I needed to be cooler.

"Fine" I couldn't look at him. I think I was meant to be happy he was here. So why was I feeling so confrontational?

"Look Jess, I can see you're not fine. It was important and I will explain, but not now. Now, I want us to do what we do best and have fun"

Silently, I stared and willed him to be more forthcoming. I didn't want to be nosy, or pushy, but I got this feeling he was holding back on me.

That letter I thought. *Why was I so paranoid?*

"More important than meeting your fiancé?" I anxiously snapped. And then like some nagging fish-wife I asked, "Where were you exactly?". I knew by the tone of my voice and the look on his face that I was behaving a little 'unhinged'.

He drew a blank face "Just attending to some business like I said. It's boring band stuff. To be honest I'm drained by it and don't feel like sharing at the minute. I just want you and pure escapism." I could tell his usual warmth was masked by something else. *Was I losing him?*

I sceptically rolled my eyes. 'Why so evasive, you got something to hide?'

What the hell was up with me? I might have not had much experience with men and fiancés, but I knew I needed to cool it. I was pushing for an argument.

His usually calm, beautiful face darkened. "Errrm, where did that come from? I said I was sorry, and I've explained how I feel. Lay off it please. Don't spoil this. Trust Jessie. You need to learn some if we are going to do this."

Shit. He was right, newly engaged, with no ring, was no way to have our first argument. I felt so desperate. I could feel the security I had wrapped myself up in was precariously in the balance. The thing was, I didn't know if it was my paranoia or his laidback attitude that was worse. Maybe I did need to learn how to trust. After all, my only point of reference of relationships until now was how unreliable and disruptive they could be.

What was I doing pushing it? I really did not want to become one of 'those' women.

"Jessie, it was just business. Anyway, being possessive doesn't suit my wife to be.' He laughed.

I could tell he was trying to ease the unfamiliar tension between us. He was right, I needed to work on my trust issues. And I was back in the room. The here and now, and we were together – living for the moment. Smiling broadly, I took his hand across the table and stroked his palm. His warm and intense grin stared back at me. The green pools becoming darker with desire. His other hand trapped mine, like an oyster within its shell.

"I'm sorry, I am being silly. I was missing you and I've had a long shift. I'm not getting much sleep you know" He laughed again. More warmly and knowingly this time.

I exhaled a long breath and smiled. I wanted to ease things. "You know that, well you've said it yourself, that we wish that we could be together all day, every day. I guess I'm learning that I'm not that patient!" I laughed now at my honesty and bravery – where had the quiet and hard-faced girl from Leeds gone?

"Even when we are married, we will still have to work, live, spend time apart. But you're right, not like this!"

"I love you"

"And I love you too. Like you wouldn't believe. I've never felt like this..." and he looked deep into my eyes. That same penetrating gaze I'd felt on that first encounter. It was like a magnet drawing me in. My whole body fizzed and responded.

"Now then, I'm hungry for food and for you...and not necessarily in that order"

My goodness he had a one-track mind.

"I've an idea anyway. It's hot tonight isn't it?"

"Hotter than it has been yes. Spiros said it will be hotter still by the weekend."

"Well, with your lack of sleep and evident tension, I think you need cooling off. Fancy a skinny-dip?"

"Not here and what about food?" I did actually but I was being practical, and I didn't want Maria or her father to see me on the beach being brazen and naked. I'd never be able to face them again.

"Of course, not here! Privacy is needed. I know a little cove down the coast. We can go on my moped and we can grab a souvlaki take-out on the way. Light a fire? Take blankets? Not that it's cold.... It just makes it – "

"More romantic. That's you Mr Romantic." And he wondered why I wanted to be with him every second? He was my dream man.

Minutes later the moped was packed, and we sped off into the sultry night. We didn't sleep fully, just dozed under a blanket of stars. We stayed until sunrise and yet another perfect memory was filed in my inner library labelled 'Corfu 1996'.

TORN

Corfu 1996
The Next Morning

After sunrise we made our way back to my apartment. I needed some sort of sleep so I could face a shift at the taverna. I awoke later to the unwelcome blaring of my alarm clock and to find him gone. However, he had left me a lovely note promising dinner later that evening and a trip to Corfu town on my day off – signed *The Love of Your Life*. The bunny-boiler side of my brain was taunting me with theories to where he had gone, as he hadn't mentioned having to be anywhere. Whereas, my chilled and sensible side was placating me with the knowledge that he did have a life away from me. Plus, a man who was up-to-no-good, would not be leaving notes with promises of dinner and day trips (I was seriously hoping that the trip might be a for ring).

So, with a steel resolution, I opened my shutters onto the brilliant blue bay and soaked up the glorious view. It never did get old. I wrapped myself in these lucky thoughts as I prepared to get ready for the day shift in the taverna.

Maria was on form. Bouncing around the place singing and grinning. I had no idea where she got all her energy from. I was dead on my feet. Spiros was preparing the coffee as I went in. Music blaring loudly from the speakers. The beat was too deep for the likes of our customers. Her father, Spiros, who had a face like thunder, strode into the table area where Maria was dancing and shouted.

"Maria! What have I told you!"

'Good God', I thought! I'd warned her but when she had it on her Maria could be so bullish and loud.

"Papa! What do you know! This is music, this is life."

"It is noise Maria. We are not Kavos and our customers don't need their...what are the ear instruments called Jessie?"

Oh god, he was dragging me into it!

"Ear drums"

"That is it Maria, you will destroy their eardrums!"

Maria rolled her eyes and smiled at me

"That'll be us tonight Jessie! Banging our eardrums at the full moon beach party"

Shit, I'd forgotten. I was knackered.

My face must have told her something and she began to look at me with those piecing dark eyes of hers.

"Jessie, you know you promised. Last week. I bought the tickets and..."

"Yes, I am sorry, but I forgot. I am meant to be meeting–ʺ

She cut me off, the palm of her hand raised towards me. There was no point arguing with her. She had such a fiery temper and that was one of the reasons I loved her. She was so protective and passionate about everything. I didn't know until I'd arrived in Corfu, but I had needed that.

"I know, I bet you have forgotten, and you are meeting your sexy guitarist fiancé! Is this how it is going to be now?"

ʺerr, no! I'm sorry. I really am. I will make it up to you" She turned away and shrugged her shoulders. I knew this wasn't over yet. She was playing the long game and I had to play it too – all day!

We spent the rest of the day ignoring each other (well she did, I kept leaving messages of I'm sorry on her order pad. And I even wrote it in chocolate sauce on some pancakes and ice cream I'd made her for our afternoon snack). She was having none of it though and when her shift ended, she shot off home on her moped without a word.

I'd upset my best friend. She'd been there for me since day one of us meeting. I felt so guilty.

FORGIVEN

BEFORE THEN
Jessie

Corfu 1996
Later That Day

The perfect turquoise waters had begun to darken, as the sun melted into the Ionian's inky depths. Yet another sunset. Yet another day living the dream. I really did have to pinch myself that I was living in this paradise. Me, a job, a small apartment – would all look but reasonably doable back in Leeds. However, with the added bonus of living and breathing this scenery every day and having the most gorgeous fiancé on the island, well, I wouldn't have managed that in Leeds.

Guilt was niggling though. First upsetting Maria and then I had called Mam earlier; she sounded quiet and distant. I knew I'd upset her by leaving for the summer, but she'd practically forced me to take a chance 'before I got tied to something else'. She was petrified of me becoming her. Struggling and scraping some sort of living, whilst the dull grey city world just kept moving without her. She'd once had dreams – I was sure of it. She wasn't stupid and I knew she was all set for college before she met our dad. Now she was tied to him and all that came with him. Maybe she felt bitter towards me? Maybe my news and excitement had been a step too far? Our lives – one in monochrome, the other a brilliant kaleidoscope of colourful possibilities. Maybe she'd had a bad day? She would never tell me if dad had been up to no good or if one of the others had caused her grief. I knew what she had sacrificed so I could be here. Maybe she was regretting it?

Maria's moped pulled up beside the taverna. She was all Denim shorts and neon crop-top.

Spiros will have a fit!

Her barely-there appearance would undoubtedly cause our customers to raise an eyebrow or two. She looked up at the balcony at me and gave me a small wave.

Forgiven then?

"Come up" I smiled. "I'm sure we've got time for a drink!". She ran straight up the side stairs grinning and I knew I was forgiven.

"I'm glad you said that Jessie. You have been so distant with me lately. Too busy – and I am not, what you say, bunny boiler. I just miss our crazy nights out! Me and my crazy British friend"

"Me crazy", I giggled "Jesus Maria, you are where that term came from!"

"Yes well. I miss you. Where is he anyway?"

"He isn't here yet. He should be here soon though. Why don't we have some of this ouzo whilst I wait for him and you wait for your lift to the beach party?"

"Excellent ideas" and we clinked our ouzo.

"*Yammas!*" we cheered.

It was like the old days (well six weeks ago). We laughed, we drank. Maria told me ridiculous stories about growing up in a large Greek family. They'd never had anything either. They'd grown up being grateful and helping each other. Not turning their backs on each other and raising hell on every path which they made. There was simply pure love. You only had to look at the way Spiros treated Maria – even when she had pushed it too far. There was always a warmth in his eyes that I could never remember seeing in my own father's.

"You are lucky you know. To have found someone so young!

I can never imagine finding a man who looks at me like Papa looked at Mama"

"It must make you sad. What do you remember? Or do you mind me asking? Don't answer if it is too painful" I checked her expression.

"No, not painful, I like to talk about her. Papa doesn't always want to. I have to get him in the right mood. My siblings too. As I am the youngest, they all remember more than me. Had her for longer"

"He always buy Mama flowers! Even now, every week he takes them to the cemetery. He keeps her flame burning without fail – even when he had the flu last winter." She looked wistful and I could see her eyes were a little glassy. "He would always be surprising her with little gifts. And there was always laughter and dancing. We were happy"

"You're happy now, aren't you? Yes, but it is different happy. There can be a shadow..."

"It must be hard to have had a love like that and for it then to be lost?"

"Yes, and it is a lot to live up to. Finding a man with that level of passion for his wife. He used to look at her like she was a goddess" She said rolling her eyes to the heavens. "This is a tall order no? To find such admiration. Is that the right word?"

"Adoration maybe? Adoring somebody and putting them on a pedestal. That's a little how I feel" (well a lot but I didn't want to compare my short relationship to what Maria's parents had had)

Her eyes cleared with the slight shift in subject.

"Do you think you've found him though? You are still young"

"I think so. He certainly says all the right things"

"And does them I bet!"

I started to go red and was glad of the evening glow. However, I was glad of the lightness of the conversation. It had been getting very serious and that would not do.

"Where is the sexy guitarist anyway?"

I looked at my watch and realised I'd been sitting on the balcony for an hour and a half.

"Late. That's where he is!" I noticed that an edge had come back to my voice.

All those feelings of guilt from earlier began to dissipate and were replaced with my old friends: jealousy and insecurity.

"Where was so important that you blew me out anyway?"

"Just dinner."

"Dinner? Pah! You are in you prime Jessie, you can eat for the rest of your life."

"I know, but, oh you wouldn't understand..." *What a shit excuse.*

"What? That you want to spend time with your sexy guitarist, and he has stood you up!" She was laughing at me and a sharpness to her tone told me that I wasn't completely forgiven after all.

"Stop calling him that and he has not stood me up! He will be busy with band business." (Even I didn't believe that line). But I couldn't be disloyal – especially after all we'd discussed last night about trust.

"Pffft! Band business, when his hot fiancé is already here looking gorgeous and ready to go out. I will take you instead. Not to dinner though, that would be silly. We can grab a gyros from downstairs – Papa will insist and then we will get the lift to the beach."

"What about..."

"We shall leave Noel Gallagher, or whatever he thinks he is, a note. He can find you at the party. You should keep him on his toes!"

She was right but I felt I needed to defend him anyway, "Why are you being so mean about him?"

"Because he stand up my gorgeous best British friend and that I do not like. Would Papa have stood Mama up? No! Jessie, it is like I said, I am doomed. Who will ever look at me like he looked at her?"

"It's fine. I'm sure it's fine and I know you worry but please don't. You're right though, I'm too young to be sitting here like a fisherman's wife waiting for him to come back from sea. We'll leave him a note and it'll serve him right for being late again!" She was right and I really needed to grow back that northern backbone.

"Again? The *Malakas!* He has done this before? This is all the more reason why you need to show him who is boss."

PARADISE LOST

BEFORE THEN
Jessie

Corfu 1996
The Morning After

"Ouch Maria, my feet are killing me!" we were hobbling towards my apartment in our highly inappropriate shoes. In Leeds I'd have taken them off, being barefoot in Greece is shameful – they think you have no money! When I'd first suggested it, Maria had gasped and told me that her *Yiayia* would never speak to us again. So, with our feet close to bleeding, and leaning on each other, we made our way slowly down the promenade. We were still dressed in our beach party wear. Both in denim hot-pants and crop tops – very little clothing was seen as less shameful in Greece apparently, although, I wasn't sure what her *Yiayia* would say about this.

Maria stopped and took a breath.

"Look Jessie, isn't it beautiful?" Maria was grinning and had her arms extended out towards to sea, the beach and the mountains. "I never forget how lucky we are. This beauty, it is like paradise, no?" She looked at home and that made me feel at home. It felt so good to feel part of something. I couldn't ever remember feeling happy at being part of something. Never fitting in as I had no money, wasn't dysfunctional, because I wouldn't conform to the state norm. I'd always felt odd. Coming here had changed all that.

I thought about the scenery back home. The grey tower blocks. The lack of colour. "Oh yes, not like where I come from – Leeds. Yorkshire might be what they call God's own country, but it can be very grey, very cold and very depressing at times. I can't imagine anyone getting depressed living here"

"No? in winter it rains, rains and rains. Do not be fooled Jessie!"

We stopped and looked out over the mountains. The sky a sizzling cool blue, melted into the lush green peaks which peppered them. The sun was rising over the tops, casting lengthy shadows onto the bay. The heat was already in the air; even in the shade. Spiros had been correct, it was getting hotter.

"Well, it looks pretty good to me! We might have the beautiful, rugged, rolling moors but it's cold up the top of Ilkley Moor – well for about most of the year! You are lucky". I meant it. I'd take all that rain any day over going home."

"Do not talk about leaving me! It feels like we have so much fun to have and you are my sidekick no? Anyway, you know we get snow in the winter?" she raised her eyebrows. "Anyway, the sun is rising and that means we are to work soon! We best shower at yours and get ready before Papa arrives at the taverna"

"Oh Maria, I'm between knackered and thrilled! What a night! I am so glad that you persuaded me to go. And I hope he does feel guilty for standing me up. His loss; he missed out on the best night"

She raised her eyebrows "Knackered?"

I laughed "Tired. Well more than - exhausted" I clarified.

At that moment I didn't care he'd not turned up. Maybe it was the ouzo, but Maria had been right, I was being too subservient! In a matter of weeks, I'd dropped the carefree persona I'd picked up partying with Maria at the beginning of the season. Instead I'd turned into a Stepford-Wife waiting for her husband to come home every day. The nineteen-year-old me was secretly cringing. Somewhere between our fourth and fifth ouzo, I'd decided to live it up like there was no tomorrow. Bravado. Trust? I needed real commitment, not promises. I'd tell him when he eventually turned up that he needed to step up and show me some respect.

It's amazing what ouzo could make you feel like

As the sun rose, such bravado was beginning to wear off – good job as we had a shift to do at the taverna. I doubted Spiros would be happy with us breathing fumes over our customers whilst they ate their breakfasts and lunchtime gyros.

But the beach party had been worth it. Revelations, revelry, and the tribal rhythm mixed by the DJs. The atmosphere had been on fire. The music had been pumping and the energy was electric! It took me back to when I first came out to Corfu and Maria and I went to all the opening parties around the island. Only this had been better. I felt like I belonged. That I was part of the community – not just a tourist there for a week. We danced and partied, and I met so many people. I felt so free and young.

"Yes, well, I am not often wrong" she grinned. "I am also not wrong about Papa, he will be thinking we were with boys and drinking all night"

"Well you were!"

Maria raised her eyebrows again at me, "And you weren't?"

I must have coloured because Maria laughed "Do not worry, I will not tell your sexy guitarist. He deserves a bit of payback"

"You don't think that's where he was do you? And I did nothing wrong!" I really hadn't but I still felt the dread creeping in. It had been a perfect and wild night. I felt guilty for behaving with such freedom, when I had a fiancé waiting for me. But where had he been?

"Stop worrying! I pull your leg – as you say in England. All is good and what happens at the Full Moon Beach Party, stays at the..."

"Maria, nothing happened! Just because you were off with Maximus – "

"Maxi! He is not a arse unlike your..."

"Stop! Enough!" I was tired and all this ribbing was getting too much. It fed the fear and I wanted to minimise the all-nighter comedown guilt as much as possible.

A sweaty Maria must have sensed my unease and came in for a hug. If I smelt as bed as she did then we definitely needed to sort out our hygiene before opening. She apologised and she agreed to me being first in the shower. We were filthy after hours of dancing.

"Oh Jessie, I am knackered and thrilled also!" She giggled.

As we approached my apartment, Maria had a sharp intake of breath. "*Skata!* Papa is there. His car is outside. He will see us, and we will be killed and locked in the cellar"

"Well if he kills us, the cellar won't matter will it! Anyway, he is your Papa, not mine"

She laughed dryly "You think this matters?"

She had a point. My stomach dropped and we agreed to sneak around the side and to the staircase up to my rooms. Although, as we got to the foot of my stairs there was a "*Koritsia! Ella*"

Maria pulled a face. "He's heard us, we can't run"

We went to face our execution

PART THREE

I THEE WED

THE BACKPACKER

BEFORE THEN
Aimee

Thailand
New Year's Eve 1999

"Jump!"

"...I can't" I squealed looking down fearfully at the sheer drop.

"Why?"

Like he didn't know! I rolled my eyes.

"I know you can. I've seen how brave you are lass. All that sass with the locals, and you busting them down from all that haggling they do! That girl is scared of nothing!"

"That's different" I laughed nervously. "That girl' says no to tat that 'she' doesn't need. She also doesn't need to jump off a what? 40ft cliff face. They are two different things entirely!"

"She still says strong. She still says brave"

Forty feet up, that 'brave' girl's knees were buckling and betraying... I wobbled and began to feel dizzy.

"...It's so high." My lack of balance illustrating my point. He grabbed me and steadied my position.

"Breathe Aims. You're nowhere near the edge." I reflected at my predicament, looking down at the calm turquoise waters below us.

Inviting and perfect they might be. Safe? Who knows?

I had to focus. I cast my gaze back up to the picture postcard dream shot in front of me. The white sandy bay opposite sat like icing on a Christmas tree jungle. *Who knew what lurked in there?*

Beauty can be skin deep, I thought. *This is what facing your fears does to you, it makes you paranoid.*

"Idyllic isn't it? This really is paradise. I can see why Alex Garland wrote that book though. Who knows what lies beneath any of this beauty? It's an Eden, and we know how that turned out don't we?"

"You wanted adventure. Hedonism. The Aimee I've got to know would love this adrenaline fuelled trip"

"Stop talking about me like I'm not here!"

"Eejit! Take'n a hold of yourself and submit. You know you want to"

He was right. It was the phone call's earlier fault, tinged by a slight hangover from last night. 'The Fear' was creeping in and spoiling my equilibrium. I'd let home invade my new world. I needed to forget that and put my focus elsewhere. I pushed away my feelings into my 'when it's time to go home suitcase'.

"I'm glad we moved on from Haad Rin, it wasn't what I wanted – too full on." I took in the unspoilt horizon "Brash. I didn't want to paint it. It didn't feel real. I felt I didn't see the real Thailand"

"Well yeah. But Jesus, forget about recording it; this isn't about your art A, this is about living. The here and now, you and me!"

"Maybe...I loved Bangkok though and that was full on. It was different though"

"Enough of the analysing!" He widened his arms like he was embracing the landscape. "Yeah, but now you have me here to liven things up!"

"Ha! It was pretty dramatic enough without you" I scanned the drop again. It wasn't getting any scarier. "Anyway, it's petrifying - taking the plunge."

"Taking a big step is always scary." He looked away, thought for a second and turned back with a strange look on his face "Tell you what, you trust me don't you?"

"As much as you can trust someone after knowing them,

what...?"

"Three weeks..."

"I'd say nearer two!"

"All my life it feels like Aims. But you do trust me, don't you? Think about it this way, if we jump together, hands tightly held...we are in it together. Forever bonded."

"You are such a bloody Irish romantic fool! It's also a bit of a deep and meaningful, to get me to free fall off this cliff face!"

"I mean it A. If you can trust me to hold your hand through this, I promise to hold it for the rest of our lives."

Whooh, slow down there...! My stomach flipped 360. My mouth dropped open. *What the...? Was he talking about a commitment?* My face must have spoken a thousand words as he broke into a huge heart stopping grin

"I mean it A. I've never felt this way before. You've totally swept me away with your balls, bravery and beauty. Let's do this as a symbol of our future lives. Let's not waste time. Fate brought us together on that beach three weeks ago"

"Two!"

A bit farfetched, I thought, but he was onto something. I knew he was different. We were different. From the moment he'd bounded into my life...

"A symbol of our future?"

"Yeah, a new millennium begins tomorrow. Why not plan to start a brilliant new life together?" His eyes were wild. The sun was catching flecks of green and gold and making them sparkle mischievously. "Frank and Aimee's excellent adventure!" The Irish eyes promised a future of lucky leprechauns and pots of gold.

Those eyes could cause trouble. I could get lost in those eyes.

He grabbed hold of me and kissed me deeply and passionately. Something I couldn't argue with or question.

His kiss ensnared me. I didn't really care – *is this what it would feel like forever?*

The movie reel of how-ever-many-days-and-weeks flickered vibrantly with memories. An instant attraction had drawn us together – was it only two weeks ago? And although I knew he was full of it, I couldn't resist him. I loved the way he made me feel; he had so much energy. After weeks of trauma, loneliness and caution, after an hour in his company, I had felt my edges soften. And he was working that same magic on my nerves now.

Maybe he was right? After all, you could know someone all your life and they could let you down.

After a few minutes, he broke off and grinned infectiously at me. "You can't argue with that can you? Chemistry!" he shouted, "But hey, best be careful, after that kiss, I might skip this jump, and take you somewhere else!"

I laughed. His infectious enthusiasm overcame me. He was right, I did feel less tense (anyone would after a kiss like that). But as much as I wanted to succumb to his Celtic charms, I was a strong nineties woman. I was determined that he wasn't going to have it all his way. And as appealing going somewhere else was, this was something I was secretly determined to do.

Maybe I could have it all?

"Aimee and Frank's excellent adventure."

"Really?" He laughed "Whatever you want gorgeous. But what I want right now - apart from the obvious, is for us to jump, hand in hand, together, into the depths of those crystal clear, endless turquoise waters below. What do you say?"

I thought about the life I'd left behind and the life which I'd dreamt of for as long as I could remember. Nothing is certain and being careful only ever got people to a destination of choice. There was no thrill of the journey. I had no idea what I was agreeing to at that moment. But, one thing I did know was this: I wanted something new, brave and exciting to happen to me.

"Okay. On one condition..."

******

"One, two, three..."

We leapt out gripping our hands tightly together. The air whizzed past is as we fell like kingfishers swooping down into the water (where in reality, we probably looked like two dead weights). The sky around us seemed endless. Time appeared to stop as the seconds suspended us in mid-air. Whilst, in actual reality, the g-force pulled us rapidly towards the sea and into its sparkling depths. Initially my nerves were still on the edge of that effing cliff, playing catch-up. However, sick with exhilaration and wonder, I looked out into the bay opposite. The hot white sands looked about 400 metres away – an easy swim. Free-falling, I focused on that and him. He was right... I gripped Frank's hand and realised that this was what living was. I pushed the nerves away and began to scream with the thrill of it. It was like I'd learnt a new language.

And just like that, after the rush, we entered the translucent water. Our bodies were pulled towards the seabed; pulling us down like magnets into its mysterious vaults. The water becoming darker as we plunged to its depths. Fear of being sucked away made me look up and I could see the brilliant sunshine piercing the surface. And just as the warm shallows cooled us from the intense midday heat, the further we plunged, the cooler water woke me up and cleared my Fear from my head. And just when I thought we would never rise up again, we stopped: unclamped hands, and broke for independent freedom. Kicking madly and swimming quickly, to fight our way up to break the surface. Me first. Frank second.

We'd made it!

All that fear and worry. All I could feel were the endorphins whizzing around my body.

"Wow," I exclaimed breathlessly. "That was something!" Laughter was bubbling up from the sheer adrenaline.

Frank gasped to catch his breath.

"I told you that you could trust me." He grinned, pulling me towards him. "Fancy a lifetime of this?" His laughter matching mine.

And at that moment, I did.

"Now need to keep your end of the bargain"

*****

That was it. New Year's Eve 1999. Whilst most people were watching fireworks, partying and singing *Old Lang Syne*, Frank and I were two bodies entwined passionately, on the purest sandy beach; 400 metres from where he promised to make our lives an adventure. The condition had been a promise: a night to match the thrill of the fall.

The new millennium: New Year's Eve 1999 was the beginning of everything. I've never lost that memory. It's immortalised, like a giant snow globe within my mind; sometimes I shake it to see it in all its glory. The very best of times. The rightness of our lives coming together. The feelings of love, lust and optimism for a new chapter. A magic that couldn't be explained. All set to a backdrop of hedonistic wonder and beauty.

It was like someone had walked up to me and said:

Happy Millennium! Today is the first day of the rest of your life!

The fuckers.

REWIND PART ONE
Aimee's Journey
Thailand
December 1999

Walking into that bar, two weeks previously, I'd felt a little lost. It was all right Frank saying that I was brave. I was bloody petrified. He didn't know how shell-shocked and bruised I felt.

Back in the depths of November: when the days were becoming shorter, darker and colder, I'd flown out to Asia with my friend Ellie. Not my best-friend mind you, but someone I thought I'd known long enough to join me in my escapism. Mistake Number One: She very quickly turned my trip of a lifetime, into a trip of nightmares – that would enable my mother to say, '*I told you so*'. Somebody else who would be siding with 'The Mother' (highly unusually) would have been my bestie Jenna (I really should have listened to her, but I wouldn't have it.) Who, as my luck was beginning to show, was stuck in England and couldn't fly out until after New Year.

The thing was, I'd been desperate to get away from the winter and finding a job which would 'fulfil me'. My parents had been trying to push me into this awful gallery job and I just couldn't do it. It was just so mundane, and well, if I was honest 'at home'. Finding myself living in my home town near the parents didn't cut it. I'd studied at The Royal College. My final show had been critically acclaimed, and I'd had some initial success. And then it stopped. Not the success, just my inspiration. I felt a nothingness, a void. Like a writer's block. Then, with nothing came nothing. The job was suggested, but I knew if I took it that I would just get stuck, and I would never be an artist – my dreams in dust like all the old shite in the back of the gallery. That old cliché of 'needing to find myself' was true – if I ever wanted the success I'd once craved and seen glimpses of. Also, I was desperate for freedom and hedonism. So was Jenna, but she couldn't come and join me until the New Year

Luckily (as I stupidly thought at the time) our other friend Ellie was up for it. After all, she was the one who pushed me to keep going when my parents kept trying to wear me down; filling my head with stories of backpacking doom. She said she also wanted escapism and wild nights on the best party beaches Asia had to offer (if the truth be told, I was slightly worried that she'd burn me out). She was also a woman on a mission, as she had just broken up with her boyfriend (whom she'd had since school). What was young loves loss, was Asia's gain!

We decided to start in Thailand. Like everyone, we'd read 'The Beach'. The backpackers' dystopian tale of what happens when you find utopia. It was to be first on our list. We discussed Laos, Vietnam, Nepal, Singapore...well, we just discussed them. We didn't want to tie ourselves down to an itinerary. So, on mutual agreement, we bought our flights to Bangkok and spent our remaining time kitting ourselves out and selling our cars 'for extra funds'.

All I can remember of those planning days was our intense excitement. We thought we were so invincible and cool.

However, it didn't quite work out. We flew into Bangkok, we found a hostel, had a bit of a wild night eating street food and mixing with the throngs of travellers, and then she disappeared for ten minutes. I say disappeared, but what I actually mean to say is: she went off on the pretext of calling home when in actual fact she stupidly called the ex-boyfriend who told her he still loved her, but she'd disappointed him with her recklessness and lack of direction in life. *'What were you thinking of running away to Thailand like that?'* He told her that he had instead found someone with similar goals, and they were looking at saving a deposit on a house.

"Two months Aims. Two fucking months!" she sobbed. Snot pouring out of her pretty little nose. *His loss* I thought. She could always do better.

I agreed that he hadn't let the grass grow...

"But look at us Ells! We are free and living it up in Asia. No one cares what we do! He is the loser in this story. You were always too good for him."

She frowned.

Oh, we aren't at that stage yet then - I realised I'd crossed the do-not-diss-my-boyfriend-line, too early. It was meant to sound supportive and make her remember what we were doing there. The tears which I had suspected had been threatening to fall, came gushing out with snot and all. We went back to the hostel and she refused to leave her bed for nearly a week.

*****

That first lonely week in Thailand I learnt two things about myself:

I was a survivor.

I had NO bedside manner AT ALL.

Being alone in a strange city, I felt exposed. Especially being a woman in a strange Asian country, it did nothing but feed into my parents' negativity. I felt like some spoilt rich girl who had stumbled off the path of milk and honey. It wasn't difficult to feel like that as I was experiencing something new. Whereas, I was used to London with its bustling life and Britishness. Where, even in the depths of China town, you couldn't fail to sense the underlying sense of tradition around every corner: Sunday dinner, apple pie and a fine ruby port for dessert. London, in all its cosmopolitan colours, was quintessentially English. Bangkok, in comparison, was like falling into a giant vat of Asian noodle soup – a spicy broth comprising of a million flavours and textures, which would either kill or cure you. I found it excitingly and tantalisingly scary.

Khao San Road was backpacker central. Thousands of disparate bodies swarmed like flies every day and being alone I felt not only anonymous but isolated too. It was a strange feeling to have when there were so many moving in different directions at once. You couldn't rest for a second and I spent most of my time on my guard. Bodies would knock you. Hawkers would grab you and try to thrust cheap knock-offs into your hands. Thailand is a hot country; even more so in the humidity trapped between the buildings which made up the road. After my first day of sourcing us more food and finding the lay of the land, I was ready to move on.

Unfortunately, whether it was due to the oppressive smog and heat, or because of that heartless wanker back in England, Ellie got sick. She couldn't leave our shared room for nearly a week. Admittedly, she didn't look well, and she had been sick. However, I'm not sure that being holed up in a tiny poorly air-conditioned space and nibbling on bits of street food that I ferried back to her, helped either. And the fact that she was still writing long and dreary letters to her 'Gary', meant my sympathy was in short supply.

It was meant to be our thrill of a lifetime and three days in I was caring for a melancholic recluse who was refusing to be coaxed out of our tiny pit-of-a-room. I was pissed off. My patience was wearing thin and even as I waved fake designer gear in front of her nose (she was a label junkie), like tiny crumbs, to lead her out of the room, she just wasn't bothered.

There was nothing for it but to do Bangkok alone and gear us up for leg two of the Thai tour. After all, after looking at all the amazing images at the ticket office, I couldn't imagine anyone not wanting to be out under those skies and on those white sandy stretches of beach. I was also desperate to head to the full moon beach party in Koh Pa Ngan. So, I braved it up and ballsed it out. I made friends with some other travellers in the hostel, and I tried to pack in as much as possible, whilst Ellie festered away in her self-imposed isolation. We did temples, partied hard in some questionable bars, and ate even more questionable foods – deep fried insects and creatures, did it all…in typical cafes. As vibrant as Bangkok was, I'd had enough by the end of the first week. I laid out options from the Lonely Planet: She wouldn't go trekking up at Chaing Mai – it was too much, and she'd never manage. She didn't want to stay in Bangkok, and she didn't want to leave Thailand yet (she'd seen nothing). So, I booked us onto the night train to the south, and I egged Ells on that it would make her feel better. After dragging, a very pale, Ellie to the train. We embarked on our next leg.

Koh Pha Ngan was everything Bangkok wasn't, but everything it was too. The vibrancy, craziness and culture, were all there but set to a backdrop of brilliant blue skies and sandy white coves. It had a heighted and mysterious quality, that captured the imagination. The beauty of the place threatened, with a sense of an undercurrent running beneath the paradisiacal scenery. Thailand was perfect; too perfect. Our days were spent exploring and soaking up the atmosphere of the disparate people coming together at some mass place of worship. Ells was good company at first, but after a couple of parties, she holed herself up again in her bungalow (I'd insisted on separate ones after all the shit in Bangkok). *Here we go again!* I remember thinking. However, it wasn't that.

She emerged one day, at the end of our third week since leaving England and introduced me to Kurt. Who, she promptly jumped ship with to the 'unmanageable' Chaing Mai; with swift apologies and promises that she'd catch up with me soon. Yeah, I was half-heartedly invited. Yeah, I could come back...*not for me* I thought, I was a survivor now and no third wheel. I happily stayed put where I was. I might have been angry but there were worse places to be abandoned.

Have you ever been deserted on a beach in Thailand? Well, it is a double-edged sword. I remember awakening that first morning – all alone - and wondering what I was going to do. Then I realised, I could suit myself. What did I want to do? It was early December and I really did like the vibes around the place. It was quite busy and due to being a single white female, I thought it was best not to go searching for that 'utopian beach'. The parties were good; and I had tentatively started to make some friends. I decided to stay put for a while – well at least until Jenna arrived. Therefore, step one on my list was to stay. I was going to unfurl from my westernised ways and become one with nature and the sea.

Step two was to get a routine. I'd never been laid back and couldn't really sit still for long. I was going to explore, socialise and build painting into my everyday routine. Since leaving England, I'd only taken some pictures and done the odd sketch since arriving and that felt like a crying shame. I'd been so busy pleasing and looking after Ellie, that I had lost the point of who I was and why I was travelling.

I spent long idyllic days alternating between eating, swimming, sketching, painting etc. and meeting passers-by. By night I would party with the best of them. Most people I went out with were staying around my beach bungalow. They'd see me working and come over to see what I was doing. Striking up conversations about what I am seeing. I became quite a minor celebrity in those days of 'enlightenment' as I like to call them now. My interpretations of my life. Some real. Some more abstract. I experimented with colour and form, and my style began to go into a new direction. I began to look differently at what was around me. The detritus from the sea was anything but and I started to play around with shells and drift wood. Looking at how I could make it into something to wear, or to decorate a space. I found customers who wanted to buy my art. I made friends who admired and critiqued it too. *This was what I came to Thailand for – fuck Ellie.*

One such friend, a Spanish girl called Beatrice, convinced me that my 'new direction' was saleable to the masses. She put herself in charge of marketing and within a short space of time, she was trading my 'work' on the market. I'd make wind chime style structures, jewellery and personalised postcards – my independence knew no bounds. I was loving life.

Another success was the way my colour work was developing. In a certain light, the sea could look like glass and the white sand would melt into it. Hours snorkelling revealed the technicolour coral reefs, which surrounded the islands. These glorious sights had to be captured in a different way. I looked at my sketches and figured I could begin to layer colours and treat the paintings like stained glass. A sort of cross between

Batik style and Picasso. Sort of like Chris Offilli with the elephant dung. Another lesson learnt in Thailand: to be free and run with it.

And after nearly a month, I felt like I had finally arrived.

It was then I met Frank.

REWIND PART TWO
When Aimee Met Frank
December 1999

At first, I barely noticed him. Not that he was easy to miss with his dark Celtic looks and swagger. It was just that I was so caught up in being creative that I just didn't 'see him'. As I said, people often stopped to talk to me. So, when this neon painted man approached me at Haad Rin beach one night, I was bowled over. He seemed to know all about me, and I knew nothing about him.

Bea had noticed him watching me. Don't get me wrong, neither of us were particularly alert to any weirdness. We had a radar for that (you had to as a single woman travelling – we stuck together) and he didn't give us 'any of those vibes'. He was drinking a beer and staring straight at me. Once I locked eyes with him, he flashed back with the warmest and most captivating smile I had ever been under the spotlight from. I know it sounds mad (and sickeningly corny) That moment something in me shifted and I felt like I'd known him forever. My brain flickered like a picture reel, and even though I can say it with hindsight, I saw our whole future together flickering past me as he held my gaze.

At first, we didn't speak. He came over and held out his hand to me. I took it and we started to dance. The beat was deep and trancey and we were soon in some sort of rhythmic mating dance. Even now, when I look back at that night, I remember the intense energy that fizzed between us. Ridiculous as we looked – painted in neon, we worshipped the beats and each other until the sun began to rise and uncover the mysteries from the night before.

The sun burst onto its stage as we began to tire. Neither of us wanted to end whatever had happened in the depths of the party, so we moved over into the shade and made introductions. Bizarre isn't it? We didn't know anything about each other (well I knew nothing about him) but yet we had 'come together' at a party at its height of hedonism. Further proof that Thailand was the right thing for me and my journey.

As the morning heat intensified, we laid sheltered beneath the cooling fronds of the palm trees. Frank explained he'd been watching me for days. He described the painting I was currently working on in intense detail and blew me away with his understanding. I should have felt spooked, but he wasn't like that – all weird and stuff – he was thoughtful and had a calmness about him.

"Are you an artist too? Your understanding is mad"

"No, but I get art. I am an artist as such though – I'm a musician in a band"

"Oh, so you must get it - about feeling, tone and depth?" *A soul mate maybe?* I was getting a bit deep from lack of sleep.

He nodded through my understanding. "Yeah, just like you see it and try to recreate it through your mediums, I try to capture the same stuff through beats and sometimes I write the words too"

This intrigued me. I'd met so many 'artists' at college and none of them seemed to have the depth that I craved. Or, if they did, they were too bloody serious and bored me to death. Frank did not bore me – far from it and the fact that he was gorgeous was a massive plus too!

"Who are you though? You seem to know a lot about me, but I know nothing about you!"

"What do you mean?" he questioned coyly.

"Well you've seen my work! I have never heard yours"

"Well, you might have done...well more in Oz than anywhere else"

"Really? Try me, I like me music"

"The Helios Kings"

"Oh god, I know them! They were playing some of their music in Bangkok on some of the bootleg stalls. I must admit, they aren't on my radar in England, but I liked what I heard at the stall"

He laughed "How do you know it was me? It might have

been some dodgy band pretending to be us! Thank you though, we are yet to chart anywhere else"

I laughed and playfully punched him on the arm "Ouch Aimee, are you always this rough on a first date?"

"Is that what this is?"

Wow, bloody hell. What am I getting myself into here?

"Yes. If you want it to be. I know I do" Those bloody eyes were drawing me in. Of course, I wanted it to be...I deflected to keep him thinking. One thing I wasn't was a push over.

"Oz?"

"Huh, oh yeah! That's where we got a contract. We went out there in 1996. We toured, got picked up and released an album. I co-wrote it with the lead singer 'Gene'. Some success meant we were sent to the old US of A – hated it, but it taught us some valuable lessons – we were a bit cocky after the success in Oz."

Bonafede rock star then! "An album, cool. And what do you do...apart from the writing?"

Play it cool girl. He's an Australian rock God – well Irish!

"Guitar. To be honest, I prefer to write the instrumentals than the lyrics, but hey, it's all part of the process" He pulled me back into the sand and laid down next to me.

"Enough about me. We've danced all night, told each other our back stories, read the album sleeves, and now we need to see if it works"

"What works?"

"You've still not answered my question you beautiful English water nymph. Is this a first date?"

He called me beautiful "Yes" I managed to croak – either through lack of sleep or nervousness.

"Then come here and let's see if that chemistry is as intense as I think it might be."

I DO

Thailand
January 2000

The sun was setting the horizon on fire with pinks and golds. If I could have had my ideal sunset delivered for today – it would have looked like this. The cicadas were out in full force and chanting their ritualistic rhyme to my heartbeat. Even though nothing had ever felt so right, I felt intense nerves bubbling up inside. Who wouldn't?

On the beach there were just a handful of people. Bea and her boyfriend Jorge, plus the entire 'The Helios Kings'. *Who has a band at their wedding?* I can remember thinking. And then I thought: *me!* After all, I was marrying, what I thought was a rock god. An undiscovered rock god, but so what?

That evening has forever been etched on my mind. To help me retain it, I even sketched my memories in the following days – trying to commit as much as possible to myself - an aide memoir as such. For me it was the perfect wedding. What happened, how we felt, it was real.

First and foremost, it was filled with love. There was no ubiquitous white meringue, but a simple white beach dress and a necklace which I'd made from my shell collection. Frank had his denim shorts and a loud shirt on, plus a homemade matching shell necklace too. All of which gave him a sexy and laid-back vibe. We all wore garlands of fresh flowers around our heads and necks. When we said our vows, we both cried.

We laughed, danced, and the band played for hours. Frank had written an instrumental ballad for me which he played instead of a speech.

If I could paint perfection and beauty, that would be it. However, I have never come close. I know we sometimes look back with rose-tinted glasses, but I do believe, I have to believe, that there was a time when everything felt perfect. There were no shadows, stains or scars on the horizon. You see, for a time, we were happy.

RETURN OF THE PRODIGAL

BEFORE THEN
Jessica

June 2001
Leeds

In Loving Memory of Sheila Elizabeth Frost
Born on 24th May 1956
She fell asleep on 11th December 1996
aged 40 years.
Beloved wife, mother and grandmother.

Fell asleep? Bullshit boys. And all that beloved shit - not to everyone! We might have loved her but Dad and Stace took the piss. God, I'd been back in the shit-smog five minutes and already I was swearing like an old pro.

I had to be though, didn't I? That was the real me. The common skank who scratched around for a life for too long...

And there I was, five years later...dressed like a princess, with a huge rock on her finger and a Mercedes Benz sports outside the cemetery gates.

Can the real Jessica Frost please stand up?

Yeah, so I'd made it. Anyone who spotted the immaculately dressed woman, would be hard pressed to recognise her as Jessie Frost. They would never know what I had done to get so far in the past five years. Education, work, grit, determination, finding the right man...and so what if it has meant taking from others?

Mam died in the December after I'd returned from Corfu. Those months were possibly the worst of my entire life.

At first, as soon as I got home, I could think about nothing else but Mam. She was so sick and needed so much care, it fell to me to be the one that gave it. I practically slept at the hospital; in between, I rushed home to sort everything out for her coming home. Of course, our Dad was wallowing in self-pity

I despised the way he'd mourn her illness, full of repent and lies. "I could've done more Jessie, and why *our mam*? She's one of the best" he'd slur into his bitter. Guilt written all over his sorry face.

And although I couldn't disagree with his logic, his pure laziness and lack of emotional support meant I couldn't talk to him either. The words I wanted to shout into his pathetic face, crumbled like ashes in my boiling mouth. It wasn't just him though, I was so angry with them all; including Mam. *Why had she been so weak to let this happen?*

James, had for all his faults, stepped up for once though. His 'cash flow' seemed to be 'flowing' so I managed to make the house comfortable. I daren't even ask him where it was coming from, I just felt somewhat secure that it was one thing less for me to worry about. We needed money and Mam and I couldn't work...the others were fucking useless.

And then there was Frank.

Initially, all I could think about was for her to pull through. I still had some of money left from my very generous wages from Spiros. Selfishly, I kept them hidden and was secretly hoping I could go back to Corfu. Then, although I knew Mam was settled, I realised she wasn't getting any better. I could feel my chances slipping away. My mind wandered back to what I'd left behind. Guilt and duty jostled for the top spot in my mind. I was desperate for him to contact me. I was desperate to be rescued.

Radio silence.

Then, after a few days. when I realised he hadn't, I began to worry. After all, Maria and Spiros had promised to pass my letter on. True it was hastily written, but I felt sure they'd have explained.

After the worry, I became more anxious and wild thoughts would run through my mind. Was he with someone else? Had the reason he'd been a bit aloof with me before I left was because he'd found someone better? Or maybe he was ill? Had there been in an accident and because it was Greece and I wasn't his official next of kin...?   I started to wonder what was happening and wrote to Maria. I told her how Mam was not really improving and asked her about Frank. She had written to say everything was fine and that Frank hadn't been about for a couple of weeks. Moved on maybe? Or, naively, I hoped in my deepest dreams, that he was making his way to surprise me. Those thoughts and Mam's health plagued me in the darkest hours. I had never felt so alone. My hopes and dreams, from the beginning of the year, had begun to drift away, along with the sun kissed and water marked memories from the summer.

Eventually, our Mam came home. At first, she seemed to come to life. She wanted to breathe in the early autumn air, and I got a sense that she was fighting for something. I'd take her to the park to see the golden and russet leaves making a kaleidoscope on the floor.

She would comment on the beauty of it and how we used to make our own as kids. "Remember those Jessie? We made them out of coloured paper and sequins. '

"My favourite times Mam"

She'd smile and look far away. "You've always be attracted to beautiful and sparkly things. Don't let anyone take those dreams away from you. Especially me"

"Don't be bloody daft." I joked. She could always see into my soul. I also felt that was she preparing me for something. Our

Nana used to call her later years her 'autumn years'. Mam was too young for that, she'd only had her fortieth in the February before. Her worldly wisdom and wistfulness were scaring me. It was like she knew.

During the days and weeks which passed, the brilliance and show of autumn made way for death to creep its way in. Empty, skeletal, boughs, exposed ugly black crows cawing in their nests. The once honied carpet became a mulchy mire. The landscape was now stark. And as nature withered, Mam retreated too. She started refusing to go out - it was almost that she did not want death to stare her in the face. Everything became bleak. I'd wake up in a morning and feel the dread, a dead weight on me, as soon as I opened my eyes. I could sense that I was losing something significant - not just Mam, but the new shoots of hope, I had grown and nurtured from the beginning of 1996, had also succumbed to the harshness of winter too. Then, as the days grew shorter, my future became darker: there was no Frank, no glorious future and come December, my reason for success had gone too.

Your grief is something only you can explain. Don't get me wrong, we all feel it, but we all have different experiences. That Christmas, New Year, winter...I felt like I was cloaked in an iron lung. I was breathing, living, but I couldn't move and didn't think I was going to live. It was like my whole life had been extinguished and along with it, so had the only real love I'd ever felt. Frank's and Mam's - six months ago I felt swaddled in it. Suddenly, I was alone.

Days passed. I hid away in my room. I barely left it and let my dad fester in his own pity party. I had no energy left for him. He, in turn, seemed to be of the same feeling and came nowhere near.

James would occasionally turn up, trying to tempt me with some wine, chips, sometimes drugs. I wasn't interested. I couldn't think of a single thing which could numb the pain inside my chest. I felt obsolete and useless.

It was our Stace, funnily enough, who pulled me out of it. She'd had the new baby 'Brandon' just before *our mam* passed. We were all so worried about how she'd cope with two and all her 'issues'. Don't get me wrong, I was in no rush to help, but I couldn't face the children suffering. I'm not that hard faced! However, Mam going did something to her. She seemed to throw all her grief and regrets into the children. She kicked the boyfriend out, along with her bad habits, and became the estate's answer to 'Supermum'. On the rare occasion that I left my room, she'd turn up with two, obviously well fed, clean and happy children. It was like a Christian miracle. Only we weren't the religious types and had no idea how long it was going to last (It didn't but...) Even I noticed how patient she'd become with them, and Dad. It was like Mam's spirit had visited her as overnight she'd become this domestic marvel; placating the kids whilst whipping up our Dad some egg and chips. And whilst this miracle happened? There I'd be, slumped, staring and starving to death in the chair. I no longer had to will to do anything. And Stace meanwhile: it was like Mam had been reincarnated.

Too fucking late Stace.

But, for all my seething resentment, deep down I began to see that she was trying. *Why should she get another fucking chance?* I'd think in bed at night.

Obviously, now I realise that you make your own luck and mistakes. You are in charge of your own destiny. It is just a shame that I failed to realise this until the age of nearly forty...

These thoughts rattled around relentlessly, until one night James got me really pissed. He caught me at a particular low point, where I was going through my box of memories from Greece. Letters, gifts, pictures...I was debating whether to burn the lot (Like my self-pitying dreams) when he walked in with a litre of vodka.

"Sis, we need to talk"

I had no words. I wasn't going to argue, and the vodka looked like a good idea. My brain had emptied itself. I was numb (I now I know about all this stuff, I know my brain had shut down). I was out of everything. I just sat there and listened whilst he went on about *'his brilliant little sis!'* And *'making life matter'* I had no idea what he was talking about.

...I'd snapped at some point. Third or fourth glass in.

"She's so fucking perfect no Stress Stace' only where was she eh?"

I must have shocked him as he choked on his drink. "What are you talking about? I'm talking about you. For fucks sake Jess!"

James explained how worried he had been about me. Dad and Stace had said something too. How I was the one who was meant to be setting the world on fire. The high hopes they'd all had for the 'boffin of the family'.

Fuck me, I remember thinking. There was some sort of love there somewhere. Underneath all the filth and grime. I had no idea.

He wanted to know what was in my box. He knew something had happened to me in Corfu.

"No one comes back glowing like you without a story to tell!"

Vodka has always been my truth serum. That's why I've not drank it since that night. I told James everything.

At first, he wanted to rip apart Greece looking for that *'fucker Frank'*. But after we agreed that was one option, but not possible, (we didn't even know where he was anymore anyway. After all it was winter there and all shut up). We talked about my plan A - before the missing fiancé and *our mam.*

The next morning dad found us asleep at the kitchen table. He had a good laugh at us *'chips off the old block'.*

My God! I'd turned into him – drinking myself to sleep to numb the pain. The thought disgusted me. I was better than this, I thought, better than the lot of them!

James made me breakfast whilst I showered. I made my face up and put on some decent clothes. He drove me out of that house, and we agreed never to discuss what I'd told him with each other, or anyone else, again.

By September, with my errant and lawless brother's help, I had a clean flat in a safe district and a much longed for place at uni.

Thinking about my brother always makes me sad. It didn't then. At first, I used to secretly meet up with him. I couldn't be doing with the others. Dad was no better and all my love and sympathy had dried up long since. Stace meanwhile, had met someone else and they were expecting baby number three. I had no idea and didn't care if she was happy or not. It wasn't that I didn't love her, but we were on our own very difficult journeys. I felt the babies were there to fill a void in her. It was like she needed something small and helpless to constantly love. James said that if that was the case, she'd be better off at the dog rescue. I had to agree.

But, as his dealings became murkier, he started to cut ties. He explained that he was protecting me.

"You are the one good thing in my life Jessie. I'm so proud of the person you are and will later become. You have no idea of how strong you are."

He must have known something was happening. Upon reflection, I felt that he was setting me up for something else. A few weeks later he stopped answering his phone. He disappeared and just like that, I never saw him again.

There were many theories, but I chose to believe he was living a good simple life on a beach somewhere. Hiding out and living off all his ill-gotten gains. One day, I hoped he would contact me. As far as I was concerned, he was my only family member I had left.

If you could see me now! Big brother

In an ideal world I'd want him to give me away on Saturday. He turned out to be my white knight, anyone or thing that's come along since has not matched up to my brother. Instead, I present myself as 'Orphan Jessie', whose Father-in-Law to be is to give her away. My new family – The Greens – now treat me like the daughter they never had. They treat me like gold and with the purest white kid gloves.

They have no idea about me.

IN THE WINGS

BEFORE THEN
Jessica

North Yorkshire
June 2001

Have you ever wondered how you finally find yourself in some unimaginable situation? What I mean by that is, when I imagined myself getting married five years ago, I never thought it would have looked like this. My first engagement, although a short one, was a flurry of excitement and romance. It was hedonistic and I was prepared to marry right there and then, in a white bikini, on the sands of an empty beach. All for love. No planning and forethought; I was acting on instinct. Fast forward, and on Saturday 23rd June 2001, I find I was about to do the exact opposite.

Waterford Hall was a vast stately home in the depths of the North Yorkshire moors. The Franklins, who have had in their family for well over two hundred years, had fallen foul to huge repair bills and costs to heat the enormous old palace of a place. Therefore, like all other like-minded people in their position, they decided to invest the little they had left and upgraded it to a five-star luxury hotel. It was Bride magazine's feature of the month, and that's why I was there sipping champagne and playing the role of socialite, and lady-to-be, on my wedding day.

Sumptuous. There was no other word for it. The grand 18th century pile was like something out of a Jane Austin novel. And when Patrick gave me the option of the Waterford Hall as a wedding venue – well I couldn't resist (the old romantic in me was still stirring inside – not completely dead then). Restored to its former glory, the Hall stood in twenty-five acres of a patchwork of land – the estate lending itself to shoots, fishing, riding and some farm land also. The interior, as you would expect, held a charm of a bygone era and time. Where, as you entered the Great Hall, you gained a sense of divine purpose and glamour. To put it another way, if I'd have entered five years ago, I would have been scurrying to the basement to begin scrubbing the floors. Now, as I'd learnt to behave, I swanned in with my rehearsed sense of entitlement and (soon to be) new badge as a 'Green' - *I am the most important person in the Hall.*

The bridal suite was what you could call palatial. High corniced ceilings and huge picture windows framed the rolling moorland outside. A large antique queen-sized bed stood in the centre of the large suite, which, if I'm being really honest, could have fitted the entire ground floor of my childhood home within it; the dressing room, surpassing the size of my old bedroom and the bathroom equally so. The grandness, the history, the opulence – well, no wonder I was drinking so much champagne at ten in the morning – it was so incredibly surreal – like I was in a dream. I was waiting for my mother to kick me out of bed and tell me to wake up.

Only, as you know, that was not possible.

That old cliché 'this is the first day of the rest of my life' sprung to mind as I stared at my reflection in the gold gilded mirror. The young woman looking back at me was not that same tattered girl from Leeds, and certainly not that carefree girl, who fought for her independence and freedom, five years ago. The face, albeit with a few minor adjustments, was exactly the same. However, what was ticking inside was completely different.

There was a soft knock on the door. The type of knock that only someone with money and breeding would give. A knock

I had been learning to perfect.

"Jessica *darling*, can I do anything to help you?"

It was Patrick's mother Diane. The glamourous matriarch of the empire (as Patrick's father liked to call her). But like most glossy and beautiful things, what lay beneath could be very different. Although, in her defence, from what Patrick later disclosed to me about his upbringing, it was no surprise that Diane had 'an edge'. As a result, Patrick was fiercely protective of his mother back then. Life moves on though, and things can change over time...

"Oh Diane, how lovely of you to come and find me!" *My accent and diction were also something rehearsed.*

"Mummy Di, please! And where else would I be on my son's wedding day? You need me today more than ever. I cannot imagine how tough it must be to, well, be without your parents"

She was half-right. I was missing Mam, but as for dad – not really. I couldn't see him fitting in with the whole shebang. Pissed up and rolling down the aisle with me, as the celloist played tasteful music, and the sit-down meal costing more than a years' rent to the council. Plus, they didn't seem to serve bitter in flutes.

"Thank you, and yes" I feigned a regretful face and channelled my emotions into how let down I felt. It must have worked as a single tear managed to escape from the corner of my eye.

"Now now sweetheart." And she passed me a clean pressed handkerchief. I dabbed my eyes and took another sip of the bubbles.

"Diane (I really couldn't call her Mummy Di) please have a glass of fizz with me, I feel so incredibly nervous and it would be nice for us to share." *God I was good at this. It was becoming second nature to me.*

She beamed at me.

"Oh, *darling girl*, you are just so lovely. I can't believe Patrick has decided to settle down and with such a beautiful person too. You are going to be so happy! How could you not? You looked so in love last night at the dinner."

Maybe it was because I wouldn't let go of his hand because of her antics?

Diane liked to witter on. Patrick said it was because his father paid her little attention, with just a bit of lip service when needed. So, for that reason, I often gave her more time than I actually would have liked. Don't get me wrong, she could be so sweet and kind, but underneath that saccharin outer, there could be a bitter centre – like that tempting chocolate which then spoils itself by being a centre of Turkish Delight. The previous night, at the aforementioned dinner, we had been given a glimpse of that bitterness, so I was on my extra best behaviour that morning – I didn't need finding out, not after I had come this far.

BUT HOW DID I GET HERE?

BEFORE THEN
Jessica

Leeds
1999 -2000

I'd met Patrick when I was on a placement with his company 'Greens Leisure Ltd.' during my final year at university. I had been working studiously hard for the duration of my degree and was predicted a first in economics. My addition to Patrick's team, was a step in the right direction of my career advancement. His family company had the style and glamour I craved. And although I enjoyed working for the modern and forward-thinking Patrick, his father liked to keep it in the past. My plans were for success. Therefore, I had my sights set on future, higher goals.

I remember the first time we actually met. I'd been so nervous entering the stainless-steel ice structure of an office block, that I'd tripped over my discount designer heels, as I strode purposely into 'Green Leisure Ltd.' Throughout uni. I'd fantasised about being the epitome of corporate chic. I wanted the success, but I equally wanted to look the part too. I'd spend my Saturday afternoons dreaming myself around Harvey Nicks and planning what my future would look like. It was all about the looks – the substance was less important. After all, who could be miserable in the glossy centre-spread page of a perfect world? My other favourite down-time activity was dreaming about how I'd become obsessed with being a smart and sassy 'career woman'. I would watch Sex in the City and Ally McBeal and create fantasy scenarios in my head about 'having it all'. The sharp suit and heels were part of the image I wanted to create for myself. It was the first step towards painting out the old me and creating a new veneer. However, the strong independent female role went out of the window, when I tripped over my own feet and went face first onto the reception floor. Patrick's first encounter with me was him picking me up off the floor and getting me a strong coffee to settle my nerves. I can remember thinking that I had failed at my 'new act' at the first hurdle. Already I was needy and weak.

But, Patrick and me: It was a slow burn thing. And although we both admitted later on that we instantly found each other attractive, it was not love at first sight. Initially, he would drop in on me to check how I was getting on (another ploy to see me he later said). He would sometimes ask me to have coffee with him and he'd show me the projects he was working on. He'd offer to take me out on 'field trips', to some of his business interests. He would explain how they worked and fitted into the structure of the company. It wasn't the London Stock Exchange, or Wall Street, but it afforded me an insight into his worth. I played it cool.

Later, when I was working the last week of my placement, he asked me for a date. Dinner he said – to say thank you! I replied that I should be thanking him. He was attractive, but it felt wrong somehow – going out with the boss (even though he was loaded). He took me to an award-winning restaurant where they had more silverware and glassware on the table than I had in my entire kitchen. I bluffed the bits I didn't quite understand – him and the array of tableware (I wasn't stupid, I wanted this kind of life for myself) and we had a really lovely time. We got on and surprisingly (although, if I'm honest, I'd spent more than I could afford on my tight little dress), at the end of the evening he told me I was beautiful and that he thought we'd be good together. The kiss sealed it. There was no love, but plenty of lust. I'd have been blind if I didn't find him attractive, and I did enjoy his company; he was interesting and a real gentleman. And, as of that afternoon, I no longer worked for him. *Why not?* I remember thinking.

Then, the biggest achievement of my life was confirmed – a first! He was so excited and stepped things up calling me his 'brilliant girlfriend'. I had no idea we were anything other than just 'dating'. He kept telling me how proud of me he was. How I had proved to have 'beauty and brains' (something he felt he'd never encountered with all the 'bimbos' who homed in on him like bees around a honeypot, throughout his bachelor life so far).

We were twenty-three and felt so grown up. He surprised me and took me away to Rome for a long weekend. It was amazing: I felt like Cinderella going to the ball! Money was no object and I felt like a golden princess. Right there and then, I believed I could have it all. Alright, I was really attracted to him and by now I found out that our chemistry was something else – we just worked in bed. But I didn't 'love' him. He wasn't Frank. And as much as I tried to push away those old feelings, I knew that no man would ever make me feel that way again. But Patrick was coming a close second. His attentiveness and generosity made things easy. There was no stress and I didn't have to count the cost all the time. His interest in me gave me options, and when you've been dealt a hand like me in life, you need to build up those options.

*****

"*Jessica* (pronounced *Jessie-car*) *darling*, what time are your bridesmaids arriving?"

This had been tricky. I would have liked some old friends maybe – but I'd lost touch with the 'Grammar' lot. I also didn't need shadows of the past ruining my day and backstory. I did contemplate asking Maria (we had stayed in touch and I had spent a brief summer back there working for them) but that would have opened up a whole new can of worms. This was my new shiny platinum life and I had to cut any ties. Furthermore, just like I wanted my brother James here, even if I could have found him, I would have had some explaining to do on both sides. So, when we discussed bridesmaids, I said something about painful memories and that I would ask my flatmates. When I asked Rachael and Helen, (well, if they were surprised, they didn't really say so). We were hardly close, but we did spend the odd night out together. If I'm really honest with myself, we were all a bit nerdy. I had to be – it was the safest option to get where I wanted to be. There was no room for error back then and spending time with wild and reckless people was not part of the plan. We were a house of geeks and that suited me for a change.

If they raised their eyebrows when I asked them, I chose to ignore it. After all, we did spend a great deal of time together – never mind it was at the library or in the quiet of our shared house. Additionally, they were both obsessed with the stories of where Patrick would take me and presents he would buy me. For a short time, we all lived vicariously through my 're-lationship' with him. I say we all, because very clearly to me, I felt like a little girl watching a fairy-tale movie: it all felt so abstract and unreal.

Quiet geeks aside, we did manage a fun hen party at the cocktail bar in town. In fact, if my memory serves me correct, we were quite wild (something I did not know Rachael and Helen had in them). I often think back to that night of shots and dancing and wonder if we'd have been closer, less focused and more fun, if we'd done that when we first met – waiting until I was about to marry seems such a waste of youth now. Although, thinking back now, I know that at the time, I was hiding away. If was self-preservation and it was the only way, I'd learnt to cope. If I didn't invest too much in love and friendships – my feelings, I would never feel hurt again. My heart had been broken and a consequence was scarring; I did not want to open up myself to anyone again – even making new friends.

Marrying Patrick was different. I'd calculated the risks and benefits and knew it made good business sense. He asked the 'bright, quiet, beauty' to marry him. I posed no threat. 'Lonely Orphan Jessica' it was. Whether Patrick's family saw me as no threat or an asset to the empire, I'll never know – but brains and beauty had been mentioned at various times. And although Patrick was vocal about these latter points, he also admitted (much later on) that he needed me.

His parents' marriage had, as I later found out, been a sham. The previous night's events had been the first time I saw the cracks in the perfectly veneered smiles.

THE NIGHT BEFORE: MEET THE OUT-LAWS

BEFORE THEN
Jessica

June 2001
North Yorkshire

Diane and Jonny Green were the perfect hosts for the bride and groom to be. Greeting the small wedding party of close family and friends, they held court over cocktails and then the starter course of wild Scottish Salmon pate, served with rocket leaves and horseradish cream. The next course was to be a light chicken fricassee and wild rice. I'd been helped (very strongly) in choosing the pre-wedding dinner by Di. This opulent evening was meant to be a small intimate affair for us all to relax before the huge extravaganza in the morning. Only the Greens didn't really do 'relaxed' and where I'd have truthfully liked room service and a movie in my huge room, I was now amongst a carefully chosen group of strangers on the eve of my momentous day.

Of course, we'd had two to three aperitifs: 'Martini cocktails' before we'd even reached the table and the crisp white sauvignon served with the salmon only added to the boozy levels of the celebratory dinner. The first inkling I sensed something was wrong was when we approached the dining table and Diane changed the pre-arranged settings. I wasn't sure what she was doing at first when I saw her swiftly switching place cards, but I was so nervous that someone would call me out for my hidden past – Dynasty style, that I kept my head down and carried myself over to me place against Patrick. I know I was shaking because Patrick must have sensed my unease and squeezed my hand; reassuringly, he told me all was good. If I saw his father raise his eyebrows, when he sat next to Roberta Fitzgerald and Diane flash him a triumphant smile, I also chose to pretend I didn't see. I'd grown up on Alexis and Blake Carrington, and I suddenly sensed that maybe I was marrying into a dynasty of similar dynamics. However, what I couldn't ignore was the instant feeling of tension from Patrick's body and his brother's deep sigh echoing it.

The salmon was beautiful and light, but something about the tension meant that I was struggling to digest it. When I looked around the table, it looked like I wasn't the only one. In fact, the only people who seemed to enjoy their starters were Di, and her new dining partner, Peter Fitzgerald. What was going down well though was the white wine...

Now, I might have been new to swanky dinners and posh families, but I knew what too much alcohol could do. I could feel a storm brewing on the horizon. Living with my lot all those years put me in good standing for sniffing out trouble and I could write it before it happened. The Greens might have played it differently, but I soon realised that no family was without its dark areas and issues. So, as the plates were cleared, I could feel the air becoming thicker and taught – it was like we were all suspended in time awaiting the first break in the oppressive air.

We didn't have to wait long.

"Friends and family" announced Di, with a slight ringing of her spoon on her empty wine glass. "My husband would like to make a short speech about the journey and sanctity of marriage"

Jonny's poker face never moved. However, his hands were fiddling with his cigarettes on the table. *He needed a prop to stabilise him* I thought.

"He, more than anyone, should be able to tell you all the secret of a thirty-year marriage. Isn't that right Roberta?"

The table fell silent. A distinct weightiness smothered the air. For the first time I wondered: *What the fuck was I getting myself into?* Again, the power of the American soap opera was edging into my thoughts.

Jonny lit his cigarette and inhaled deeply. Patrick put his head down.

Di held her glass. Peter filled it.

"To happy marriages" she toasted.

We had no option but to toast this weirdly loaded sentiment.

"To happy marriages!" we chorused.

Jonny cleared his throat to break the silence.

"Thank you dearest" (said in the sweetest voice dripping with sarcasm I think I have ever heard) "So like you to steal my moment! That's my wife, she likes to be in charge. That's the secret Patrick, let Jessica think she is winning. Give her the world and she will never question the small print! Works well in business too" He started laughing. With the tension strung tighter than a piano wire, we felt we should do the same. Thankfully, his unfunny joke released some of the pressure.

"Seriously, joking aside. My advice would be that marriage is a partnership. You might be full of lust and love now, but that will undoubtedly fade over time. What you really need to keep going is an understanding, a togetherness, and to remember to have a jolly good time! Isn't that right darling?" He raised his glass to Di, and she coloured slightly. I had no idea what was going on. Up until half an hour ago, I thought they were a Hello! Glossy mid-page spread, perfect family.

"To Patrick and Jessica, may you have a long and lasting marriage"

A roar of *here!* and cheers went up. Patrick squeezed my hand and was subdued until the coffees and liquors when he perked up and wandered off to speak to Di in hushed tones. He was telling her off. I felt shut out and abandoned. And to this day, I still believe their god-awful shit-show was what cursed us from the beginning.

APPARENTLY, I DO

BEFORE THEN
Jessica

North Yorkshire
June 2001

Two hours later and I was, yet again, standing in front of the full-length mirror, admiring my gown, hair and make-up.

"Oh Jessica, you look simply stunning" Di drawled. Maybe slurred? After all, she had rung for more champagne and I'd barely touched it. The girls had arrived, and they'd only had a small glass each. By my calculation, she'd had at least well over a bottle.

I did. I looked fucking amazing! My chocolate brown hair had been blow dried to an inch of its life. Loretta Lawn, celebrity hairdresser, had been drafted in and she had swept it up into an elegant chignon. Not content with us 'struggling along by ourselves *darling*', she also arranged for Mazza Karlfield to come and airbrush out any 'little imperfections'. All this alongside the Vera Wang gown and Jimmy Choos, meant that I had finally vanquished the evil trolls and my happy ever after was being finally written. But life isn't like in fairy tales. They fail to acknowledge the fallibility of life. Masculinity challenges feminism, real life takes over. Therefore, my perfect ending was inevitably flawed.

My wedding was just a new shiny beginning. The past was erased, and I had plans for the future. I was going to be Jessica Green – a beautiful rich wife of one of Yorkshire's most eligible bachelors. I'd be looked after for life. So, what if I had to act a little?

PART FOUR

THE BOOK OF REVELATION

ISOLATION

THEN
Aimee

Saltness
November 2016

Winter had arrived. A bitter north-easterly was rolling in from the Balkans. The iron grey North Sea was beating itself against the rocks; a kind of a metaphor for how I was feeling.

Sandra Dee Dog and I were taking a long morning walk on the beach. We needed it – freezing cold or not. She wouldn't settle for me for the remainder of the day, and I needed to wake up and refresh my sluggish brain. Sleep, like the population of Saltness, had been eluding me.

How had it come to this?

First and foremost, I didn't believe I had done anything wrong. Whatever the gossips knew (or thought they knew), nothing had passed between me and Paddy. It was just an ill-misjudged friendship (because that is all it was) that branded a bloody marriage wrecker and calculating bitch.

You had to wonder if anyone had ever really known me? Then again, I was never one for school-gate politics.

Since the Ice Queen began spreading her nasty rumours, the school gates had become frostier than Siberia. And if that wasn't bad enough (I might not have joined in, but I certainly was part of the community), Jenna was swerving my calls. The children and I were becoming isolated from a network we had relied upon since losing Frank.

How the hell had it come to this?

As I become more energised from the invigorating air, I rolled around the scenarios in my head – conversations which I knew must have occurred; the quietness of my social media was eerie; as were the play-date invites.

It was the latter which killed me as I hated that my children were suffering because of this. Not just that but they missed hanging out with Oli and Toby. They were confused and I was angry on their behalf. After all, when I think about the amount of times I had ignored rumours...being a loyal mum and friend to others. Now we were being cold shouldered by those I had stood by. And, on top of all that, my parents, who had always been a bit unreliable, were away in Australia until next year. The isolation made me very alone and vulnerable. More to the point, career and financially wise, I had no idea how I was going to solve my other problem.

Just after Halloween-Gate, I received a phone call from a gallery in Wakefield called The Hepworth Gallery. The gallery, being named after the Yorkshire artist of the same name, was to hold an exhibition for local artists. The idea was to celebrate and publicise the talent in the county. As well as giving us an opportunity to make some (much needed in my case) money from our art. It was sheer luck how they'd found me. My career had been stagnating for so long. Although I had a steady stream of summer work from the tourists, plus the odd local commission, family constraints and grief put a stopper on my once fierce ambitions. The gallery found me because one of the curators had brought her young family for a day at the sea. They'd wandered into our town pavilion and seen some of my work being displayed.

To say I was thrilled was an understatement. The call was like a shaft of sunlight piercing through an otherwise grey autumn day. As soon as they'd called me, I had wanted to tell someone. Unfortunately, I thought of Paddy straight away; especially as he had been so enthusiastic about the family piece on my wall. However, 'The fucker' then flitted through my mind and I quickly disregarded him and decided I did not need his arrogant opinion anyway. So, I text Jenna as she was my appointed cheerleader and adopted sister in life. I received a cool 'well done' (only one X) and no further questions. And for the second time in five minutes I thought 'The fucker'.

Luckily (well I say that, but they rarely took interest in anything I did anymore) my parents were more forthcoming and unusually excited (at this point I would like to say that this says more about them than me) as finally they'd be able to boast about their daughter's talents (the ones I had always had but they'd chosen to ignore up until this point). Instead of the way that 'Yes, she hasn't really amounted to much' and 'let's look at our latest holiday snaps instead.' Their sheer pride (and need to brag) meant that initially I had lots of help from them with the children: Phoebs and Haz were stunned.

"Whaddya mean we are going to Nan and Grandad's for tea?" questioned a confused Phoebe.

Hazza's sweet little face was punctuated by high eyebrows "They are actually picking us up?"

They did and the children were somewhat a mix of apprehension and excitement at the same time. However, when they returned, they weren't so sure about this new development in their little world. My parents are nothing like me and are very straight. Apparently, Mum wasn't keen on her plant pots being made into goal posts. Dad wouldn't let them watch 'certain programmes' (which Phoebe retold me with inverted commas). But, credit to them all as they found a way to meet on common ground. So, teething problems aside, Mum taught them both how to make some lovely scones and bread, and this meant that we all had a rather pleasant afternoon tea together. Dad (who I think I might secretly have inherited the creative gene from) had helped them make decorations for it – this thoroughly shocked me as he never did anything like that with me as a child. And, to my secret joy (even though I still smouldered at the times they had ignored us) Mum and Dad actually seemed to take great happiness from all of this; laughing at and lighting up as the children chattered and giggled.

All good things came to an end; the planned tea party preluding a goodbye. They were to be off in Australia until February. The realisation that they were going to miss the opening of the exhibition hit them quite hard – and for once seemed that they were genuinely sorry. They also admitted that they were very sad at leaving the children. I told them that they needed to spend more time with them – especially when they got back.

Mum said something like 'Oh Aimee, we've tried in the past' – I didn't understand this and made a mental note to find out at a less highly charged time. Plus, I couldn't remember the exact quote as Harry was handing over a list of all the things he wanted bringing back from Oz: a koala, a boomerang, a kangaroo, and some edible bugs and things like on *I'm a Celeb...* Dad was too busy loudly laughing.

'My lordy me,' I remember thinking *'I can't believe the difference in them all!'*

Dad must have caught the exchange between myself and my mum as he told her to shush and muttered something quietly about 'water under bridge'. Which gave me a flash of anger. Giving me a sense that they were blaming me for the distance in our relationships; something else I need to think about and put straight – whatever the issue. However, right then, apart from the children, my main priority was to get exhibition ready. How I was going to prepare when no one seemed to be speaking to me, I had no idea!

The theme for my collection was to be 'Freedom'. It had taken a while and many hours with SDD on the beach to find my inspiration. After all, I was a mature artist now and I needed to think about what I had learnt in life. This was my opportunity to show some depth and make a statement about how I was and am. I thought back to that strong and independently willed young girl who went against her parents' wishes and pushed forward with her dreams. I thought about Frank's role in all that and how he had clipped my wings. All that freedom of travel but I was pinioned to him and his career. He was so desperate to succeed, and my art was just something I did along the way. I wondered what would have happened had I not have met him? But I had to file that sickening thought away as I wouldn't have my precious children without him.

I found it from my muses. It was one day when the children and I were on the beach. It was a wild squally day and the waves were crashing in against the rocky shore. The children and SDD playing chicken with the encroaching waters. They were winning at the game. Only SDD had been caught a couple of times – the problem of becoming an ageing arthritic dog. However, the children were becoming braver; their bravado making them more reckless. Suddenly, a large swell came from nowhere and washed them with an iron curtain of sea water. There was screams and I remember thinking '*shit!*'. And then there was laughter as they ran to me – arms out stretched and full of joy that the icy cold burst had given them. They looked so alive in fits of giggles and threatening to go back for more. Their cheeks red and healthy. They looked so carefree. And then I realised what it meant to be free – freedom being a state of mind rather than a state of being.

This took me back again to those early years and I looked at them through a new lens. I thought about uni, about Thailand, and the places I had been which made me feel alive and free. I thought about the feeling of the outdoors and how confining life could be. I wanted to bring people outdoors and show them the freedom of being alive. Death had been overhanging in our lives for too long...

As hedonistic these ideas were, I had no idea how I would get it all done in time. I did have some previous works squirreled away which would work, but I had an idea for a series connected to people. I wanted to do some studies with different lettings and people of varying ages. I had the children, I had the vibrancy of some of my travels. I even had some work of Frank performing – where he looked so free and alive that I thought they would fit nicely. I needed something more though – a centrepiece – something which would tie it all together. I thought about it day and night, but I needed time and support. And there I was: I was alone and shunned. It was only that morning that I heard the latest bits of gossip. Hushed whispers behind my back and what I like to call (un)knowing looks.

Angela Clerkenwell, the resident Hyacinth Bucket, was at it was usual. Her little upturned nose in the air, an overly super-cilious stance adopted: "I have in on good authority – " then going silent as I rounded the corner.

A half smile from another one: Sharissa Fox, who I had stuck up for only the other week, when they were all pointing fin-gers at her, after the ridiculous rumours that she'd slept with her boss to get the promotion *'They say she was all over him at the summer barbeque...'*

What I wanted to say was *'What do you have on good authority Andrea?'* Instead I looked at their scared little provincial faces and felt pity for their tiny lives. *'Well fuck em!'* I decided *'What do they know?'*

I was so angry with Paddy. How he had ruined everything. The hands of friendship that we'd bizarrely held, were broken by his ridiculous arrogance. However, as angry as I was with Paddy, I was more upset with myself. *How had I let this happen?* I wondered. I had built such a wall around myself and the chil-dren, that at the first opportunity, with the least likely can-didate, I had let my carefully built defences down. *Why had I done that?*

Sickeningly, I knew why: I was secretly flattered that he would want to spend time with me. It was like I had won some sort of competition – a man like Patrick Green had put all his pretentious antics to one side and wanted my friendship. The fact that he was very attractive had nothing to do with it, I told myself. But I had missed him more that I cared to admit to myself. I'd had my fingers burnt and that was that. What-ever the secretly jealous, the witches' coven would cow about at the school gates, I had nothing to be ashamed of as he'd let himself down at the final hour.

SDD galloped (like a sturdy soft fudge-like Shetland) across the rocky shore and towards the incoming tide. I watched her as she played chicken with the freezing November water. She was living her best life and I felt myself smile. *Thank the lord for dogs!* I thought. Their faithfulness couldn't be matched, and neither could their unconditional love and loyalty. Sandra Dee Dog was, most possibly, the best thing Frank ever did for me. Yes, we had the children, but SDD got me through some very bleak moments in life. Hours we've walked on the beach. She got me out when I wanted to hide away; when I found my days could be so long after the children started school. I'd miss them and the empty void their dad had left. Unable to face my work, I centred myself around the children bookending my day and SDD providing the filling. Then, it was about putting one foot in front of the other.

In and out sea was moving; the consoling beat of the rhythm of life. I watched: there was a small sea bird hovering above the white horses, minding its own business. SDD had her inbuilt senses locked on it - so intently, that as the wild waves became bigger, they pushed in mightily, energised by a large gust of wind, and swamped her in salty iced sea spray. I couldn't help but laugh.

She ran to me like a little girl wanting a kiss better. I gave her a good fuss, wetting myself in the process, and felt myself regain some equilibrium. I needed to stop worrying and make things work. I had the children and the dog. I didn't need anyone else.

LOST

Saltness
November 2016

Before I start, I need to state to you - the judge and jury - that I am no stalker. When I chose to walk to the beach, it wasn't because I had seen Aimee strut down there with her Sandra Dee Dog – I was planning on going anyway. My car was in the garage and I was on foot that morning – I relished the thinking time. So what if I hung back in the shadows – so to speak? If truth be told, I was scared.

It was a great iron fist of a day. The mighty North Sea doing its upmost to remind the world who was boss. I love days like those. They put me in my place and remind me of what is significant. Funny, I'd worked all my life; been in the family business – even before I left school, and I'd rarely taken my eye off the ball. Success and family honour were what drove me to make my choices. Even my personal life was dictated by clever moves for image and aspirations to be the best. However, living in what some would call, a run-down northern coastal town, suited me. It is the only place I felt like me. I liked the feeling of living on the edge. Of being able to look out and see endless slate grey waters. It made me feel alive.

You might wonder why I felt scared. A very successful (rich) man hurtling towards forty. I was wealthy enough to retire and could set my destiny on a course of my choosing. Well, I had recently come to a crossroads – one where I had to decide if I wanted to begin a new project – it would mean that I was going to be fixed into the business for at least another five to ten years.

Power. That double edged sword where you have the tools to make anything possible. But you don't always know what that possible is. You don't always know where possible leads. Don't get me wrong, I had taken many risks in business. Calculated risks, which had led me in various directions. I'd made money and I have lost it too. No one is infallible – even if those of us arrogant ones say differently. This said, I had always kept a cool head. But when you're wanting change – personal change – things aren't always so simple.

Aimee's shoulders were sagging as she made away across the sand and to the rocks. SDD was circling and loving the freedom that an empty beach affords. Freddie was straining as he could see them way out in front. I couldn't risk letting him go as it would have broken Aimee's mood. Even from far way and with my insensitive soul, I could sense the sadness. I had an overwhelming urge to run to her and reach out some kindness.

The thought scared me.

I wasn't sure when the feelings began to develop. However, I did know they were something alien to me. I found them intoxicating and exciting. I'd think of her laughing and see the mischief and edge in her sparkling eyes, and I would want to be the person to make her do that. When she'd turned up with that Jenna bird, I was filthy jealous of their closeness. *I was supposed to be the one responsible for that joy and happiness.* And then I'd remember I couldn't.

Watching her struggling with something killed me. And I knew that if I went anywhere near, she would tell me where to go. It wasn't just the pass I'd made – I think I could have bluffed out of that one (not that I wanted to). Aimee would never take me as a complication in her life. I knew this as that was her. She had spent too long being strong and independent. Sleeping with a married man with a terrible reputation would do her no good. In fact, I think I would hate her if she did.

The reason I felt that way is because she was who she was. No nonsense.

All that aside, it is what Jessica has done since that had caused so much pain. The rumours and exclusion wall which had put up around her. I knew this. That is what my wife was good at; good at manipulating and isolating. I should have known, I'd had it for fifteen years.

My wife. Marry in haste and repent at leisure. That's the old proverb and so true it was too. Sometimes I have to cast my mind back to my motivation for being so desperate to get her to marry me. When I first met her, she was so vulnerable. She had an edge of being a survivor (like Aimee) but she was young, and I could tell there was a story too. When I first saw her, I was hit by her beauty, and then pretty soon, I learnt how clever she was. Her work ethic impressed me: she worked so hard and was so keen to progress. But she wasn't cocky, flirty, or rude; she was different. I liked different. I was attracted to her intelligence and the strength of her character. This might have surprised people – even then. I was bored of the money grabbers and needed an equal. I respected her and felt we'd be a good match. For all this I just had to get her to feel the same.

It took a while – the courting. We didn't rush things and I learnt that her serious character was due to being orphaned. She had no one. My family embraced her because of this. I felt like I had struck gold. I was so proud of her when she graduated. I took her away and rained on her with gifts; I couldn't spoil her enough. She just took it all in her stride. She was quite sweet back then – in her own quiet way. Just before we married, I made her get rid of her old second-hand car and bought her a brand-new red Mercedes sports car. She was so embarrassed, and I felt so lucky to have found someone so different from all the others.

There was only one cloud on the horizon...the love. Did I love her? and did she love me? Naivety, plus youth, made me think we did. However, as time progressed, I realised that I'd fallen in love with an illusion – I didn't really know her. She was never who she said she was; she wore a mask.

At times I could get under that mask. We were particularly good in bed as we were both so ambitious and driven. So that helped smooth over many cracks in the early days. Once the children came along, we were kept busy with them. I tried to be a good husband – in those days I was still trying to prove a point to my philandering parents, but to my shame, and even though many believe I'd been up to no good for years, it was only about five or six years ago that I started to stray.

I had become lonely. I had begun to realise that I had been alone for a long, long time. Although, Jessica had become almost glacial (The mask was up and there was no way in). The silence was deafening. I felt completely adrift in a plotline that no one had given me a script for. I had no idea what changed her so drastically, but whatever it was, it killed the only spark of warmth that kept our marriage alive for so long.

I'd been lost for so long.

SDD dog was racing at the sea. Aimee had stopped walking. I wanted her to turn. I wanted to hold her to me; to say that *'whatever it is, I'll help.'* At the same time, I didn't want her to see me. I realised the absurdity of the situation: I'd been following her for about half an hour and suddenly felt absolutely ridiculous.

What if she saw me? She'd know.

SDD was in stalking mode. A huge wave sprayed SDD and she ran to her mistress for some love.

Lucky girl.

I hastily retreated over into the dunes. I needed to find a way. I had admitted to myself about my fears and I knew that I could not live in a web of lies and loneliness anymore. Only, the problem was that webs aren't easy to get out of. They trap you. I needed to find a way out.

THE VISITORS

THEN
Aimee

Saltness
November 2016

"Hello and take this. Quick, it's freezing out here"

Jenna was holding out a bag of what looked like wine and snacks. I gingerly took them off her and wondered what had prompted the impromptu visit.

"And then these are for you too!" at which point she pulled out a lovely bunch of yellow roses "for friendship. Although, I've been a shit one recently"

"You know what I'd have done to Frank if he'd have bought me flowers when he'd upset me, don't you?"

"Yes, but – "

"Auntie Jenna!!!!" was screamed by both of my children as they shot down the stairs to the front door. Reluctantly, I took all her things and let her inhale her godchildren's heads.

"Oh, my Phoebs, you've groan like a foot in the last few weeks! And Haz, look at you! Just as gorgeous as ever. What have you got to tell me?"

They dragged her, one on each arm into the living room, amid a wave of chatter.

I guess she's staying then.

I let the trio catch up. I might have some questions for my 'best friend' but the children had clearly missed her. They'd suffered as much as me and were missing their community. I emptied the bag and found not only wine, but snacks for us to graze on: olives, cheese, posh crisps, lovely little bits from the deli...'grovelling food' I thought. And two beautifully wrapped boxes with a P and a H on.

"Are these for now?" I waved over to Jenna. To be honest I wanted the whole 'Fairy Godmother' performance over so I could drill her about her ghosting me.

"Oh yes, guys, I got you something"

"ooh!" they swooped in like a pair of red kites and went to grab them. Reminding them of their manners, they kissed their Auntie Jenna and opened their little boxes.

"They're bells look Mummy!"

"With our faces on. Look!" insisted Harry whilst thrusting it into my face.

"Wow, they are pretty' I conceded 'What are they for?"

Jenna explained they were Christmas bells. They were to hang them up on the fire place and they would alert Santa if there were any issues with Phoebe and Harry's behaviour.

"What, so like he's watching us?" asked Harry.

"He's always watching" I smiled.

Phoebe didn't look convinced. I realised that she was at that age where she didn't not want to believe but she had serious questions regarding logistics and the number of parcels which would arrive before the big day. She must have decided that whatever the real answer was, that she still needed to be on her best behaviour.

"Thank you, I love it Auntie Jenna" and she kissed her on the cheek.

Quick as a flash H was in there – never one to miss out "And me. I'll kiss you too"

"Hazza, you're the only man for me!"

The children had obviously forgiven her for her absence (short memories). I suspected I would too, I never could stay mad at her for long. I was sure she had her reasons - I needed the children in bed and to speak to her frankly.

"Right children, hang up your bells and say goodnight now"

"Awh, can't we stay up? We haven't seen Auntie Jenna for

ages!" Phoebe moaned.

"No, not tonight"

"That's right kids. I need to speak to your mum. But, if it's alright with her and you, I could take you out on Saturday? Give her some peace?"

"Yes! The Winter Ice Rink is open. Can we go there?" exclaimed Phoebs.

"Please" echoed Harry, falling to his knees.

"Please" pleaded Phoebe.

"Please" They were both chorusing now and, on their knees, as in prayer.

"OK, stop!" I snapped. I shouldn't have. I was getting impatient. I wanted to know why she'd been ghosting me. They just wouldn't leave it sometimes. Even though I didn't know what she was going to say, I would let them. I needed time to work. Uninterrupted. Plus, whatever was going on between us, she loved them, and they needed her.

"Alright then. Now go to bed and don't forget to brush your teeth. I will be up in five to check you are tucked in. You can read, but no electronics!"

In a flurry of kisses, they slowly dragged themselves upstairs, like explorers clinging to the bannister as if it was the highest and steepest mountain, they'd even experienced.

"Like two cute sloths" joked Jenna.

Only they still weren't done with her...

"Can you help Auntie Jenna?" whined Harry.

Phoebs yawned dramatically, "We are so tired, and I don't think either of us is able to hold the toothbrush up and turn our sheets back"

I rolled my eyes at the sheer drama of them all.

"Go on then, it'll give your mum a break"

Then with a miraculous recovery, the sloths sped up as she chased them to the bathroom.

*****

"So, go on then, where you been?" Now the children were settled I was not going to piss about.

"You know where I've been Aims, work has been mental!"

"That I appreciate, but we've never gone longer than a week before. Well...apart from when I was travelling"

"...and brought yourself a husband back!"

"Yes, I did, didn't I. See what happens when you leave me alone!"

"Frank loved you Aims" She smiled.

"But we both know that he was in no way perfect. You, my oldest – "

She interrupted. "Less of that bitch!"

"Oldest friend" I laughed "knows more than anyone what he could be like"

Jenna laughed and looked away. She was all very well and good laughing, when she was the one who used to prop me up when he was being unpredictable.

"Look, stop avoiding the question. Where have you been? I have barely spoken to you since that party"

"Well, yes, that is true." She looked a bit shifty "Honestly?"

"We don't do anything other do we?"

She shifted uncomfortably in her seat. She looked straight at me, "Right. Well, I was jealous and hurt. It felt like you had been having an affair behind my back"

"An affair? Not you too!"

"What do you mean? Me too?"

"That's the rumour. The one started by that bitch of his wife Jessica. I have no idea why she could think such a thing. Apart from anything else, she is supermodel stunning, and I, well I'm just me – I've no idea how anyone believes it! It must be a slow news week around here."

"Shut up! Stop that. You are not 'just' anything. You are beautiful – you've never understood, I think that is why...anyway, maybe she had reason to be jealous too"

"How?" *Jenna with her theories. Everyone jumping to conclu-*

sions when all we were was two lonely parents whose children liked hanging out.

"Seriously. You, you don't see it do you?"

"What? That people think I am one capable, and two that he would ever look at me?"

"Cop on, as Frank would have said, you seriously think he's not attracted? He wanted you all to himself. I was there you know – saw the way he was watching you."

I flushed. I remembered his eyes on me. "He was drunk" I reminded her. I will not tell her about the pass. "Anyway, I would never cheat on you Jen"

"Ha, I know! You couldn't even manage a trip abroad with Ellie. Remember her?"

"Yes, Ellie the Fair-weather friend. She's living in Australia now. Married with two children and living on a sheep farm with some man she met in Vietnam"

"She made it there then? I stopped caring after she dumped you unceremoniously"

"Yeah, she managed to rinse enough people to help her 'backpack'..."

"She was never cut out for that was she?"

"Nope. Big mistake! I think the sheep guy got her pregnant and they headed to his family farm in New South Wales. Not my thing – being trapped by some bloke in her early twenties"

"Erm, that's EXACTLY what happened!" she laughed.

"No, it did not!" Only Jenna could say that to me. She had the right as she had been there through everything. But I knew I was different to Ellie "Although we married early Jen, we travelled – a lot! It gave me a certain amount of freedom" Even though, I knew deep down this wasn't the case, I wasn't ready to reveal my recent revelations just yet, "and we didn't have a child for six years. There was no trapping going on!"

She cast her eyes down "I know, I know. Sorry. But you are deflecting this Paddy stuff" She said this last part with raised eyebrows.

"Yes, well, you are most certainly wrong" I was not going to tell her.

"Are you telling me that nothing happened when I left?"

I've never been a good liar, so I busied myself with the snacks and put four olives and posh crisps into my mouth at once. That can't have been enough though.

"It did, didn't it? Stop pretending by shoving stuff into your mouth."

She knows me too well.

I couldn't talk as my mouth was crammed. I took a large drink of the wine to wash it down.

"I know you Aimee O'Donnell, tell me!"

I could feel my colour rising. She could always do this to me.

"It was nothing"

"Clearly not, by the lengths you are going to avoid my question!"

"He was drunk and pissed off. I was just a face"

"He kissed you?" She fist pumped the air "Oh my god, that's one in the eye for that bitch of an ice queen!"

"Not quite. I didn't let him. Anyway, he threw up." She howled out at that. "And I left furious; I felt like he was taking the piss. After all, I am nothing like his wife and it was surely tit for tat"

Jenna's face froze. "What do you mean tit for tat?"

"Nothing really. I shouldn't really be saying this, it's very gossipy of me, and I am only saying this as you are my 'oldest'"

"Piss off oldest: bestest would do"

"Bestest friend who has recently deserted me."

"Sorry a million times" she smiled earnestly.

"Well, their marriage isn't the happiest. It's quite sad really. I get the sense that there's no love there and she is barely around, not that I am judging. He tells me he has been an absolute knob to her. But, as earnest as he is being, I feel like they play games with each other"

"That is quite toxic Aims. And sad"

"I know, so I think his drunken pass was part of their games.

Does that make sense?"

"After all you've told me, I can't understand how you could actually make friends with that eejit?" There's the Irish again. Sometimes, it is like Frank is still here with us.

"You channelling your inner Frank again?"

"I am only saying what he would have said. Only he would have never let things go as far as they did"

"Meaning?"

"It is obvious isn't it? Men and women can't be friends. That is why you're the hot gossip. And that was why I was jealous. I just felt excluded."

"I know. I can see why you must have felt like you did. I didn't mean to mislead you – or hold things back" Or *had I?* I remembered the way I had not told her the full details of the party. *Was I really hiding something?*

"Yeah well. I am sorry to for being a Prima Donna."

"You're not. You ARE a Prima Donna for fuck's sake!"

"Cheers to that!" She laughed and we downed our wine. More snacks were shoved into our mouths. We quietened as we munched away in a companionable silence.

"So why did you become friendly?"

We are still on Patrick then. I rolled my eyes and took a deep breath. I suppose I'd asked for this.

"It just happened. We met on the school run."

I filled her in about Jessica being away and how the children were friendly.

"You're not his usual type though" she smiled.

"Type?" *Here we go again...*

"Yes, type! He usually hangs around with rich knobs who like to give it the Jonny-big-bananas." She was laughing now. This was better, we were on familiar territory now – pissing about.

"Ha-ha! Are you implying I've not got the balls required to hang around with him?" I grinned. "I've also got plenty of bananas" I was gesturing to my fruit bowl. "Look plenty!" I laughed.

Jen was bubbling with laughter now. I took a large mouthful of wine.

"Oh Aims, you've always had the balls, but the banana, well – is it just a knob on your head!" She picked up the required fruit and was trying to model the balls and banana look for me. Her balls kept rolling off the chair.

"I can't control me balls" She howled.

She looked hilarious. Laughter erupted from within me, causing me to inhale the wine; forcing it out through my nose, squeezing tears out of my eyes. Jen fell apart: tears were now streaming down both our faces.

Hiccup.

I couldn't catch my breath. Jen was doubled up and attempting to pat me on my back, but her balls and bananas fell onto the floor and that set us off even more. I kept hiccupping and Jen was on the floor in stitches. Neither of us could move for laughter.

Like old times.

It felt so good after the stress of the last couple of weeks.

True to form, it took us a long time of trying to recover. Our success being hindered due to the constant presence of the offending fruit, which we were forced to hide it behind the sofa. This setting us off again with howls of 'hide the banana' and 'search me where it's gone!' Hilarious as we were, we eventually managed to stifle the laughter long enough to refill our glasses and shove more crisps and olives into our mouths, without them being a choking hazard.

"Anyway, seriously." I didn't want to do seriously, I wanted to do the funny. "I still say there's something there. There's chemistry you know" argued Jenna whilst shoving a mini quiche into her mouth.

I needed to stop this (not the shoving of food, just this topic of conversation) "Look Jenna, I know you mean well, but let's drop it. We aren't talking anymore and I've bigger fish to fry. Married men – attractive/attracted, or not, I have a career to kick-start"

Jen nodded. She knew me well enough to know when I was done. "You win." She grinned. She knew I'd had enough.

"Anyway, I have career news…"

For the next two hours, we drank to 'us' and we ate our own body weight in all the snacks she'd arrived with (there were also nuts, scotch eggs, the mini quiches too - she had also been to M and S and I was grateful for the luxury in my Aldi inspired kitchen). Plus, she'd brought a box of Ferrero Rocher (these had been our staple since we met in school) *'So sophisticated, even the Ambassador has them at his parties!'* We'd giggle.

We caught up with each other and Jen cried when I explained about the kick-starting of my career and told her how I was struggling with the exhibition. At which point she offered 'all my services' (not that she had much time as she was a very busy lady) to help me complete the work. That roughly meant spoiling Phoeb and Hazza with a full food and entertainments package, (which I could never provide to her scale – I was budget hotel, Jen was five-star cruise services) whilst I would hide away in my studio. Motherhood nil, career one (That was my guilty conscience working and not Phoebe and Harry, who would be ecstatic with the prospect of being ruined by Jen).

Happily reconciled, Jen went about elevenish. I was merrily tipsy, but not drunk. With it being a Thursday and being very busy – Friday was to be another full-on day with all the sodding work I had yet to complete - I decided to go into my kitchen and get some water.

A pint of water and some tablets would do the trick and would help me sleep.

However, just as I went into the kitchen, and was about to turn the light on, I spotted a shadow moving near the back window.

Shit

I went to take my phone out of my pocket; then I remembered it was on charge in the living room. I didn't dare move. I anxiously watched the shadow – after all, I didn't know if it was my eyes playing tricks...*was it a tree? A cat? Or was it something more sinister?* My heart was rapidly thumping in my throat.

Where the fuck are you now Frank?

You were channelling Jen earlier when I didn't need you...

I began to shake. I was all alone with only an ageing Lab for protection. A million scenarios flashed through my mind. I felt so sick. At least the children were asleep.

The shadow moved again, followed by a small yelping noise; alerting SDD from her ageing slumber. She managed to muster up the energy to make it to the back door and start barking. The shadow moved forward. I grabbed the first thing I could (a *whisk, what the hell?*) Flung the door open with my now excited dog and hit the shadow with my cheap egg whisk.

"Ouch, what you do that for? SDD was suddenly very excited, like one of her 'friends' were visiting. She was running rings around her 'friends'. I just stood, whisk in hand, opened mouthed and stared.

"Patrick Green explain yourself!"

HIROSHIMA

THEN
Patrick

Saltness
November 2016

People think they knew me. The big flashy businessman, who apparently owns half of Yorkshire. An arrogant, pushy and wealthy bastard, whose reputation is as big as his ego. No one had ever bothered to look beyond that. It could be very lonely...

And, being given little option in life, I had spent years playing up to that role. It wasn't always that way though.

It is a little-known fact about me: If I hadn't had been pushed into the family business, I'd have liked to have been a scholar - history and politics. Springing from a fascination, as a child, with what was going on in the news. I have vague memories of the Falklands; our constant fear and paranoia of Russia; the impact of Thatcherism...And where most children were bored to tears by the evening news, not me, I was hungry to see what was going on. I'd watch the IRA bombings and try to understand why? And, why were dictators so desperate to control? Whereas, there were children starving in Africa. I could never understand why my mother and father weren't as horrified or interested as me.

My inquisitiveness, as a child, used to drive my parents mad. '*The questions!*', they would laugh, thinking I was merely being a pain and that I didn't require any answers to these important matters – after all I was just a child. The nature of their lives being far more important: unfortunately, for Charles and me, they weren't interested in anything other than themselves.

Growing up in the eighties meant there was no internet to feed my curiosity, and my parents were 'very busy people'. Therefore, we would spend hours with our grandparents. Nan would take us to the library – laughing at our strange choices of books. Me: history, dystopian fiction, and spy novels. Charles – how the body works and books about Darwin (he was destined to become a doctor). My main topic of fixation was war and the struggle for power. I wanted to understand how these world leaders and warlords used power and influence as weapons to win. And how, when that didn't work, they resorted to real weapons.

Why were they so intent on destroying lives?

My grandpa would sometimes tell me some things of his own experiences. He was a silently intelligent man who had seen more than anyone would ever want to imagine. However, as a veteran of World War Two, he would not often speak from experience. But what he would emphatically talk about was human nature: he understood what made men tick. He told me that ambition, as far as he could see, came from some negative feeling of fear or anger. Which inevitably, would come full circle when these people reached their ambitions and realise that it had not solved their wanting; leaving them afraid and angry again. Grandpa said that it was better to make calculated risks which did not require any hurt to fuel them. That way we could all rest easy at night. *Why do you think they all end up dead?* He would argue.

So, I took that to mean that I had grown up to be a good person. I had to be focused and make decisions for the greater good. After all, Dad needed me to be ambitious to run the business. And as much as I wanted to go off and study, I quickly realised that it would kill my 'very serious I want to be a doctor' brother; therefore, I took one for the team. He'd never have coped with Dad's antics and I knew that it would kill him. He had dreamed of being a doctor since we were in the playroom at the ages of 4 and 6 respectively. After all, back then I was a better person, believing that I could be and ethical businessman and make a difference – I would not be like my father. Once I had made the decision, I also realised that my knowledge of social history and politics could be applied to our business to make it grow.

My company (Dad signed it over to me when we had Oli) is in leisure. What we do is hotels, restaurants, gyms, spas... anything that requires health and luxury – we do it. We have a chain of 'boutique' hotels in the most salubrious locations in Britain – and it all started with our large seafront hotel in Saltness. My grandparents opened it after the war, handing it to dad when they decided to retire early. By then they had bought two more guest houses, a restaurant and a caravan park from the profits. After all, the fifties were a golden age for seaside resorts - no one went to Spain on a plane in those days! My dad just continued to grow the company – ruthlessly at times.

The present problem was, the new plans which would lock me in even more, no longer excited me. We had plans to expand into France, Spain and Italy. No doubt we would be successful – but did I want it? Plus, with our ten health spas, gym franchises all over, and Eat Forest Green; restaurant chain, I appeared quite successful and wealthy, but it had all started to leave me cold. I was just babysitting it.

There was still some pride though: my amazing team. My team of trouble shooters were the ones who had made me into the success I had become. It was an idea I had years ago. Dad wasn't convinced but he gave me twelve months for my 'project'. Which, to his utter shock became one of the areas of the company with the least outgoings, but the most incoming cash on our books. And as I was particularly instrumental in setting up, it settled his mind about the future of Green Leisure Ltd. And was the reason he signed it all over to me. I had finally proved myself.

With the whole company at my disposal, I restructured, built myself a stronger team, who came from (poached) some of the best in the business. With the offer of a good wage, travel and share options, it was easy to get them on board – that and the fact that it was going to be an exciting new challenge – got them interested straight away. Ultimately, the largest part of our income came from our consultancy side of the business and that took us to another level.

It worked like this:

A chain of hotels (or restaurants, gyms etc.) would employ us as consultants. We would go in and look at how we could move the business forward. We would look at the current business model - staff, profit, design and how to modernise and keep abreast of trends. All with the aim of them making maximum profits and keeping a happy, loyal workforce.

Yes, there could be blood lost along the way, but we prided ourselves on being ethical and kind. I found top experts in their fields: tech people, accountants, writers, lifestyle gurus...One of my team was a trained psychologist and he was able to work out the temperature of feelings and be to somewhat manipulate the team we were working on into submission. He'd teach techniques and workshops, which would then show them how to behave towards the customers and the business. Also, I struck lucky when I employed Dani, my tech whizz. She was on her way back from a placement at Microsoft in Seattle, when I grabbed her. She was light years ahead of anyone else I knew in the industry. I was also careful when choosing my numbers guy, interior designer and publicity expert. My job was to head up the team.

All my hard work paid off when we won business of the year three years in a row. Professionally, this had been the proudest part of my career. I'd buried myself in it – travelling all over (sometimes overseas), becoming even more successful. All to fill that empty void inside of me.

Fortunately, it was this business model that enabled me to apply all my knowledge. I knew about life, why we are here. I knew about cultures and what made people tick. I also knew that if I kept my cool, then I wouldn't become like one of those people who Grandpa warned me about – after all none of my ambition came from fear. Or did it? It wasn't until recently, until I had had to spend time with the children, that I had taken a back seat from eighteen-hour days, that I realised what that was exactly what I happened – I'd been most scared of my home-life.

Recently, I'd been feeling so guilty. Spending time with the boys had made me wince about the amount of time I had lost with them. Furthermore, spending time with Aimee had taught me something – it made me think about how simple life could be. Not that she was simple (best not say that to her) far from it! But - she made things seem easy and simple. Like coming home – if that even makes sense? And, not that I am comparing but Jessica never made me feel like that. Instead, we seemed to have fallen into a cold war state where each one was calculating the other's move. Both not knowing what the other had in their arsenal.

These realisations knocked me for six. It came around the time she arrived home and found me with the empty JD bottle next to the side of my bed. We'd not seen each other for weeks and all I could feel between us was ice and the gleam of tri-umph I saw in her viper stare which said 'check'.

Being caught on the 'house-is-a-mess-and-I-am-very-hung-over' backfoot, meant I could not securely throw any comments at her about 'abandonment' and 'injustice'. I under-stood immediately that I had lost that particular battle and was so mad. I had calculated all the moves for when she re-turned. It was like she'd sent recognisance in whilst I was not looking. And that set me up for a mighty loss.

Bitch.

So, looking at my marriage and business, I realised that to be successful, had made me want to win no matter what. The need for power was born from negativity – greed and the fear of losing – not money, but face within my family and community. *What had I become?*

Maybe then, it was this fear that made me hunker down into my trench and find a way to nuke everything. I felt that I was losing, and I needed to do something drastic. Maybe it wasn't just Jessica who I wanted to shock, but me too. God knows, we needed it! But as with Hiroshima, the fall out would inevitably affect many innocent people – Aimee, our children, family...But, that day, when chance handed me my nuclear weapon, I told myself that I was fighting for the greater good.

What did I think she'd do? Fall into my arms?

⁕⁕⁕⁕⁕

I had laid low for about three weeks. I was beginning to think that I would be stuck in this limbo forever. Jessica barely talking to me. Aimee just a lovely distant memory, and me back working eighteen-hour days, and planning the new year trip out to France to look at possible sites. But my heart wasn't in it. Following Aimee earlier that morning, I felt so despondent. I didn't recognise the Patrick who wouldn't approach her and tell her to forgive him or else. I was losing my bottle.

Truth was, I could feel myself heading into a ravine. Mid-life crisis? Maybe, but surely, we have them for a reason? I couldn't face work (which was so unlike me) so I took Freddie home and we settled down in my bed and put a shit film on. I needed to wallow and felt like I needed a lifeline.

I wasn't meant to be there.

I was just laid there praying, with Freddie's head on my stomach (we looked like a sorry pair of old men – a tableau for the future) when the doorbell chimed. I couldn't be arsed to answer it (I'm telling you I was seriously losing it) and decided that they'd come back, when I heard two voices outside – one being Jessica, *oh god she was home; I wanted peace not tension,* and another one which sounded oddly familiar. Carefully (I was thinking about sneaking out before she saw me skiving and causing another argument) I looked out of the window. Jessica was back and she was talking to that loud friend of Aimee's – Jenna.

What did she want?

I heard a muffled "You'd better come in then"

And they moved in through the front door. I was intrigued and my miserable self-pitying lethargy escaped me as I crept out of our room and towards the landing. They were directly below me and glowering at each other like a pair of alley cats.

"I'm telling you to sort it"

"Telling me? Fuck's sake,"

Hell, Jessica is swearing. What is Jenna asking her to do?

"You bitch. I am not answerable to you" *That's Jessica, always thinks she's boss.*

"Really. Well I know something about you, and I am sure you wouldn't want it getting out" Threatened Jenna.

Blackmail! Fucking Hell, this is better than Desperate Housewives!

"What? You don't even know me" She was not just swearing, she was raising her voice.

My appreciation for Jenna multiplied: blackmail and the ability to rile up the Ice Queen – maybe I'd got her wrong. She was great at upsetting my wife.

And then she dropped the first bomb.

"Look, I know this awful thing, and believe me I was prepared to take this to the grave to protect the best person I know, but I know you were with Frank the night he died. And now you think it is fine to try and ruin her reputation as well"

There was a suspension of silence. Neither of them spoke. I must have been holding my breath as I started to become really dizzy and had to hold the banister. I felt like I'd been hit over the head and I was seeing a million stars around my head.

What the fuck?

I didn't know how to feel. Too much information.

"What?" Jessica managed to croak out.

"Yes, I saw you both. And if you think you can use my

best friend in your toxic power struggles then you've another thing coming!"

It started to sink in. *Saw them? Jessica and Frank?* I couldn't believe what I was hearing.

"That's why you've been spreading rumours and Patrick has been making a weird friendship with her isn't it? Payback"

Weird friendship?

I nearly shouted out that she had no idea but stopped myself in time.

"He doesn't know"

"Really? About the night he died? Come off it, why else…?"

"None of it" I could hear a wobble in her voice. So unlike my wife. She didn't do emotions other than faking it and nasty comments.

"Well why the sudden interest in Aimee? What has she done apart from being a widow to an unfaithful husband – who by the way – I never told her about to protect her? I hate the fact we are even having this conversation"

"There isn't really. I avoided her for years. I have no idea how they palled up, but they did. Imagine how I felt?"

"Felt? I don't really care about your feelings. I don't know the details, but I do know she doesn't deserve any of this. Why are you now trying to destroy her? After all you've done?"

"She must have known. That's why she'd manipulated herself into my family's life – payback"

Had she? I didn't think so and evidently neither did Jenna. Strangely reassuring that we both felt the same.

"Not her style and no, she doesn't know. That's your paranoia. Guilty conscience maybe? Two wrongs don't make a right. They might in your fucked-up world, but not mine. I'm straight up"

"So straight up you've been hiding this from you best friend for five years?"

Ouch, Jessica was trying to regain the moral high ground. Although, after observing them I realised that Jenna could go back in with a cracking left hook.

"You tell me what I should have done? She was grieving with two small children. You think I should have said '*oh and by the way, your beloved Frank was cheating on you with that icy rich bitch Green.*' That says more about you than me"

Well played Jenna. Exposing her for what she is. If only I'd had the balls...

She quietened down. She was silent and I could feel a slight shift in her stance – *maybe there was a conscience in that cold void somewhere?*

"He told me she knew and wouldn't let him go"

"Ha! That was him all over. A romantic Irish fool. He would have said something like that. You didn't know him very well did you?"

"I thought I did. We'd loved each other forever" she croaked.

"Sorry Jessica, but the only thing Frank loved was himself and the idea of being in love."

"You're lying"

"Really? Why do you think I've never married? I can't trust men and I have spent all my adult life protecting my best friend because she married a fool. I knew him better than anyone. I had to – Aimee and the children relied on me. Frank did too – to some extent. I was his Jiminy Cricket"

I wanted to laugh at the absurdity of it all. I felt slightly hysterical and realised that I was probably in shock and needed to make some space between us all. Only they had no idea I was there. My car wasn't there, and Jessica would have assumed I was at work.

They both went quiet.

"I think you better go" Jessica demanded in a cool icy tone. Only me, who thought I knew her better than anyone, could detect a tremor of something awful underneath.

"Me going doesn't solve anything, only you can do that"

"I will stop the rumours"

"Thank you. I think it's the least you can do"

So gracious. I was waiting for a Dynasty type bitch fight. I was severely disappointed.

"About the other stuff?"

"Not now. Find me on Facebook: Jenna Davis"

And she was gone.

Right then I remember thinking that I was going to offer Jenna a job as my chief negotiator. She would be a fabulous asset to the company. Only, in this instance, her weapon of choice was particularly poisonous; the fallout causing untold damage.

Weapon of choice – I could end it all now.

I quickly realised that I needed to hide. Jessica couldn't know what I had heard. From downstairs, I could hear instant muffled sobs and my caring part of me wanted to go and hug her. It was awful. No matter how I felt about her, it sounded like her heart was breaking – like hearing an animal suffering in pain. But...the other part of my brain took over, *'what the fuck? Jessica had an affair with Frank before he died!'*

I listened for a bit, my brain ticking on overtime. She eventually went out for a drive. Relieved, I quickly grabbed Freddie and made my escape. I decided to go up to the beach for another walk. I needed to think. Two things struck me. One: my lack of feelings about the affair. Two: How I could use this to win our cold war.

THE SECOND VISITOR'S CONFESSION

THEN
Aimee

Saltness
November 2016

Fucking Patrick Green.

"What do you think you are doing creeping around in my garden at nearly midnight?"

"I needed to shee yoush"

Oh fuck, he's drunk.

I raised my eyebrows and crossed my arms.

What on earth did he think he was playing at? It would certainly fuel the rumours…

He swayed slightly and crashed into the recycling bin.

"For fuck's sake Patrick, be quiet. The children are asleep."

Ignoring my appeal "That," He wobbled. Steadying himself against my door frame "my lovely Annie, is why I am in your back garden. I didn't want to ring the bell"

"Text?"

"As if your stony face would answer! Ha, anyway, that Jenna – who my opinion has somewhat changed about – does she want a job by the way? -"

"Jenna? And err no?"

"Yes, I saw you chatting away and eating many olives"

"Spying? *'She probably won't answer?'* So instead you took some notion about espionage and stalkering – all at the same time!"

The dogs were getting a little silly by now; starting to career and bark - a bit of happiness at being reunited.

"Fred, SDD, come here" I half-whispered.

I bundled them and him into my warm kitchen and gave the furry ones some treats. They ran off happily and settled themselves in from of the aga in companionable chomping. God, I wished it was that easy!

I looked at Patrick who was slumped over the table and drinking from the dregs of the wine bottle. He looked a glorious mess. His good looks all ruddy and wild. I'd never seen him so bright faced and alive. However, the crumpled mess of him and the fact he was turning into Saltness's resident wino contradicted this. My resolve softened at this thought.

What had put him in this state?

"Coffee?"

"Haven't you got anything stronger?"

"No, you need something to sober you up. What on earth has happened?"

Purposefully, I put the kettle on and began spooning coffee into the mugs. There was a quiet hum in the room. Patrick had his face in his hands. He must have sensed me looking at him. He smiled.

"Thank youse" he slurred.

"What for?" I had no idea why he was thanking me. After all, I was very pissed off with him. He was a mess though and I could see he needed some sort of help.

"Letting me in"

"I couldn't have you stumbling around in my garden, falling into all the shite around the back door. I'd have become even more 'persona non grata' than I am already"

"I don't mean that but thank you for that also. I mean for letting me into your wonderful life. You are also not 'persona non grata' and if you are those people are wankers"

I didn't know what he meant. "Letting me into this wonderful life?"

"Yes. Being a friend. A real one. I don't really have anyone like that. You let me, and my children, and my dog, in." He nodded towards a dozing content Freddie nestled into SDD. "They look happy together, don't they? They fit"

If I didn't know him better, I would say that he was going all misty eyed.

"They fit" he repeated. "I thought I could make Jessica and me fit all those years ago. You can't make love happen though – even with all the key ingredients"

I did not want to get involved in his marriage again.

"Look Patrick, as much as I would like to help you, I feel really awkward about having this discussion"

"But that's the thing Aimee. I need you to understand how I feel more than anyone. If you don't understand then all this would have been for nothing"

"All this?" His drunken logic was losing me.

"Yes, what I have learnt, how I feel, you see I have something to tell you"

NAGASAKI

THEN
Patrick

Saltness
November 2016

If me finding out about Jessica and Frank's betrayal was Hiroshima, I was about to make things worse. Two dramatic, but well-intentioned bombs dropped in near succession, to end what was an impossible stalemate. There was a war and I wanted to finish it. I wanted peace time.

"Well?"

She was looking at me impatiently. I was stumbling over my words and I could tell she still wasn't thawed out. I went into my pocket and fished out my hip flask. David at 'The Sailor's Inn' had kindly filled it before he chucked me out '*I have got to close Paddy.*' He'd reminded me (David and I had become firm friends that afternoon and I had invited him to call me Paddy).

"Err, what are you doing?" I was tipping a large measure into my coffee.

"Want some Aims?"

"No, and you shouldn't either" a laugh formed under that frosty veneer. That was the thing I'd learnt about her – she didn't nurture grudges.

"Why are you laughing Annie? Anyway, I need the Dutch courage"

"The absurdity. If anyone had said to me, six months ago, that Patrick Green would be sitting in my kitchen slurring his words and being a prize dick, I wouldn't have believed them!"

"Yeah you would. You've always thought I've been a dick"

We both laughed.

"True. You have always been a dick"

This broke more ice. The iron fortress which had met me at the door, was now opening up and was looking more welcoming.

God, that felt so good. Seeing her light up.

"That's better. I like it when you smile"

"Shut up! Stop soft soaping me. What's wrong?"

"I mean it. Well actually I don't because I love it when you smile"

Silence. She looked away. I knew she could feel it – there was a tension in the air. Just like the night I tried to make a stupid pass. And now, there I was again, drunk and making statements (*please don't let me throw up again*) I should really be making sober. I couldn't stop myself though.

"I mean it. That's what is wrong. I miss it, I miss you"

"Is this going to be another drunken pass? Because, I'm telling you now, adultery isn't my thing."

God she can read me.

And then I don't know why I said it – probably the drink which had lit the arrogant side of my brain. It had empowered me to jump six months into the future. To second guess a woman who I had no business of doing so to. To implicate her in my decisions. The true depth of my feelings came tumbling out:

"No, because I'm leaving Jessica for you"

"Don't be so ridiculous." She laughed. She looked at my serious face. I was not laughing "What makes you think I'd even want you?" she looked furious. I thought she could feel it too. I needed her to. I couldn't stop thinking about her. She filled all my head space. Even when I was making decisions I would think '*what would Aimee say?*'

How had this crept up on me?

Anxiously, I looked at her beautifully naked face – no make-up. Nowhere to hide. She didn't need any of it. She had this naturally sexy glow of strength and independence. She didn't need anybody. I wanted to get to know her more than anything else in life. At that moment it was all so clear to me: I wasn't being ridiculous, for the first time in years, I was being totally honest.

How could she not feel the same?

"I know you want me because it can't be possible to feel so much for someone without them feeling it in return. I have never felt like this before. Me Patrick Green – what is going on when I can't stop thinking about this strange artistic and sometimes caustically witted woman. One who paints and walks her dog. Has lovely children. Faces the world head on. Someone who doesn't realise how beautiful and sexy she is. Well that's who I want to fill my life with." I was rambling now. It was getting a bit embarrassing as she was just staring at me.

Silence. We locked eyes and I noticed her cheeks were flushed. She looked across the room biting her lip. She was staring at an old family photo of them all. I could sense that I was getting somewhere. My clumsy attempts were beginning to work. But then the drink loosened my mouth further – but in the wrong direction.

"Look Patrick. I can't do this. I know it is five years since Frank died"

"Saint Frank" - I couldn't help myself. That fucker had ruined too many lives. He was the real catalyst to the decline of my marriage. And here she was worshipping the fucker.

Her face hardened.

"No, not Saint Frank and you have no right...he was no saint, anyway"

All of a sudden, I thought I did have a right. Bringing him up had ignited a flame that had been smouldering since lunchtime. "I fucking know all about his 'unsaintly ways' don't you worry"

"What's that meant to mean?" she hissed.

Why couldn't she see it? Be in the same place as me. I wanted to press fast forward, get her through all that pain and have her fall into my arms like some damaged damsel in distress. I wanted to rescue her, and she didn't want rescuing. I was getting more garbled and desperate. I think that's what made me say it.

"Ask Jenna"

"Jenna, what's she got to do with it?"

"Ask her"

"About what? You are talking shit again Patrick. Come on, I think you need to get yourself home"

She stood up to rally Freddie and get me into my coat. I was desperate. I needed her to understand, to feel like me. I'd do anything to stop the impasse. To move forward from the torture. To move into peace time.

"Ask her why she was at mine earlier, threatening Jessica"

"What? Threatening Jessica. She never said…"

"No, she wouldn't, would she?"

"I am sorry Patrick, unless you want to stop talking in riddles and shit, I am going to have to ask you to leave. I admit, and I will tell you this, so you understand where I am coming from, that I do feel…" I was losing the thread of what she was saying. My mind was wandering.

What was I telling her again? Oh yes, about Frank, Jessica, Jenna knew something.

"Yes, threatened her. She saw them together the night he died"

What was she going to say? She does feel…?

"Who?"

"Frank and Jessica"

PART FIVE

TO LOVE, HONOUR AND OBEY

AFTER THE HAPPILY EVER AFTER...

BEFORE THEN
Jessica

Leeds to Saltness
September 2006

When I was first married, I went back to work for Patrick. I think about that time fondly, proudly even: we were quite the formidable force in those days. We ran the 'Firm' with focus and diligence, bringing it more into the new millennium. Old Jonny Green might have been good in his day, and to some extent he was still a great weapon in our arsenal, but his forward thinking had stalled somewhere before the birth of the internet. Much to his dismay, he was becoming old-school. Patrick, his young-gun protégé, had been fighting out the merits of new technology with his father. Jonny firmly believed in the face-to-face side of the industry – customer facing, legacy loyalty, and all that...his old-school short-sightedness having its place, but meaning we were in danger of getting behind in the game.

Our marriage worked best in the boardroom. We'd get a kick out of making a project a success. Patrick and I were always better at the business side of our relationship. It was where our passions mostly lay. We'd work extremely hard and enjoyed reaping the rewards together. It fuelled our physical relationship when we clinched a deal or managed to maximise our profits. In those days; in our twenties; before the children; we were successful and infallible. We were the dream team of Green Leisure LTD, and Jonny knew it.

We began to pull in big deals. Between us, we managed to manipulate the business to our modern planning strategy. I learnt about how to use the multiple business platforms available to us through the growing technology industry. Armed with my research and reports, I'd blind Jonny with figures, and he released (with lots of persuasion) a budget for me to develop that side of the company. Meanwhile, Patrick was looking into consultancy. It was the first time we'd worked solely on separate projects. I was excited and so driven, and honestly? It was the best time of my life. Plus, my new role gave me my own self-respect. I wasn't just the boss's wife: A Green. I was proving my worth.

I began with the company brand and our websites for our various businesses. I introduced text services – way before you could check in on an app and have a concierge service LIVE on your phone. I did virtual tours of our hotels and gyms. And as the new iPhone was released – I saw the potential game changing way it would further modernise the way we did business. I read all the technology news and I travelled to Google's office in Ireland, to understand more about how the world was developing.

In those days, my husband would laugh and tell me *I was obsessive about my career.* I loved it though. I lived off pure adrenaline and I knew I was good at what I did. Both Jonny and Patrick treated me as an equal, or so I thought, in a man's world of commerce and economics. I remember feeling strong and independent, like I'd grown up from the naïve little girl who pleased everybody. Finally, I was pleasing myself. Also, I felt so lucky in my marriage as he treated me as an equal - I always knew Patrick respected my head for business and my drive. And, the little geek inside of me felt good to be recognised by his father – the formidable Mr Green Senior.

However, nothing is ever perfect. Like I said, we worked hard, and we partied hard. Our rest and relaxation were taken in the best locations, all over the UK and the world. After all, our job was the leisure industry and we needed to see what everyone else was doing. Every trip was research and enabled us to adjust our business models. We were at the top of our game and had the best of everything. And for the first time in my life, money was never really an issue. We enjoyed each other's company and had the time of our lives. But, as much as I tried, I knew that the deep love I should have felt for my husband, wasn't there.

For a time, I lied to myself what love was. I almost believed it. But, deep down I knew that the only time I'd ever felt what I thought love should feel like, was in Corfu back in 1996. But that was a different Jessica. That was Jessie. And that young, quiet girl, could not be found in the face of the polished new me. Only I knew she was there - deep down. It was her desperation which scared me: her struggle for a better life. Her hunger for love. The little girl lost, missing her mum.

Sometimes, I had to focus so much on the present, so that I could block out the emotions which threatened to expose a different me. When I fell pregnant with Oli, I really struggled to keep a lid on it. Luckily, (I say luckily, but losing your mother to cancer at forty is not lucky) I could blame my distress on being an 'orphan'. Of course, the Greens couldn't do enough to protect me, and I felt grateful for their support. But, since the breakdown of sorts I had after Mam's death and Frank's abandonment, I had learnt to focus on work. My focus dulled all the other senses – the sheer adrenaline of achieving and going above and beyond. I was what they call 'A Workaholic'. In fact, on the morning before I gave birth to Oli, I was overseeing the development of an app which would enable our customers to manage their stay from their phone. At the time we didn't know if it would work. However, what I was doing turned out to be revolutionary to the way we did customer service. Our reviews went through the roof and bookings went up by 20%. I was successful and I prayed Mam was looking down.

But like I say, nothing is ever perfect.

After Oli was born, I really struggled with my conscience at leaving him. Patrick and I employed a nanny, and at first it seemed like a fantastic idea. However, I wasn't prepared to jet off here, there and everywhere, to enjoy the lavish lifestyle I'd once enjoyed. I explained my issues with my husband, and he was surprisingly very supportive. He suggested I work part-time, enjoy Oli, spend our well-earned money on the large house we'd just bought in Headingly. I knew this made sense, after all, the city apartment was a great deal smaller and someone had to make the new house a home – Oli had and would invariably change our lifestyle for good (babies do that I told Patrick when he was moaning that I wouldn't be able to fly to Dubai with him for business, as I was breast feeding).

A few weeks later, when I was juggling a breast pump and reading through a contract, I asked him to help out more with Oli. The bastard (that was how I felt right then and now) told me that all I had to do was 'manage my time better' and promptly flew off to Ireland to look at an old hotel, which needed his team to 'inject some life into'.

What could I say though? People looking in through the window of my life would think I had it all: a (mostly) supportive husband; a bonnie baby boy; a large house; money, and a career (which I was hanging onto by my fingernails). But I knew they were wrong. What I had begun to learn in my life was that people make assumptions on what they want to see. No one ever really knows you – then again, I was pretty closed as a person back then. All I wanted was to be valued. As I took to my new domesticated life, I felt myself losing my newly built identity. I didn't want to change again and become another 'Jessica', I wanted to be the strong and independent one. I loved her; she was the best fit. I was fighting for breath in what was emerging as a man's world.

The final nail in the coffin came on Jonny's sixtieth birthday, when he was expected to be signing over the business to us as a nod to retirement. To get to that point, we were to endure some god-awful birthday weekend to celebrate. We had to go to the North Yorkshire coast, to Saltness - *the place where it all began*. The glorious flagship of 'The White Cliff's Hotel'.

If not a little tired, it was incredibly charming hotel (the fact that it needed a refurb did not deter Jonny from choosing this venue – he liked to show how far he'd come). He had booked out his whole (negligible) five-star cliffside hotel for the weekend. This was to be the first time our young family of three would all go away together. I was nervous and so I could relax a little, Diane had arranged for a trusted family friend to childmind Oli for us during the 'Big Event' (something told me that Patrick wouldn't be very helpful that night, so I readily agreed). We were also to meet Charles's new fiancé – another trainee doctor called Moira. Of course, he'd invited loads of other people from Jonny's 'Trusted Close-Knit Community' (as they liked to call it – I secretly called them old lecherous pissheads). With the self-smug Fitzgeralds as their oldest friends and guests of honour, heading the guest list.

The entire weekend had been mapped out. We had little freedom to do anything – well it appeared I didn't anyway. Whilst Patrick was expected to schmooze Jonny's so called 'friends', I was literally left holding the baby. And as adoring as Diane was, she didn't offer to look after Oli at all. Oh no, it would have interfered with all her busy social activities like golf, tennis, and drinking endless G and T's with her own 'Circle of Friends'. I was bored shitless, with only Moira (the new fiancé) for company. Whom, as lovely as she was, was quiet and a little aloof. I suspected she thought I was like the rest of them – shallow and empty headed (all everyone would talk about was where they'd been and what they'd bought). With a major baby brain still, it appeared that neither of us had anything in common. Conversations limped and time hung heavy. I felt like a Victorian bride waiting for her death photography shoot. This thought inspired me and led me to mention the wedding, thinking I could help her with venues and suppliers (I didn't actually care but it was something to say). She shut the conversation down quite quickly telling me that

'Charles and I will not even consider marriage until we are in our chosen roles: him in surgery, and me in practice.'

And that she could see herself having sweet babies like Oli, once she'd proved herself. That stung; I'd proved myself, or so I thought I had, but Oli seemed to have topped trumped my career and it had come to a stop whilst Patrick had no such issues. Not for the first time, I thought that men should be made to breastfeed and carry a small child inside them for nine months – *they'd never cope!* I craved the equality that we once had. In hindsight, I wanted the opportunity to have the strength of vision to have made Patrick wait for children.

The pinnacle of the weekend was a dinner dance in the hotel's (once) Grand Ballroom. Surprisingly, the room looked gorgeous. It had been opulently decorated by the very best event co-ordinator this side of the Humber Estuary. Diane had masterminded the whole 'look'. It was black-tie, and always inspired by all things 'Audrey Hepburn' and 'celebrity' (believing herself to be a local one) that Truman Capote's famous 1966 Black and White ball should be replicated. That, and the fact it was the 40th anniversary of the party of the century. Diane was determined that it would go down in history as the greatest spectacular the North had ever seen.

I needed to be at my best. I'd been fighting the weight loss since before I'd given birth. I knew Oli was going to be born about three months before the big event, and I felt the dread creeping in as the weight piled on during the third trimester. Stupid as it sounds now, I started dieting. I cut out carbs, exercised daily, and ate small healthy salads and fruit – all little and often. Then, within two weeks of giving birth, I was out running. If I wasn't running, I'd be taking Oli for lengthy walks around Headingly, in his Bugaboo (Gwyneth Paltrow had nothing on me). I tackled the 'pre-baby body plan' like I tackled my work – I focused and didn't take my eye off the ball for a second. Also, I wasn't stupid, Patrick (although at that point the affairs hadn't started) was a flirt and I didn't want to give him a reason to stray like his father had throughout his lengthy marriage. Additionally, and superficially, I'd had my eye on the most glorious white Dior gown, since I'd been six months pregnant. I knew I'd need pouring into it, even pre-pregnancy, but I was so driven with the idea of all eyes being on me when Jonny was to make his (anticipated) announcement, that my days revolved around being super fit and healthy. I wanted Patrick and I to look every inch the 'power couple'. I felt the retirement speech would launch our next phase and would propel us to even bigger success. Patrick was convinced we'd be made equal partners. He'd talked about it all year.

That night, in September 2006, he certainly did make an unforgettable speech. One that would change our lives forever.

AND THEN...

Patrick

Saltness
September 2006

The first shift in our relationship was when we went back to my home town of Saltness for Dad's sixtieth. Obviously, prior to that, Jessica had given birth to our beautiful Oli! My god, I was so proud of her, my gorgeous wife giving birth to our perfect son. All his mother's beautiful dark brown hair tufting out of his head. Clear blue eyes I could drown in. I'd never felt anything like it before – my son! He was a Green and it was instant love. I'd never felt so happy. Back then, I felt like I had it all.

Jessica took instantly to motherhood and seamlessly recovered back to her old self within weeks. She had lost the baby weight immediately – she'd hardly put much on in the first place. Plus, she was out and about in no time – I expected nothing less, being my uber organised wife – I had no doubt that I was right in marrying her. She was just perfect.

That was why I was not surprised that she was so eager to go back to work within four weeks. However, reality was she just hated leaving Oli. We'd employed a nanny, but she was breastfeeding and forever having to pump. It was exhausting her. Jessica felt like she was losing control of her personal and professional lives – I could tell. I told her to do whatever she liked. I told her she could work part time, spend money, enjoy Oli, make our new house a home (out old apartment and lifestyle was out the window for the foreseeable) – whatever made her happy. I'd have done anything for her in those days. She'd given me Oli, and that was the greatest gift I'd ever been given.

That Friday morning, when we drove across the moorland, I felt so smug. Like I had earned the label as the happiest and most self-satisfied man alive. I was nearing thirty and I had nailed it: an angelic son, a beautiful wife, and my business (I was already calling it mine in my head) was making more money than it ever had done. I was also feeling sure that he'd be relinquishing it to me and Jessica. After all, we'd brought it into the millennium – kicking and screaming and had made the difference in its finances, between drifting along and powering forward.

I remember looking at Jessica, her eyes closed – power napping she called it – whilst I swung our new family Mercedes People Carrier across the moors and around the hairpin bends. I was indestructible. Nothing scared me anymore. I felt very smug and couldn't wait to show them both off. I wanted to show them the town I grew up in. We were now going to make our own path and show them all how it's done. I intended to spend all weekend with my new family. I wanted to indulge Jessica and spoil Oli. After all, I was feeling some guilt about the trips to Dubai and Ireland – I knew I had some making up to do.

My Father, Jonny Green had other ideas. Entrenched in old-school etiquette, he'd invited his top business connections and cronies, to his 'family celebration'. So along with Charles and Moira, Jessica and I were outnumbered. As soon as I stepped foot into the marbled reception, Dad was ready with the scotch and introductions to be made to his 'Inner Circle'. Of course, I knew most of them, but I had a feeling that this was to be the unofficial handover to me that weekend. This thought I relished. And as guilty as I felt (again) letting Jessica settle in with Oli and taking the parenting reins, I promised myself I'd make it up to them the following day.

Only I didn't. I let her spend time with Moira, whilst

Charles played the 'academic one', impressing Dad's acquaintances with his qualifications and aspirations. Dad was showing us off and I knew it. So, I let Jessica bond with Moira – her future sister-in-law, I drank lots of scotch, played golf, and held court at the hotel bar. Any guilt I felt was pushed away telling her that we had to do this for Dad as the company was nearly ours. I told her that we'd worked hard and once this weekend was over that we could make our own choices and be answerable to no one.

The only blot on our horizon were the bloody Fitzgeralds. I knew Jessica felt the same – they were awful people and I didn't know why my parents spent so much time with them. He was a retired MP, and she was his society wife. Both from old money (as Dad would say) and both taught to sponge off any whiff of new money. I sensed that Peter might have helped Dad a few times during his political career. When I spotted them in the bar on that first afternoon, Mum was sharing a G and T with them, whilst Jessica was managing Oli's needs. I was a bit put out that she hadn't rushed to help Jessica and thought she'd have been a bit more hands on with her first grandson. I felt disappointed and stuck – I was mid-discussion and did not want to be rude to the man I was talking to – he'd made a fortune in away days and that was something I wanted to add to our portfolio. So, I cursed my mother and the guilt stacked up towards Jessica.

Little did I know that Diane was so distracted and full of gin, that she had bigger fish to fry. Peter, now recommissioned to the women due to his retirement and lack of usefulness to my father, was sitting there between the two women, his red and bulbous drinker's nose shining like a beacon of failure. Roberta flanked one side dressed for Cannes in white trousers and a Breton top. She had glorious red wedge sandals that I'm sure I'd seen Jessica wearing (Roberta probably saw her in them and wanted that look – she was always quite a jealous and greedy woman) and was sitting back from Peter and looking at me with a smile plastered across her face. Mum sat straight backed to his other side (she never slouches, even when she is soaked in gin) looking flushed from what was probably her fourth gin. She was more demurely dressed in a smart navy shift dress and pearls; looking every inch the Stepford Wife. Thinking back now at my ramrod straight pained mother, and the carefree nautical Roberta, I should have guessed something was going on. Anyway, I remember thinking, their weird friendship wasn't my problem. I swapped pleasantries and went and arsed myself around (that is what Jessica called it when she was mad at me, I prefer to say, 'work the crowd') the marauding crowds around the welcome drinks' reception, of our 'Close Knit Circle'.

SISTER SUFFRAGE

Jessica

Saltness
September 2006
The Ball:

I know I've mentioned it before, but to really understand Patrick's family, I will have to make Dynasty as my point of reference. It's all big revelations, affairs, throwing each other under a bus, money and grand gestures. The blood line is highly important and so is 'The Firm'. It is central to everything. To be a Green is to be successful, preferably in business and marry advantageously – there's no room for dead wood. Each of us would serve a purpose. Each thriving off their allotted role.

For a time, I did too. I was good at what I did and had the respect of 'The Firm'. It was what drove us to survive on five hours sleep and still be able to close deals. It was thrilling in those early days and we were such a force to be reckoned with.

No one messed with The Greens.

That was why the sheer opulence of the ball just rolled off me like night is day. It no longer awed me. More often than not it bored me. Don't get me wrong, I didn't take it for granted, it just no longer impressed me. I found Diane's taste vulgar and outdated (obviously I'd never tell her that) but it was true.

The 'Look' for the ball wasn't so bad. Large swags of black and white material were hung from the ceiling; gathering from the chandeliers which glittered like brilliant stars in the night sky. Giving the appearance of an Indian tented palace (in reality it was hiding a much-needed lick of paint). Black and white balloons reaching up the tented ceiling, from the rounds which framed the polished dancefloor. White lilies and roses were entwined with gypsophila and berries, which had been dyed black; the black falling over the pure white heavenly scented flowers like a widow's veil. The effect was chillingly beautiful; a foreshadowment of this macabre celebration of life. The only hint of any other colour on the table was the golden rings around the black linen napkins.

A sultry jazz band played on the stage, inviting couples to take to the floor. They played Duke Ellington, Louis Armstrong...bodies swaying in an old-fashioned timeless way. The whole scene held a type of elegance. Men and woman dressed in nothing but black and white. Guests wore an ensemble of masks - all competing for the top spot for the best dressed. All very tasteful, retro, and totally over the top – all, I guessed, was born from the stylist's vision from Diane's ostentatious need to show everyone the Greens' obvious wealth. However, what you could also see was where Diane had made her mark for independence too.

She was of a different generation. Equality seemingly had passed her by. She had made the waitresses on drinks duty to dress like Playboy Bunnies. All black and white tuxedo leotards and fishnet tights. Men were invited into the Ballroom bar area for cigars and after dinner port. Ladies were entered into the competition of the 'Best Dressed', and she made the judging panel Jonny, Patrick and Charles. All her outdated notions of female subservient meant that finally Moira and I found common ground to agree on. We were both silently outraged, until after and uncharacteristically, she'd had too many welcome champagnes asked: 'Has she always been a misogynist enabler?'. I laughed and told her she'd seen nothing yet and enquired if she'd yet met the Fitzgeralds. By the knowing nod I realised she knew exactly what I was talking about. We tended to stick together after that – united by our shared anger at Diane setting women's rights back thirty years.

"Next we'll catch the men slapping the girls' bottoms and calling them game lassies!" drily observed Moira.

If only that had been our only problem that night. It was worse than that.

The menu had been carefully crafted. All Jonny's favourites but with a twist. So, after the 'Playboy Bunnies' had served a trio of canapes: Mini Yorkshire puddings filled with a small serving of carpaccio of beef and a whisper of horseradish; chicken liver pate served with balsamic and shallot chutney, on mini melba toasts; and mini sundried tomatoes stuffed with mozzarella and olives. We were seated in a very carefully orchestrated seating plan for the 'Main Event' (Only it wasn't). We began with Welsh Rarebit, served with shots of Bloody Mary. The main was Haddock and Chips, served with fresh minted crushed peas and homemade tartar sauce. Concluding with a trio of desserts and the ubiquitous cheeseboard. It was comfort food and tasted so good. I'd had months of starvation to get into my Dior gown. I threw caution to the wind and decided to loosen up. With the added ingredient of alcohol, Moira and I bonded over a shared love of reading.

"I have to say Moira," I was laughing and trying to breathe in my increasingly tight dress. "I've had to move heaven and earth to get into this dress for this evening. Jonny's feast might have undone all that good work!"

She laughed at my honesty "Ha, I was wondering. You've done incredibly well. I've patients who've had wee ones and would scratch your eyes out to get that figure back in what – four months?"

"Three, and it wasn't easy!"

"I bet. You look good though. I hope when I finally get to that stage that I manage. I am prone to carrying it on my hips - child bearing hips my granny always says"

I appraised Moira in her slinky black gown that clung to all the right places. Her red hair piled into an elegant chignon, held by a diamante clasp. Her Celtic green eyes twinkling in the sea of black and white. She was a glorious riot of warmth and colour in the monochrome world Diane had created.

"I'd say you've got it all going on. You're beautiful Moira. A breath of fresh air for this family. I won't feel so outnumbered anymore!"

"Och, get away with ya! Thank you though. I was worried about meeting you. Charles always painted this picture of this determined and dynamic woman."

I nearly spat my wine out (not very ladylike I know). "Me? Charles did? I suppose I am very driven, and I do enjoy working hard. But what I do doesn't compare to what you do."

"Even so, I bet you have to stick up for yourself, no?"

I nodded.

"I think" gestured Moira around the room "That we are both women fighting for our place in a man's world"

She was very perceptive. I held up my glass. "Let's drink to that!"

"Cheers!"

"Anyway, men aside, I like to feel good for me. Plus, I felt it important to look good tonight"

"Ah yes, the 'Big Reveal!' As Charles keeps calling it"

"Does he mind? I did say to Patrick to talk to him. After all, he is a Green more than me"

"Yes, but you do know that Patrick saved him. He took on his dad and the business so Charles could follow his dream. Admirable really: save for the massive fortune it's worth!"

"He has his share option and Patrick respects him enormously for what he has achieved."

"I know, I'm joking. They're like chalk and cheese, aren't they? But fiercely loyal to each other. Have you got any brothers and sisters?"

I was used to this question by now, but it never stopped that splinter of a pause. I didn't like lying to my warm and intelligent new ally, but I had no choice. "No. I have no family..."

"Oh, I'm sorry. Tell me to shut up. Charles says it's the clinician in me – I can be so direct. Unlike this lot" She nodded towards the rest of the family. Moira and I (plus the brothers) were sitting on the table next to Jonny, Diane and their crew.

I knew what she meant "Ha-ha" I laughed "Yes, they are all smoke and mirrors aren't they?"

"Charles told me earlier, that you have turned about their internet business. I have to say Jessica, I owe you an apology"

I looked at her, the question in my eyes.

"Yes, at first, I had you down as one of those trophy wives."

"More direct speaking! You must be a very good doctor – I bet you soon get it out of people what you need to know"

"Yes, like I say I'm sorry. I didn't realise what you had actually done, until Charles explained and then I was slightly in awe, like I said earlier – both of you to get Jonny to drop his old-school ways. She gestured around her to the bunnies and the smell emanating from the 'cigar' room already. "And, not yet. I will be though"

I understood where she was coming from. I could have been hurt, but I liked her honesty and the fact she understood who I actually was and not just Patrick's wife – who, up until now I had been addressed as such, with my boobs very much the focal point of the conversation.

"Thank you. Yeah, I might have married the boss, but I work hard. Finding it difficult with Oli, but it's worth it. I've earned the success as much as Patrick. I suspect you'll do the same with Charles. Neither of us will end up like these." I motioned towards Diane and Roberta.

"That's the plan. I'm not giving up any independence when I get married. Partnership. That's why I shut you down earlier about the wedding"

I shot her a look.

"I know. It was just that I thought you might be in cahoots with Diane. She's been ringing non-stop about venues and dresses…"

"Yep, that's Diane! She's a steamroller"

"Yes well, she is in for a shock. I'll tell you because I've decided I quite like you. Charles put me straight on one or two things this afternoon – he thinks highly of you, you know?"

"Does he? We barely speak"

"Yes, well, that's Charles. However, he does know how his brother has met his match with you and he likes that. He thinks you will keep him on the straight and narrow, unlike..."

"Ladies and Gentlemen, may you be upstanding for mine host Mr Jonny Green"

A loud cheer and round of applause went up as we stood and did, what felt like, a million toasts for Jonny. I caught Patrick's eye and he grinned at me. I felt we were finally beginning and that although it was all work, play and sex, for a long time. We were finally becoming a true partnership. The speech was coming, and I finally felt like I was going to be a true Green.

AND THE WINNER IS...

Patrick

Saltness
September 2006
The Ball:

Dad was standing up and arranging his papers in front of us. I sat down and held Jessica's hand under the table. This was very un-us, but since becoming parents, and with the anticipation of Dad's speech, I felt closer to her than ever before.

"Good evening friends, family, and countrymen"
Trust him to begin like Julius Caesar. Both ruthless.
There followed a little laughter and Dad cleared his throat.
"*As you all know, we are here this evening to celebrate my sixtieth year. And what sixty years it's been!*

As you all know, it started here, in this very hotel, a year after the war ended. My father came home from the far east and I was his welcome home present nine months later."
This solicited another laugh and then with an exaggerated aside he added "*Some of you might not know this but my dearly departed mother actually gave birth to me in the penthouse suite upstairs. Only, it wasn't called that then, it was our family home*"
This was so like Dad, he liked to play the 'humble beginnings' card. Fact was, his parents were wealthy, and he just worked hard to maintain and finally improve that.
He looked down at his sheets and continued.
"*My family, as many of you know is very important to me. As*

was the way with my mother and father, we have always worked hard for our success. I helped my father build his empire, as I grew up. He handed it to me in the seventies, and Patrick has done the same for me since his teens. Supported by his mother Diane, his brother Charles, and later his beautiful wife Jessica, he has grown into a son to be proud of – well they both have" he nodded over to us both. I was so glad he'd mentioned Charles. He had achieved so much and without Dad's constant support. He'd gone out alone and been successful in his own right.

"Over the past ten years Patrick has taken this company from strength to strength. He has dragged it into the modern era, against my old-school ways as he likes to call them." We all laughed. He'd heard us then! *"And now tells other companies what to do! He is a credit to this family and I'm sure him and Jessica will continue to raise my first grandson Oliver to be a true Green too!"*

I knew it was coming. I squeezed Jessica's hand. To be honest, I was a bit wrapped up in myself at that moment and failed to notice he had omitted Jessica from the company's present success.

"Therefore, this evening, I would like to officially announce that I am handing over Green Leisure Ltd to my son and heir Patrick Green! Whilst I am going to retire and enjoy my old age whilst I still can! Thank you, Patrick, for making me proud and making a success of modernising my company. A toast for my son Patrick!"

He'd done it. The whole room stood up and cheered, clapped and banged on the tables, to congratulate my success. Dad proposed a toast and I felt proud. I'd finally done it – I'd gained his respect and trust. I looked at him and smiled and then glanced at Jessica. She was smiling but there were tears brimming in her eyes. Stupidly I mistook it for emotion. I took her in my arms and held her for a moment. She was shaking slightly, and I remember thinking how overwhelmed she must have felt. Again, it never really registered that he'd only mentioned her child bearing success rather than her professional success. I knew as well as she did that, we'd done it together – fifty/fifty.

But, when you finally get everything you want, you can become blind to any problems. Blinkered vision can mean you neglect to notice what is going on around you. I suppose now that my arrogant ignorance was the beginning of the end.

ALEXIS AND CRYSTAL

Jessica

Saltness
September 2006
The Ball:

Of course, he'd not mentioned me. Well, he'd grouped me in with Diane and Charles. The three musketeers, or puppet masters, who helped Patrick up the success ladder. Deep down, I knew that was unfair on my husband, it was my jealousy talking – since then, I'm not so forgiving of him. But at that time, I knew we'd all sacrificed more than just being a side-line to Patrick's success.

They toasted and generously cheered and applauded my husband. I managed to keep myself in one piece for that. There were congratulations and some joking from Charles about being disinherited *'I better do as he says from now on'*. Patrick said that *'Charles would never win a fight ever again!'* I knew Patrick would do nothing of the sort, he'd keep the share options safe and that he loved and respected his brother more than most.

After all the chatter had died down, the 'men' were going off for cigars and other bullshit, and I was able to make my excuses to get away. Always the professional – even at being the model wife (as I had now decided was all Jonny thought I was good for) I held my head high, put on a glittering smile, and sashayed out of the ballroom on the pretence of going to check on the childminder and Oli.

It wasn't until I made it outside in the cooling September air, that I let the tears come. I promised myself that I was allowed a few before I checked on Oli and repaired the damage to my face. I eyed the doorway to the back staircase and knew I could go to our room without being seen. I felt incredibly abandoned and stupid. Why did I feel so slighted by Jonny? After all, there was no pre-nup; we were equal. But that wasn't it. It was nothing to do with the money. I wanted to be acknowledged for what I had achieved. I'd put the company first – at times before my marriage and having a family – because it's what Patrick and I knew needed to happen. He'd told me on the way up here that he couldn't have done it without me and that his dad knew that. He felt sure I'd be rewarded. However, as much as I knew that we were seriously rich now, the only thing he'd acknowledged in his 'Main Event' speech was that fact I'd had a bloody baby. A baby that I'd left at four weeks, so I could go back to work and finish the app deal, which was worth a great deal of money. I had to leave him with his nanny, whilst I pumped at my desk so he could get the 'best start possible', and it killed me. I'd never felt so torn. Even Patrick had recognised that, encouraging me to do whatever felt right. There was no pressure. But, clumsy as his attempts were to rectify the situation, I knew he had no idea really. He left it all to me and he just carried on as normal.

The garden stood at the edge of the cliff, teetering over the hostile North Sea. I looked over at the black vastness of water stretching out towards the rest of Europe. There was a whole world out there, I thought. More opportunities, different paths and multitudes of futures all brimming with possibilities. I reminded myself of my insignificance. Of how I was just a tiny speck on the planet. And I was nothing. None of it should matter. And if I didn't matter, neither did Jonny's opinion of me. I took large gulps of the briny air coming in from the sea and tried to restore my equilibrium. *I could do this.* The silent tears began to dry up and I started to stiffen my resolve.

Breathless, a calm soft voice came up behind me "Jessica, there you are, I've been trying to find you. You've got to come and help me, it's Diane and…"

It was Moira. I quickly spun round and hoped the dark would hide my dishevelled appearance.

"Oh, I did wonder. He's a bastard anyway, you think what he's done to you is bad?" *More honesty. Stand down Jessica.* "Anyway, you need to come now, I'll help you later. It's what we do in A and E – we take the worst cases first"

"What…" my voice croaked.

"He might have slighted you – I know, he's an absolute twat and I'm sure Charles, and his blinkered brother will agree, but what he has done to Diane is a great deal worse"

As we went in, Moira steered me towards a small library room in the hotel. The swing band had finished, and a more upbeat band was playing now. Mostly rock and pop hits. Probably to cater for the younger crowd. They were playing that Aerosmith song from *Armageddon*, which always reminded me of wedding discos. *How apt!* I remember thinking. *The night had that fatalistic feeling to it.*

The room was quiet and tucked away next to the main bar. It was what once was called a reading room and was full of books and newspapers. Big leather Chesterfields flanked the fire and there was a desk and chair in the corner with a green table lamp and baize top. All very traditional and gentlemen's club. No doubt styled by Jonny himself. A dishevelled figure encased in black and white stripes was curled up in a ball on one of the sofas. A bottle of brandy in her hand.

"Diane?"

She looked up and took a large swig from the bottle.

"Don't look at me like that *darling*. Brandy, it's good for shock"

"Shock"

"Yes, your *bar-stard* of a father-in-law has finally done it"

"What?"

"Come on girl," She pronounced it gel. "You've more in

you than one-word answers. And don't think I don't understand what his little speech was about. We were all slighted. Charles might be a doctor, but he's still a disappointment as he snubbed 'The Firm'. And you and me? well, we are baby makers. Like fillies being stabled and fed to breed good stock." She took another large gulp from the bottle. "All we are good for *darling.*"

She looked at me. Her glistening eyes taking in my elegant gown and bereft face "You know, I was like you once: beautiful, hardworking, loyal – oh yes, I started life as his secretary you know? Nothing as grand as you, but times are changing, aren't they? Only, things were different in our day." Another slug "And when we married, I stopped managing his office and went on to manage his parties and work life, like the good little hostess that I was. No thanks though. No pay check at the end of the month to do as I pleased with. He just expected it of me. Just like he won't acknowledge what you have done for the company."

I must have raised my eyebrows, but I was so shocked at her sudden out-of-character outburst, that I was numb.

"I know you all think it, but I'm not stupid. I've watched you Jessica. You're a grafter and that means something to me – and my husband – not that he'd ever admit it! *Bastard.* That's why he let you marry"

"Let me marry?"

"Yes, you made a good match and he knew you'd earn your place." She nodded at Moira "Don't let anyone ever tell you it's easy being a Green wife."

What an earth had happened? This wasn't about me. What else had he done?

She burst into a round of tears and took another swig.

Moira was trying to manage her prospective mother-in-law's uncharacteristic behaviour. I had a million questions and hadn't a clue where to start. "Diane, have a wee bit of water. That won't cure anything" she offered.

"Did they teach you that in medical school *darling* Moira?

Because my old doctor always used to tell me brandy was good for shock"

"Maybe it is, but a whole bottle will just make you sick"

I felt I had to support Moira. "Look Diane, I can see your upset but it's not worth this..."

"What? You haven't told her have you Moira?"

I looked at both faces. Moira looked startled, like she was staring into the headlights of an oncoming car. Diane looked like I felt: both women wrung out by life.

"Jonny is leaving me"

Wrung out by Jonny then.

"What?"

"Yes, his sixtieth present to me was to tell me he's retiring with Roberta. They are booked on a world cruise and then they are going to see all the things we used to talk about when the boys were little. We were too busy then. This was to be our moment, but that bitch..."

"Stop! Are you telling me...*the bastard*" I muttered under my breath.

"Yes *darling*, he most certainly is. No need to whisper on my account. However, that bitch Roberta is worse. She knew the score and there she was all yesterday in the nautical gear, it was like she was rubbing it in my face"

"But surely, Peter..."

"Oh, he's too pissed to know what is going on. To be honest, that's why I've turned a blind eye for so long. I guess I felt sorry for her and let her 'share' Jonny"

"Diane, this is awful. What will Patrick say, and Charles? They'll be horrified." It sort of made my situation a bit petty. Although, it makes me think about his motivation in not recognising my impact on his business.

"They'll be upset but the boys aren't stupid. Unfortunately, I know they've always called his little secret assignations 'side-pieces'. I've always just gritted my teeth. I thought it would all end when he retired, and we finally got to spend time together. *Darling*, that's what has always happened...it's what we did."

"And now?"

"Well, he broke all the rules and it's all been for nothing"

I was incensed. *How dare he?* "Nothing? As in you don't get to spend your dotage with a man, quite frankly Diane, who walks all over you and treats you like the hired help"

There was a sharp intake of breath and Moira went to speak. *Had I gone too far?*

"Well, Jessica, I think that's the first time you've ever said anything genuinely kind to me in the past six years."

I felt ashamed. *Did she really think that?* "Really?"

"I may be stupid where it comes to letting you lot laugh at me and abuse me..."

"I've never...neither has Patrick..."

"Stop it. I know how you roll your eyes and think I'm just 'The Mother-In-Law,' but, I do know that you are right at his side and I appreciate it. Not very feminist, I agree, but you are a good wife."

Christ. Was there some truth serum in that brandy bottle?

She took another gulp.

"What do you think Moira – as a newcomer?"

"From what I've seen, I believe Jessica is right"

"Thought so. You young *gels* like to stick together. Good to know that I finally have back up." Diane took another large gup of brandy. I'd lost count of how many she'd had.

"Arh, there she is. I see you are coping in the usual way Diane"

Moira and I quickly turned around and were faced with a smug faced Roberta. All resplendent in black taffeta, like Ursula the sea witch.

She laughed something resembling an evil laugh. It was like I'd walked onto a movie set. I had to pinch myself, it was all ludicrous.

"Oh, it's you" Slurred Diane, straightening herself to her former glory. "Jessica, tell the waiting staff that there's some shit that needs cleaning up in the library please"

Moira and I gasped. So unlike Diane to use the shit word.

"Is that the best you can do Diane?" She crowed. "You know it was always me. He's been waiting to retire so he can just fuck off from you all. You know he calls you all leeches, don't you?"

She was gesturing in all our directions and I felt bad for Moira being caught up in this. Although, I should have guessed, she wouldn't care.

Not to be deterred by the witch: Moira asked "Is that right, what's your name again? Bertha?"

"Roberta" she spat.

"Well, seeing as you hardly know me, and neither does Jonny for that matter Roberta, I'd ask you to keep me out of it. And as for these two ladies – I see neither leeches or disloyal wives." She turned and smiled at us. "Unlike you!"

Moira was trying to build a united front. *I'd got that woman so wrong.*

Diane grew taller. "Thank you, Moira, you'll do quite well for my son."

She stood up and steadied herself on the back of the chair. She brushed herself off. I sensed a fire about her.

"If you think insulting Jonny's family will bode you well, you are sorely mistaken. Jonny might say shit when he is under the influence – which is when he's probably had to pre-pare himself for sleeping with you." That hurt. 'Bertha's' face smarted. "I believe they call it 'beer goggles' – is that right ladies?" She nodded towards us. I wanted to laugh. She was good at this and she was right, I'd seriously underestimated her. "In fact, I suspect, it's probably when you also got to con-vince him about leaving..."

"Oh, he wasn't drunk darling, he was very eager. He told me he couldn't wait to spend every night with me cruising around the world. Having wild sex in every port."

Moira and I locked eyes. Shit, this woman was a bitch. Diane held steady though.

"Powered by Viagra no doubt. Good luck with that one *darling*. You're perhaps doing me a favour after all…"

"Well maybe with you, but with me he doesn't have that sort of…"

I needed to stop this. I didn't want to know about Jonny's sex life and libido. I could feel the haddock and chips threatening to make an appearance. "I think that's…"

"Oh, shush yourself. Go and tell your Ken Doll husband what's happening." Sniped 'Bertha'

Diane was gathering herself. A flash of venom flickered in her eyes.

"Insult me but never insult my family" she took a step towards her nemesis. She was at full height.

"Oh good, but darling, I don't need your permission to do anything"

I noticed that she was slightly swaying. She was as intoxicated as Diane then. I looked at one to the other. *What the hell was Jonny thinking? Swapping one lush for another?*

There was a suspension in time. Neither spoke. It was like before a storm where the air becomes heavy and tight, where you are willing it to break as it becomes unbearable.

"What was I saying? Oh yes, the sex. That was what clinched it. He said that at the end of the day he couldn't bring himself to take his frigid wife around the world. I don't think you realise how much he needs it do you?"

This was worse than catching your parents having sex (not that I ever had). They were all ready to collect their pensions and all they could talk about was the bedroom. Moira caught my eye and I could see she felt the same – it was all so ridiculous that I wanted to laugh and cry at the same time.

Only, that last comment did it. Diane broke the storm as she lunged forward and slapped Roberta around the face.

The band had moved from soft rock ballads to a cover of the new Kaiser Chiefs track 'I Predict a Riot'. *The irony*. Within seconds the lushes took it as an instruction and followed suit.

Watching the people get lairy

Egged on by the slap, Roberta grabbed Diane's hair and got her into some sort of choke hold. Diane fought back by kicking her in the shins. Before long they were rolling around in front of the fireplace like the two naked men in that old Oliver Reed movie.

I predict a riot
I predict a riot
I predict a riot
I predict a riot

I saw, and heard, flashes of teeth (I think Diane bit her). There were screams and at one point I saw real hair flying. Moira and I must have silently agreed to let them have their moment – after all, I wanted Diane to give her one – the bitch deserved it.

It's not very pretty I tell thee

The music played on and I heard fabric rip, then as Roberta was spitting in Diane's face. Accusations fell like punches. Slaps and scratches tore like knives. Diane had her held down and was telling her that *she'd always thought she had bad breath* and that *her Botox made her look ridiculous.*

He said that he saw it before me
And wants to get things a bit gory
Girls scrabble round with no clothes on
To borrow a pound for a condom

'Bertha' (as I preferred to call her thanks to Moira) was now on top, snarling in Diane's face, telling her that Jonny told her that his wife was '*dried up and gin-soaked. He no longer wants a drunken albatross for a wife!*'

"Opposed to a cheap tart and limpet with no class?" She spat back.

Whoosh! An icy bucket of water showered over them. They both shook like dogs clearing the excess water from their

209

coats. Standing there, with a discarded, and now empty, champagne bucket was Jonny. I've never felt more disgust for one person in my life, as I did for my Father-in-Law, at that moment. The bastard was laughing. I was too angry to do anything. We helped Diane up, Jonny told us all to *fuck off* (I'd never seen him so rude and ungracious), as he needed to speak to his 'Darling wife'. *Sarcastic bastard.*

And if there's anybody left in here
That doesn't want to be out there…

I wanted to be anywhere else but here. I stormed off to find Patrick and tell him what a fucking mess his parents were.

THE DRUGS DON'T WORK...

Patrick

Saltness
September 2006
The Ball:

I had to hand it to Dad, he'd played a blinder. His speech left no one in doubt about who was to be boss. I'd done it. All those hard years and sacrifice and I was now head of the business.

I cast my eyes around the room, searching for my glamourous wife; easily the most stunning woman in the room. I'd made no mistake in marrying her. She was elegant and had brains. She'd helped me climb that ladder, and together we'd made it.

Where was she?

"Well, boy wonder did it then" It was Charles laughing at me and shaking my hand. I was lucky to have him. I knew some people would wonder why there was little sibling rivalry between us – but I knew – we weren't like that. They didn't know what I'd given up. They didn't know how I'd given Charles the opportunity to pursue his dreams...Anyway, it wasn't like he'd been disinherited, Dad had told us both that he was making sure there was money there for us both.

"Yes, thank you"

"You should be thanking me! You'd have none of this if it wasn't for me!" He was still laughing. His generous warm eyes suited to my kind, focused and talented brother.

"I could never do what you do though. Seriously, I'm so proud to call you my brother"

"*Och*, as Moira would say, let's no go there. Let's drink to our success instead. We still haven't wet the *wee bairns* head yet properly. Have we?"

I laughed at his attempts to mimic his wife-to-be. My brother had always been a good impressionist. I'd missed him.

We'd invited some of the boys from our old school, to Dad's party. An assortment of professionals who had done well for themselves and who we'd drink under the table in those early days of finishing and leaving school. The only difference was that they'd all gone to university. I'd always felt jealous and slightly out of it whilst Charles and they all were scattered around various red bricks around the country. They reminded me of what I had given up. But it had given me the fire to be successful. I wanted what came from hard work and determination – I wanted respect. Now, sitting in the bar with them all, sharing the fruits of my labour, I finally felt I could hold my head high. I might not have that bit of paper like they did, but I earned more money than they could ever believe possible.

I realised that I'd made it.

I grabbed one of Jonny's bunnies and told her I wanted a bottle of champagne for each of us. Charles said that '*why stop at just a standard bottle? Why not a magnum?*'

Arrogantly, I didn't get the sense that he was quietly chastising me, I thought he was egging me on. So, fuelled by my new status and need to prove myself, I switched to magnums.

*****

Jessica came in like a swan. She was all calm on the exterior, little did I know that there was a panic going on under her serene vision of beauty. She looked beautiful in that dress. It looked like it had been made for her, and I knew all eyes were on her as she headed towards me. She had a pained expression on her face which made me think that maybe I was overdoing it a bit. She'd never been a fan of drinking games, and found loud raucous behaviour a turn off. She also wouldn't be keen that I was hanging out with David Hall. I hoped it wasn't obvious that we'd been up to old tricks again.

"Patrick," she shouted over the noise. We were singing an old rugby song and every time we got to the chorus, we'd do shots of vodka, which sat alongside all the champagne bottles I'd ordered. Charles was harmonising and rolling his eyes theatrically, and I realised that he'd drank most of the fucking bottle already. *Moira would kill me!*

"Yes my love", I replied. I wanted them all to see how amazing she looked. She'd barely given birth and she looked sensational. I wanted their jealousy. I could see David's eyes were on stalks. He'd always been a lech, right back to the time where the girls' and boys' schools used to meet up for a dance. He'd always be the first to find a girl to hide in the changing rooms with him and a warm bottle of cider.

I puffed up with pride. "Here she is the mother of my perfect son. Have I told you that she has come up trumps and provided me with a son? An heir to the Green throne!"

I could sense their eyes turning green in front of me. I had the business, the wife and now a son.

Jessica's face was unreadable. I knew she'd be pissed off about our vulgar and shitty behaviour. But it was my night...

"I was just seeing where you are *darling*"

Shit.

She smiled a smile that didn't reach her eyes. I noticed she clocked the state of my brother and nodded at Moira. They said something to each other which I didn't catch and walked away.

Fuck it.

I puffed on my cigar and had another drink.

IN THE MORNING, I KNOW YOU WON'T REMEMBER A THING...

Jessica

Saltness
September 2006
The Ball:

The music was booming out of the ballroom, and there had been a distinct shift in tempo. Both the atmosphere and the ambiance had become charged. People were drunk – spilling out all over the hotel – talk about being debauched. The posh friends of the Greens were certainly showing that they were no better than a working-class girl from the worst estate in Leeds.

God I must be drunk to be even letting myself think about that.

Usually, I lived the pretence of orphan from inside myself. It was easier. To believe the lie, is to live it...

Bodies were strewn everywhere, like a scattering of clothes on a bedroom floor. Men and women were all over each other on some of the sofas in the foyer. As I rounded the corner towards the ballroom entrance, I spotted a pairing I shouldn't have - Patrick's Uncle Gareth, with Wendy Wainwright (the Mayor's wife). I decided I'd pretend I hadn't seen that they were heading for the stairs with a bottle of champagne. There had been enough family drama, and I didn't want to be the one to break it to Diane's sister-in-law that her husband couldn't be trusted either. I think they thought they were being discreet, as they stumbled up the stairs. Luckily, the fact that most of the people scattered around the lobby, entrance and hotel bar, were up to no good, and completely pissed, meant they weren't spotted.

Pushing all these thoughts aside, I strode purposefully into the ballroom. It was smoky. A mass of bodies was dancing on the floor. I spied Patrick in the bar to the right. He was playing a drinking game with his brother and some old school friends. Initially, I softened to his boyish side. He never saw his friends. We lived in Leeds and only really saw anyone if we dragged ourselves over to Saltness for some family gathering. The hotel was the battered jewel in Green Leisure Ltd.'s crown. It represented what they were, and where they'd come from. How ironic that is was now that the Patriarch and Matriarch were unravelling within its dated walls.

Moira was hot on my heels. We needed back up. This really was not our call. Jonny needed telling and that was not our job. If we did, it wouldn't end well. We both spied out the brothers and got ready to grab them.

Only, they were both completely gone. I'd never seen either of them so drunk. Patrick was singing and Charles was doing the harmonies. Each time they reached a chorus line everyone had to take a drink. It was ridiculous but refreshing to see that they were at least united and enjoying themselves before Moira and I destroyed their worlds by telling them about their fucked-up parents.

"Patrick," I shouted.

"Yes my love" he never called me that "Here she is the mother of my perfect son. Have I told you that she has come up trumps and provided me with a son? The heir to the Green throne!"

My sympathy evaporated rapidly. I wanted to punch him

there and then. He was no better than his fucking father. My respect for the Greens was lost somewhere within the smoky dancefloor. I looked at him, skewed bowtie adrift and his eyes wild. I could see the tell-tale signs of white lines in them.

Fucking hell Patrick.

"I was just seeing where you are *darling*" I lied and smiled. Surprisingly Charles looked no better, his head lolling to one side and an empty magnum in his hand. Moira shook her head at me. She pushed her way through a mass of braying men, and after some discussion she was handed a bottle of something at the bar.

"Well, I if you canne beat them, join them, I say. We'll take this outside and work out what the fuck to do shall we?"

Moira had gone from hero to zero in the course of an evening. We linked arms and pushed our way through the dancefloor and onto the veranda. As we moved across, I could see the band more clearly. They were now belting out a Razorlight cover. The lead singer was really going for it. He sounded good. I sized him up, all six-foot Irish god of him and thought: *oh my fucking god.*

PART SIX

THE CONFESSIONAL

THE RECKONING

BEFORE THEN
Aimee

Saltness
November 2016

Grey clouds scudded across the silvery winter sky. Gulls called as they swooped down into the stone crevices serving as home for the nesting of young. The skeletal boughs hung over the footpath, which wound its way around the rocky precipice. The breaking of the waves drowning the eerie stillness of the desolate cliffs.

I'd rarely go up to the cliffs. It wasn't because I didn't want to remember and didn't miss him, it was just Frank was all about living. The plaque was just that: a plaque. A reminder for his children and his mother (who never visited anyway). But today was his reckoning and I felt he needed to at least be there in some form or another.

We sat side by side; either end of the bench. Frank's plaque fell between us; art imitating life – so to speak. The ghost of Frank conspicuous with his absence – he never could face up to things.

We'd been like that for about ten minutes. Just sitting. Just waiting. Our silence stretching like a taught tightrope.

Meeting was easy. Finding the words was difficult. I could see her out of the corner of my eye: her steely glare reflected by the silvery light creeping through the clouds. The Ice Queen.

By now, since I'd confronted Jenna about her confession and

threat to Jessica, I'd gained a clearer picture of what happened on that awful night. I knew Jessica felt betrayed – *the irony!* But I had been too, and by the two people closest to me. Although, I understood that Jenna was trying to protect me (she'd spent her whole adult life doing just that). *How could she possibly tell me about what she saw moments before he died?* Her, the other woman, crying and begging him to come back. Him running away.

But I did understand. This was more about cleaning up his mess than about me. Like I'd said before; Frank had his issues, and ones I wasn't sure she understood or knew. He was good at hiding things. I decided that as she wasn't going to talk, (it had been her idea to meet) I'd rip the plaster off quickly.

"I knew"

She let out a sharp gasp. "So, he did tell you!"

She had no idea. I was seriously fed up of all the shite I was still dealing with. Five years I'd been without Frank. AF hadn't fared much better than life BF.

"Well, not you exactly. But I knew he was with someone the night he died."

"Oh. He told me you knew – that you were the problem"

Her tone was monosyllabic. It was like she was trying to supress her emotions; pushing them down so as not to look weak. *Hurt? Wrong footed?* I had no idea, but I wasn't there to spare her feelings. I was there to put things straight – Frank's final mess.

"He would have done. He liked the drama. He would never have left me. He couldn't"

She laughed, breaking that cold veneer. But it wasn't a true laugh, it was more incredulous – at that minute, I think she believed her own fantasy. The one where the sainted Frank was a demi-god.

"How would you know? You weren't there. Our feelings went deeper and way back before…"

"Look, before you go on" cutting in as like I said, I wanted to cut the bullshit, "there were things only I knew about him. My husband. We'd been married over ten years when he died."

"You can't have known him that well if..."

"Look, I'm sorry but you need to listen. It's important. If you don't listen, I won't be able to explain. You wanted to meet..."

"To tell you the truth" She cut in angrily.

"That may be so, but..." She was staring at me. Pleading, with her eyes. Somewhere in me a pang of sympathy twanged. She had no idea. She was as much a victim in all of this as the rest of us. All we were was casualties of Frank's problems.

"I'll tell you what," It could wait, what I had to say wouldn't help her.

God knows, it won't be easy when I do.

"You go first Jessica. Say what you've got to say"

The bitch in her raised up and rolled her eyes.

God she was full of her own self-importance – no wonder she got on with my husband.

My Frank, so full of empty promises. Guessing what he might have led her to believe, I supposed she felt like she had a point to prove. Little did she know that she was on shaky ground. She was obviously used to getting her own way. She was such a match for Patrick, I was surprised their marriage wasn't working. *Maybe too similar?*

So be it. I bit my tongue and waited for her to go on.

"You see, I met him in 96. We were engaged. Way before you even met. I was working in Corfu for the season. He was this gorgeous Irish charmer who flew into my life and gave it a direction and purpose. He was the guitarist and lead singer of 'The Helios Kings'...but I suppose you know that bit?"

"The band and Corfu yes. You? He never told me about a fiancé, but then again – men don't tend to tell their new fiancé that they've been engaged before do they?" He always did like to omit certain information.

"No, I don't imagine they do." She looked sad, a hint of betrayal flashed across her face. *She thinks she is special.* "Anyway, I had to go home unexpectedly and well, there was some confusion"

She stopped. "I guess Maria was right."

I studied her face. She was deep in thought "Right?"

"Yes, about him not being straight forward."

She had been listening then. "She got that right, this Maria –
"

"Well, maybe, but …it still didn't give her the right to mess with my life"

"What did she do?"

"She kept us apart. I left a letter for him with my phone number and address in England. She never gave it to him. She said he never came back. Much later on, after we found each other again…she gave this long story and excuse about him not being reliable and that she felt she was protecting me."

"Found each other again?"

"Yes, after all those years of remembering him: my teenage-self, because thats what I was then, my feelings were once again fired up when I saw him performing one night. He came back into my life at exactly the right time. I thought he was there to rescue me. I thought it was a sign."

And then as she told me a story about a horrendous ball she attended; confirming my suspicions about Patrick's family.

THE AFTERMATH

Jessica

Saltness
September 2006

That night rocked all our worlds. After seeing Frank, I made my excuses, using Oli yet again, and told Moira I had to check on him. I did, but not before I slowly walked the long way around to the back staircase and allowed myself another cry as I made my way to him.

When I went in, he was beginning to stir. I suggested to the minder that she had a break - she had been with him a long time and the late summer evening was quite stuffy. I told her that I could settle him. She went to get some air and said she wouldn't be long.

As he stirred, I cradled him in my arms and inhaled his perfect head. I have, and always will, love the smell of babies. They are so clean and pure and untarnished by the cruelty of the world.

I got his bottle ready, as I had been pumping all week to make sure I had enough for the weekend. *Tonight's milk would need dumping.* His hunger bottomless, he took it greedily. His appetite seemed to be never ending and I laughed at him in his rush to guzzle, that it was coming out of the corner of his mouth. He was snuffling like a pig for truffles. He looked at me with those innocent knowing eyes, calming my racing pulse. I drank him in and turned over the events in my head.

Jonny's obvious slights, Patrick's arrogance; Diane's meltdown; Roberta imitating a low budget Alexis Carrington – *I mean please, she's not even attractive*; my unexpected bonding with Moira – finally someone in this fucked up family I could talk to, and then Frank.

Frank.

What the fuck? Of all the nights he chose for him to drop back into my life, he chose this one. I thought about what he looked like on that stage. Ten years on and he was still gorgeous. I still fancied him and judging by the way my heart was racing – like it had been jump started by some power leads, I still felt passionately about the man.

And then I looked at Oli. I was a mother now. A married one at that. I was married to a successful businessman who, although I didn't have the same burning desire for, I did love in my own way. On paper he was the perfect fit for Jessica. But for Jessie? The girl I knew who still lurked underneath, not quite so much. The problem was I didn't know what role I was playing anymore.

Oli's eyes were drooping as he continued to fill his big belly with milk. Still sleepily guzzling I smiled at his big tummy threatening to burst out of his onesie. His chubby arms tucked into his chest. I felt proud. I'd done that. He'd been tiny when he was born – only 5lb. But, with a combination of breast and bottle, I'd soon fattened him up and he was becoming the most contented and placid baby I had ever known. I remembered back to Stace's kids – they were screamers. I thought about the pram faces on the old estate and smiled smugly to myself. I was a good mum and that was my true role now. *Fuck Patrick, Jonny and even Frank.* I was now a mother and I knew that was the only role for me. I knew Oli would be the only man never to let me down.

When I eventually went back down to Jonny's Hades, Moira was tackling a now incoherent Diane into the lift. I felt so guilty, I should have been there helping and not wallowing in self-indulgence, in my room. Moira batted away my apologies, and we half carried/dragged Diane to her suite.

She was barely conscious as we got her onto the bed. With

her make-up smudged all over her face and her puffy eyes, I finally saw behind that mask she had worn since the first day I had met her. The formidable matriarch was just a sad and lonely post-menopausal woman. I surprised myself with my capacity to feel sympathy for her. She'd been shit on by a man who she had supported all of her life. A man who she put before her own needs and who was now dumping her as, according to Roberta, she was 'frigid'. I suspected different. I had a feeling that Jonny was a manipulative liar and that Roberta would soon come unstuck too.

In a random act of kindness, we felt we should help her feel more human. I suspected when she woke up, she'd feel like she'd been hit by a bus. We undressed her (never thought I'd have to do that to the snooty out-law) and put her into her silk pyjamas. Moira was all business like and put water and tablets next to her bed – getting her to drink some first. We cleaned her face and tucked her up. Just before we left, we thought it would be fitting to show some unity – female solidarity and all that. We shoved all of Jonny's things into a suitcase, put it outside the room and put a *Do Not Disturb* sign on the door. We agreed we'd check on her in the morning.

*****

Frank was still playing as we went back into the ballroom. They were performing some eighties power ballad, and the room smelt of debauchery. I stood at the back and took the scene in: taking quick glances at him. If I was going to put his ghost to rest, I had to settle some curiosity.

He looked the same. Maybe, closer up, he'd be a bit more rugged, but from the back of the room, he looked like my Frank. As the lyrics swayed the sweaty dancers on the dance-floor, he began to play an instrumental on his guitar. It took me right back to that summer ten years ago. To a time of hedonism and excitement. I'd had my whole life ahead of me and I realised that it had been the only time I'd been ever free of responsibility. It was all about me. And he was part of that.

I wondered what our lives would look like now – if we hadn't been parted so suddenly? And then I thought about everything I'd achieved – whatever my 'wonderful' out-law said, I wasn't prepared for him to take that from me. I thought about the life we'd built – Patrick and me. I thought about Oli. My precious boy - who I'd vowed to pour all my energy into from now on. Green Leisure Ltd could take a running jump. And Frank – I consigned him to that box of memories James had caught me with all those years ago.

*****

The next days and weeks were a blur. Once the Patrick and Charles had sobered up, we managed to tell them everything we'd witnessed the night before. They boys were horrified. The usually quiet Charles told his dad that he wasn't sure he could forgive him this time. He told him that he'd lost respect for him – after all, she was their mother and he had treated her appallingly. Meanwhile, Patrick was more subdued about that matter. I could tell he wanted to let rip, but I guessed that the money and position kept his mouth shut. Whoever said money can't buy silence? I saw his point, but I lost a bit of respect for him there. Another nail you might say.

Diane was a mess. With Charles and Moira back in Edinburgh, and Patrick playing dumb, I was in charge of piecing her back together. Jonny and 'Bertha' had been holed up in Saltness since 'Greenageddon' – and I couldn't help thanking god as I didn't even think Patrick could bare to see them as a couple. Diane just rattled around the old family home in Harewood, drinking away her days in her house-coat and slippers. Gone was the immaculately dressed formidable powerhouse, being replaced by a gin-soaked Sue Ellen character, waiting for her JR to come back and reconcile - wanting to find love again.

By Christmas, Bastard and Bertha (as Moira and I had rechristened them – God I'd been wrong about her) were sailing around the Caribbean and Diane was in the Priory. And that meant that I'd been thrust into the unlikely position of 'Mrs Green Senior'. An unpaid job role of organising the household, social calendars, family events, and dinner parties. And although I was unpaid, I had a rather large budget to look the part. Ultimately, I was turning into my own worst nightmare – a society wife. I had a first in economics and my career was over.

PREGNANT PAUSE

Jessica

Headingly, Leeds.
January 2009

The pains were awful. I felt like my back was breaking. I knew labour pains and I knew Braxton Hicks – these were definitely the former. However, I was only six months gone. I was petrified; Patrick was away, and I was on my own in the house with a sleeping Oli. Panic gripped me like the vice like pains in my back. What was I going to do?

I rang Moira.

They'd married two years earlier, on a beach in Sardinia, with just a few of us as witnesses: us three, Diane, Moira's parents, her sister and partner. Jonny 'The Bastard' had split with 'Bertha' not long after the cruise – apparently, he'd already strayed on the boat as Roberta was being too 'clingy' (Patrick had got it out of him after one too many scotches) but to Charles he was still 'persona non-gratia. So, he was conspicuous by his absence.

Anyway, I rang Moira (she was now my favourite Green) and panicked down the line. They'd moved to London by then, as Charles had gained a residency at Barts. He was now a heart surgeon and highly successful in his own right. I think Patrick was quite jealous of him. I'd begun to learn that my husband could be the jealous type and suspected that he'd been the one to put doubt in Jonny's head about my part in the modernisation of the business. Moira wanted to know why I was calling her at two in the morning and not an ambulance? I explained how scared I was and how I was alone with just Oli – her two-year-old nephew.

She talked to me calmly and I could hear her rousing Charles, who started to make calls. Within minutes an ambulance and Diane were at my door. I was glad to see her – even if I was dubious about her 'state' but I knew she'd been doing better lately, and I couldn't smell anything on her. She told me not to worry and that she'd call her son. And then I was blue lighted to Jimmy's Hospital.

Luckily, it was a false labour. The doctor and midwife were concerned though. They also said that my blood pressure was raised. They ordered complete bed rest until the baby was born. This put Patrick out enormously, worrying who was going to support him at his various functions. And more to the point, *what about next weekend's dinner party?* I wanted to say fuck off. But I'd learnt well from Diane and told him that he would have to make my excuses at the functions, and I would hire caterers for the party telling him *'I'm sure I can manage to make polite conversation at a table darling'.*

We were turning into his parents.

Only, if I'm really honest, I was my own worst enemy. Confined to doing very little for three months, Diane took over. She revelled in being needed and took on a whole new lease of life. Gone were the days of wallowing; she had a new purpose and I let her run with it.

I, on the other hand, lost my purpose. My days were spent propped up in bed, gentle walks around the garden, and shopping on the internet. Only, there was only so much shopping, only I could do. With lack of structure and time seeming to stretch out infinitely, my mind started to wander. I thought back over my life and for the first time in years I wondered what had become of my family?

This was the only part of my story that Patrick still knew noth-

ing about. I felt that it was too much to confess in one go.

I was on Facebook as Jessica Green. I had altered a great deal since my teens. For a start, I now looked expensive and shiny. Also, I only befriended people I only knew as Jessica Green. I knew no one would ever find me. I'd spent too many years covering my tracks. However, if I was to do any digging, I decided I needed to assume my old identity. I knew that's what people did. All Patrick had to do was add a couple of old school friends, and he had all sorts of people form his past 'reconnecting'. Some people, I assume Patrick wouldn't even smile at in the street. But that was the fickle world of social media: it was a false impression of one's level of success and popularity.

I created a new profile as Jessie Frost. I used a picture of 'Jess the cat' from Postman Pat (I used to get the theme tune sung to me at school) and I went searching for any names from school I could remember. I decided finding old friends would be a good way to begin.

I found some random girls from school. Disappointingly, they were all leading mundane domesticated lives. I would have thought that they'd have been more dynamic, but I guessed that they didn't have the fire or challenge. They'd grown up entrenched in privilege. They were happy to be married into it, and now seemed to be leading the ubiquitous middle-class life which, to be honest, bored me. I knew I was one to talk, but I'd worked hard – one way or another – to get to where I was – and I wasn't just coasting middle class life, I was in the upper echelon looking down. I remember this thought startling me and making me think once again that I was morphing into Diane.

Only one of my old friends, Kate, had seemed to have broken away. She was living in Adelaide, as a single parent, and lecturing English at the university. I was intrigued by this. *How strong must she be to live such a different life alone?* I felt an admiration which reminded me that I was nothing like Diane after all, and that I was still Jessica Frost – a hybrid of the two. I sent her an inbox message and enjoyed an afternoon of correspondence with her. It was weird – I strangely felt more like me than I had done in a very long time.

Over the next week I built up quite a list of 'friends'. And by the weekend, Stace had added me and sent me a private message:

```
OMG, we thought you were dead somewhere.
James said he knew different????  As good as
it is to find you are still breathing, I'm
not happy finding out you are alive through
Facefuck.
Explain.  Stace xx
```

What have I done?

I was opening up a can of worms. I had to be careful with this as I didn't want to let her know about my life. I messaged her back:

```
Sorry Stace, I really am.
After Mam passed away, I think I had some sort
of breakdown.  James helped me get away as I
couldn't stand being near dad.  I went to uni,
and then moved away from the area.  I am cur
rently living abroad, and don't know when I'll
be in England next.
I am sorry I left you all.  I am sorry if you
found out like this.  But it took me a long time
to heal.  I'm much better now.
```

I didn't know how to ask about everything. I had no right really. I'd abandoned them all and it was only because I was wallowing in my sick bed that I was even entering into this bizarre double life.

I opted for:

```
How are you?
```

I thought the rest would come.

It turned out Stace was not backwards in coming forwards. A series of messages went back and forth where she took the higher ground and I grovelled. I got a bit sick of her tone after a while, but my curiosity was piqued by now, so I kept digging and eating humble pie.

She now had four children. She'd managed to train in beauty and had worked her way up to owning her own salon. The children, she admits, she had too young and says she cringes at how she behaved when Mam was still alive. She said that Mam going and me disappearing, meant she had to grow up. She wanted to feel pride in herself. Eventually, after baby number three was born: a little blonde girl called Shelby, she threw out the dad.

He was a useless twat Jessie. He used to steal the child benefit for pot and the kids were starting to go hungry. At one time I'd have been joining him, but I realised I had responsibilities. He wouldn't/couldn't get a job because he was always stoned in bed, he never helped, and he couldn't be trusted to look after them when I had to go to the shops. I tried it once and it ended badly. So, I kicked him out.

Dad, she said, was living in a shitty flat in the tower block. She said she didn't know how he was still breathing.

I swear to god Jessie, he's a waste of space. I often wish it would have been him that died and not our Mam. He just sits there on his piss soaked sofa watching racing on the telly. The only time he goes out is for his giro money, the bookies and the offie. I avoid him.

I daren't ask about James yet. I dreaded the answer. Instead I asked about Mark. He had been successful. He might have abandoned us (who was I to talk?) but he'd quickly excelled at army life.

Mark is some hotshot in the army now. He's saving the world. You'd not recognise him. He's done tours in Iraq and Afghanistan. He's living in Cyprus now. He's a Captain or something.

I was proud of them both. Not too bad for the product of our shameless father.

I had to ask:

And James?

Oh, your fairy godfather? Living in Thailand since 2000. He's done really well for himself. He ran off there initially as he was in trouble with some local nutters. Remember the Banner twins? Well, things got nasty – a bit of a turf war. Anyway, he licked his wounds for a while, went straight, and now owns some club in Koh Pa Ngan. Best let me speak to them both before you add them though. Mark really did believe something terrible happened to you. James reassured him but even he doesn't have a clue what's happened to you now.

I realised there were tears running down my cheeks. They'd all done so well. Without me, with a shitty hand they'd pulled through and there were no horror stories. *Maybe I'd been wrong?* I'd hidden my shameless family for so long I'd made them into some monster. They weren't. I was proud. My stomach flipped and my heart dropped. *What had I done?*

As they all got in touch I listened to their stories of success. Stace sent me photos of the children (Oli had gorgeous cousins), Mark filled me in on army life, and James sent me pictures of his club and hotel. He also told me he'd met someone I knew back when he first went to Thailand. He said he punched him for me and told him that I had bigger and better things to come rather than marry a second-rate musician.

I realised he must have meant Frank.

How did you even know it was him?

The name of the band. I never forgot what you told me on that vodka night. He never deserved you. I knew he was no good.

What about me? I lied a lot and told some truths. I told them that I was living in Australia (I know – I stole Kate's story), that I was widowed but I had two children. (I killed Patrick off) and the second was yet to be born. Offers of flying out to help were quickly halted when I said how good his family were and that I would visit them as soon as the children were able to manage the flight. Luckily, they were all really busy with their lives, so they didn't take much persuading.

As the days and weeks slowly ticked by, I became more and more down. The guilt I felt for my family consumed me. Confinement didn't suit me, and it reminded me of that time after Mam had died. I'd let my two worlds merge and I couldn't differentiate which Jessica I was anymore. My dreams, which were always quite lucid when I was pregnant, were interwoven with my family and Patrick's. Stace would be living with Jonny as his new girlfriend. I was nannying all of the children and no one would help me. In one dream, Dad turned up at a family meal and threw up over Diane's best dress, I was scrubbing the floor to clean it up. Then they would kiss – Dad and Diane. All dysfunctional and all too believable. What I think I was beginning to learn was that money didn't solve the fundamentals of the seven deadly sins.

LIMBO

Jessica

Headingly, Leeds.
February 2009

Patrick had been away for a week. Not only was he away, but he was apparently 'working' in some swanky ski resort in Italy. As a practised skier, I would have normally joined him. I loved it. The adrenaline you felt when you flew down the black slopes could be phenomenal. Meanwhile, I was motionless, gathering dust in my Victorian bed chamber.

What had happened to me?

My melancholic mind cast back to times when I felt young, free and beautiful – not trapped into motherhood and surrounded by misogynist wankers and a gin soaked out-law. I felt fat, ugly and lonely. I wanted to feel like that young girl in Corfu again.

Meanwhile, life was passing me by in my ivory palace.

It was easy to find him. I knew it would be. That was why I had never looked for him before. I knew how Diane must have felt - one drink and game over. But, being nearly nine months pregnant, drinking my way to the bottom of a bottle wasn't really an option.

I started by Googling: The Helios Kings. At first, I found some articles about them in Australia. It turned out that in the late nineties, they gained some success there. A couple of top ten singles, an album that reached number 4 in the charts – I was impressed. There was also some stuff about the touring–Japan, America, Europe...but for some reason they hadn't seemed to tour for a while. Instead, the latest news was about them performing at Yorkshire Showground for a small festival. Not the headliners, but not bottom of the bill either. I could see that they were still performing in some venues. Interesting that they'd had success but not managed to quite make it.

There were plenty of pictures of him. Frank still looked the same. I remembered his scruffy dark brown hair and his magical green eyes. Most of them were of him with the band or his guitar. There was one with a pregnant blonde woman and a child. I guessed that meant he had a family. I felt sick and was overcome with an insane jealousy. I bet she wasn't stuck in her bed and alone. I bet he was looking after her and waiting on her hand and foot.

That afternoon, whilst Diane took Oli out for a walk, I sat looking at that photograph and imaging scenarios where I was her. That, or that she was a bitch who'd trapped him. It consumed me and it must have shown as Diane said I looked *'awful darling!'* when they came back, deciding to stay the night to keep an eye on me. I did feel terrible, and I had no idea why I was torturing myself about some ridiculous fantasy.

That night I tossed and turned. I just couldn't stop thinking about what could have been. I was desperate to know more. I wanted to know who she was, about the child, where they lived – was it Saltness? I wondered. After all, that was where I saw him that night.

I tried to go back there, to that night, in my head. Part of me was desperate to regain that strength of character. Part of me wished that I could turn back time and talk to him. After all, if he saw me now, he wouldn't look twice; that night I looked fucking amazing. Not the hormonal fat mess I'd since morphed into.

I logged onto my new Facebook account. I found him straight away.

Frank O'Donnell
Works at: The Helios Kings
Musician
Married to: Aimee O'Donnell
From: Galway
Lives in: Saltness North Yorkshire

The picture I'd been fixating on was his profile picture.

The latest picture on his newsfeed was of a baby boy called Harry. So, she'd had the baby then.

I scrolled through his photos. More of the band. Some of 'Aimee' and some of a little girl who looked to be about Oli's age. In all of them he was grinning that infectious grin. He looked as sexy as ever and took my actual breath away. I managed to discount her and fabricated more tales of her white-witch qualities.

My finger hovered over that add friend button. I just couldn't do it though. I had no idea what to say and where to start. Plus, he'd think I was stalking him, wouldn't he? Or was he still thinking about me like I was him? Could he remember that summer?

OPENING THE TOMB

Jessica

Headingly, Leeds
March 2009
Opening the Tomb

Toby Charles Green was born on Wednesday 4th March at 2.25am weighing 8lb 7oz. Where with Oli I was tiny, Toby's baby elephant status meant I felt huge too. Post-partum, I felt like a deflated balloon. Unlike when after I'd had Oli, I really struggled with the weight loss, self-esteem and coping. Very quickly, I began to fall into some state of post-natal depression, where I'd spend days in my pyjamas just existing.

Patrick would go to work and carry on like he had before. He was such a prick and did nothing to help. When the doctor told him I was ill (I'd made him come with me as he could be so blind and not listen) he hired another nanny. It seemed to me that my husband's default response to any problem was to throw money at it and hope it goes away.

So, the nanny helped with the boys and I would lay in bed. My depression and the nanny enabling it, meant I could spend hours stalking Frank and his perfect family. Admittedly, he didn't post much but his wife did: trips to the glorious Yorkshire beach, their dog, days out…all the things I should have been doing with my often-absent husband. And I wished that I could just turn the clock back.

I entertained fantasies of turning up in Saltness and him saying '*you're here*' and something Mills and Boon like '*I've been waiting for you all my life*' and he'd rescue me like one of those romantic heroes I used to fixate on when I was younger, before life tainted me and broke parts of my soul.

Days turned into weeks and the bitter March spring weather began to make way for the warmer early summer. I festered, dreamt wildly and cocooned myself in a half-fantasy. Patrick stayed clear. The nanny didn't have a clue what to do and instead of encouraging me to get moving, bonding with Toby and to get dressed, she would just leave me and ask me if I needed anything. I felt like some perverted version of Miss Havisham but instead of being an abandoned bride, I was like a female octopus dying and wasting away after serving the Green bloodline two sons.

My job was done.

It was Diane who kicked me up the arse. She turned up one Sunday morning stating that we hadn't cooked her lunch for weeks and she thought maybe we were siding with Jonny. Patrick wasn't in and the nanny was juggling the boys. I was in a three-day old nightie with crusty old knickers on. I was laid out like a mummy in a darkened room. I'd heard a car on the drive and the door slam. I thought it might have been Patrick back from a place in Devon which he was making 'less corporate' (To be honest I'd stopped listening. I no longer gave a shit.)

The door flew open. No knock. "Right, up you get darling!"

She flew into my bed chamber like a typhoon. Whizzing around and talking at a million miles an hour.

God, I despise you sometimes.

"Darling Jessica, this is not good enough. Do you want your husband to follow in his father's footsteps?"

I didn't care. I was exhausted and felt sick. She ripped open the drapes and tied them back. The blinds were flipped open and the windows were opened. The bright light made me flinch.

"Fresh air Jessica. That's the best thing you need. It smells like..."

"Shit Diane, it smells like shit in here." See I didn't care. I briefly wondered if I'd hurtled towards my dying days and that incontinence had started.

The sunlight was piercing and hot. I felt like a bat coming out of a cave. I felt sure I had some sort of vitamin D deficiency and expected my bones to start to crumble at any point.

"Stop being vulgar. It doesn't suit you darling. Next job, dressed"

I couldn't remember the last time I'd worn clothes. I daren't even try it. Last time I'd tried my jeans on I could only get them to the bottom of my thighs.

"Of course, you need a good bath first." And with that she waltzed into my bathroom, just like my house I realised, and started running me a deep bath using my best bath salts and my Molton Brown oil.

One thing about me is that I can be a good girl. I tend to do as I am told. The compliancy comes from being eager to please as a little girl and my Grammar school education. I had never really misbehaved and always wanted to get things right. So, even though I couldn't bare life, I did as Diane ordered me to do (I remember thinking that they should put her in charge of world peace and then they'd be no issues).

Bathed, hair washed, I went to find some clothes. I tried on a little two piece of navy capri pants and an oversized Gucci white shirt. Surprisingly they both fitted (it turned out that lying in bed like I was dying can be quite good for the waistline – but I wouldn't recommend it). She thrust my make-up bag at me, and I put on the bare minimum.

"Right. See, look at yourself. You look more like you. Now that wasn't difficult really was it *darling*?"

She was right. I looked human. My skin looked sallow still and my hair lacked its normal shine, but I'd done the unthinkable – I was clean, up and dressed.

"Right. We need a plan Jessica. You and me – lunch and we shall talk"

She drove me out to a little country pub and tried to force a prawn salad down me. My ravenous appetite from the confinement had disappeared and I could only manage a few mouthfuls. We both steered clear of the drink and for the first time in our relationship, I felt grateful for having Diane in my life.

"*Darling*. This all has to stop. Your boys need you."

I sat there mute. I wanted to laugh. *Oh, how the tables had turned!* I couldn't say much these days as nothing ever happened.

"I do know how you feel, but you need to buck up dear and find a way through."

I knew she was right "I know. I just feel so dead inside"

"And numb too I bet. I became obsessive about things. I'd fixate on something"

"You? Did you..."

"Yes, after the two boys. Jonny loathed me for it of course and that was when he started wandering. He always needed someone. He can't manage on his own and he has a high sex drive. So...he had to have a woman to fill the void. It's where our problems started"

"Oh, I had no idea"

"No, you wouldn't. The boys don't really know as they were too small. It wasn't the done thing to talk about it in my day. You were given tablets and told to get on with it. Did more harm than good though"

I raised my eyebrows.

"Yes, he found comfort elsewhere and I started on the gin. Sad really, as if I'd have had some sort of help and understanding I often wonder if things would be different?"

"Well, I've help but it doesn't help" I complained.

"You've got to want it though. Also, if I'm not mistaken, you're not on the gin and Patrick hasn't strayed. We've time yet"

I laughed.

Diane was here to sort me out. The irony – wait until I speak to Moira!

"Laugh you might my dear girl. However, your boys need

you."

Guilt spread through me. "I do know that"

"Yes well, more importantly, you need you. There's no, point in living in misery. It's taken me years to heal. Jonny leaving did me a favour – not at first admittedly as it was a messy time for us all. But later, when you and the boys helped. Charles marrying that lovely Moira. Me in the clinic – I realised what I'd been missing all these years."

"What?"

"My freedom dear. You helped me. Now it's my turn. We need to find you yours."

After, what turned out to be, a nice lunch, she forced me into a short walk around Roundhay Park. I'd not been for years – since I was dating Patrick. The trees were heading to full bloom and the flower beds were starting to burst with life. I felt like Sleeping Beauty. It was as if I'd slept through life for months; enclosed in my own dark misery of loneliness and missed chances. Like Diane, I realised, men had put me into that mess. Them and a super imbalance of hormones. The park was a riot of noise and colour and it made me feel alive.

"It has put colour in your cheeks Jessica. See, I'll have you tip top in no time darling."

But, after half an hour I was exhausted. She took me home and put me to rest. For the next couple of weeks, she took me out walking.

"Darling, let me help. Patrick will have no idea..."

She fed me small nutritious meals. We began to take the children out and she helped me bond with Toby. Some mornings she'd have to drag me out of bed. We'd write lists of what I needed to do. She got me a cleaner (I'd always been too stubborn and did it myself), cut the nanny's hours down (she'd been practically working 24 hours a day and I felt terrible) and made me tend to the boys in the night. I found it exhausting and terrifying. But one morning, at the beginning of June, I woke up and everything felt different. I finally felt alive. And Diane was right – I now needed to find my freedom.

THE STAND OFF

Jessica

Headingly, Leeds.
June 2009
The Stand Off

"Something's got to change"

Patrick had just come home, and he'd barely noticed the change in me. He'd been away for the longest time ever. His team had been working on the hotel in Devon and with it being such a long drive, he'd stayed there for the duration. I didn't blame him really. I just felt frustrated. He was so focused on the bloody business he would leave his postnatally depressed wife for nearly three weeks.

"What do you mean?"

I sighed. It seemed the older he got, the less understanding he'd become. "Well, this working away for weeks on end. It's not fair"

"Not this again? Bloody hell Jessica, who do you think keeps you in Chanel and Gucci? Me, that's who. What do you want to me to do, sell up and we live off fresh air?"

"No and hell Patrick, we would not live off fresh air. Stop being so dramatic"

"Well, I don't need my wife moaning to me when I've not drawn breath for weeks. All so I could get back to you and the boys."

"Yes, and I do appreciate you. I know how hard you work – I used to too, remember?"

"Yes, but now you've retired…"

"Retired? Christ Patrick, if this is what retiring is like, you might as well finish me off now!"

"I didn't mean it like that" He had the good grace to look guilty.

"Well, I'm not moaning, and I do understand. But you need to understand me."

"I do, don't I? Although you are a woman and you're notoriously difficult to understand as a race."

Hold your cool. I channelled my inner Diane.

"Yes, Patrick we are from Venus and you're from Mars. Now, please listen." He could be infuriating sometimes my husband. "Diane and I have been talking."

"Diane?" He sounded shocked. We'd not told him about our recent relationship change.

"Yes, your mother. She has been helping me put things into perspective. I'd forgotten how forceful she could be when she wanted. I have had a glimpse of the old Diane recently"

"Good or bad thing?"

"Mostly good although the bossiness can grate a little bit"

"Thank god. So, go on, what have you and my mother been talking about?"

I had to be honest. Not about all the Facebook stuff and Frank – that was to be my secret. And as well as I was feeling, the daily stalking was still given a portion of my time.

"I need a life"

He laughed. I wanted to call him a bastard, but I rarely swore out loud, and only brought it out for the big guns.

He could tell I wasn't laughing - he was hilarious though. He wasn't that stupid. "What do you mean? You've got a fabulous life"

"On paper maybe, but am I happy?"

"Well, the depression aside I'd say yes."

"Oh, you were aware then? About my illness? And you are so wrong Patrick."

He looked cross at me. "Why is nothing good enough for

you? You used to be so grateful…"

"Grateful? I was never grateful as I worked hard for the first six years of relationship. You know I did! And we were a team and after I had Oli, I kept running the home and your calendar. I've been your unofficial PA for the past three years. God Patrick, you talk like I just lay back and reap the bloody rewards. Have I been a shit wife, is that it?"

He looked taken aback. "Well, no, you've been supportive. But how can you not be happy?"

"Because I trained and went to uni for a career. A career which I excelled at and then packed in for you and our family. Who else would have took your mother on? After your dad dumped her and all that well…"

"I know, I know. But what to do? You could never go back to working like you did. Even you must see that in your stubborn little head"

Little head? I wanted to punch him. *Who said marrying for money was easy?*

"I want change Patrick."

"Tell me what and I'll see if I can make it happen" He liked solutions. And I knew this. That was why Diane and I had already found one.

"I'm going to refurbish and relaunch the hotel in Saltness."

"Says?"

"Diane. After Jonny gave it to her in the divorce, she's decided she wants me to modernise it."

"But it's over an hour and a half away. You'll be commuting and the children. You'll never manage"

"I will, because that's the second thing I want to change. We are moving to the seaside."

LET'S HEAR IT
FOR THE GIRLS

Jessica

Saltness
May 2010
Let's Hear it For the Girls

The early summer sun was high in the sky. Blazing hot in its beams, freezing cold in the shadows. It was that time of year where you never knew what it was safe to wear. Made doubly difficult by the sea breeze which could on the warmest day, cut through you like a knife. Where you could look out of the window and see the most perfect day and be caught out by its deceitful nature.

Anxiously, I looked out onto the dark steely North Sea, praying for a lack of storm clouds. I couldn't help be reminded of how Mam would say '*Ne'er cast a clout 'til May is out*'. I smiled and hoped she'd be looking down at me. How I'd built myself back up from all the knocks. Pushing down the stabs of guilt about my web of lies I'd woven. The sky was clear, with a bright blue expanse reaching out as far as the horizon. Just a tiny puff of cotton white punctured the sky in places.

My heart was racing. I steadied myself by taking large gulps of the fresh sea air, filling my lungs with oxygen and energy. I was petrified it would all go wrong. Steadying my breathing I decided how good it felt to be independent. However, I also had a family, and right then I wanted them there – reassuring me and holding my hand.

Patrick should have arrived half an hour ago. My stomach was flipping with nerves. I texted him. I wanted my boys by my side.

```
You won't be late will you? xxx

I'm on my way xxx

You know how important this is to me! Xx

I'm not stupid darling!  Be there soon x
```

He'd better be. I was so agitated. Today was to be my big moment. The grand reopening! It was May Day weekend and I had chosen it to relaunch the new White Cliff's Hotel. I'd sweated blood and tears to get the redesign done. It needed to be relaunched for the 21st Century. Gone was the garish eighties décor, with me bringing in a sense of style and new purpose. Freshly painted walls, sumptuous sofas and a look of opulence without trying too hard. Stage one was done: new décor. Six of the rooms refurbished (including the honeymoon suite), a new top chef and menu too. Plus, the launch of the new function side of the business. Tonight's launch centred around it. Stage two was to centre around a spa and the remainder of the rooms. Today was about showing off the progress and future to plans to all the local people of importance, and to an assortment of travel and lifestyle writers.

I looked on my phone at the time and yet again worried that Patrick wouldn't make it. Diane was here and I'd fed her what spiel she should say. But I needed my partner in crime. He was good at networking and I needed the dream team on it. Jonny's absence was conspicuous, and I didn't want to have to deal with any tricky questions about him again. I understood why people might be interested though – marrying a woman half your age and all that...

"Darling, this is simply amazing! Look at you - my clever daughter!"

I smiled and felt warmed by her words. Something else which had changed since I'd taken on this project. Since she'd pulled me out of my pit of pity, was our relationship. We'd actually grown to quite respect each other. There was certainly love there. It made me feel truly valued (more than my husband had ever done) and I surprised myself with the glow I felt with her pride shining on me.

"Thank you, Diane. Do you like the flowers?"

I gestured to all the fresh blooms which were festooned around the lobby. Expensive I knew, but essential when you want to make an impact. I'd made the hotel 'wedding ready'. I had 'Yorkshire Bridal Magazine', 'Bridal Dream', and 'Weddings' all coming to take photographs. The lobby smelt like a church, filling the air with gardenia, jasmine and lavender.

"Beautiful! Where's that son of mine?"

"Late. On his way apparently."

She raised her eyebrows. "He better be or he'll have me to answer to. The Green ladies are taking back control and he needs to see it!"

Diane had been my right-hand woman. We'd worked hard on the hotel and shared the children. We were exhausted but happy with what we'd achieved.

"Have you been into our 'wedding reception?"

"Yes, the bride and groom look wonderful. I've been and checked on the bridal suite too – it's so heavenly up there! It makes me want to marry again"

Diane had come so far. "Ha-ha! Would you?"

"He'd have to look like James Bond and have modern values. I wouldn't want to be ruled by a man again. Seeing as I don't think that is very likely, I can't see me marrying, can you?"

I thought this was a shame. Not about the marriage but giving up on life.

"That's sad."

"Would you?"

"Marry Patrick again?"

Now there's a question. How to answer? She's his mother, as

close as we'd become...

Oli and Toby bounded in from outside. *Patrick's finally here then*. "Of course," I answered, "Look at our gorgeous boys!" Safe ground. We all loved the boys dearly. Whatever tensions surrounded us all, the boys' happiness was paramount.

Diane laughed as they ran for cuddles. Oli, now four, was clutching his baby brother's hand. Always protective. Their cheeks were flushed, and I could see grass stains on Oli's knees.

I bet he's taken them to the park in their best clothes!

They looked so happy though. Patrick followed them in. He looked healthy too.

"Sorry we are late! We've just had Freddie out on the cliff path for a walk." He stopped and took in the lobby. "Wow Jessica, this looks amazing! Mum, isn't Jessica amazing?"

My plan was working. We'd moved for a better life and it was happening.

AND?

Aimee

Saltness
November 2016

I didn't know if she wanted my sympathy or admiration. I had to admit that if any other person had told me this story, I would have felt both. However, being Jessica/Jessie – whatever she wanted to call herself, I just felt angry. She'd just openly admitted being a stalker of my husband!

"Well Jessica, that was all very interesting, and I appreciate your honesty" I really did, "but I'm not sure why you feel the need to tell me all this – are you looking for sympathy? Because, if you are well – "

"No, not sympathy. I'm not completely ignorant to your feelings. I just felt that you need to understand me – so you can understand why"

"Why what? Like, why you thought you had a right to my husband?"

"Well, I wouldn't word it quite like that, but I do think you need to know the full picture. It didn't happen like you think."

"Think? I have no idea what to think"

"No, I don't suppose you do. But I do need to tell you that stealing your husband wasn't really my intention."

"Ha! Do me a favour and stop talking shite. You were effing stalking him!"

She had the good grace to look embarrassed, as her face flashed bright red.

"I know. I'm sorry. Let me explain..."

REWIND PART ONE
Jessica's Secret Journey

It didn't take much to convince Patrick into moving back to his home town. I sold the sea air to him and how it would help our boys grow into strapping lads. And as much as this was part of my motivation, the move took me further away from my newly discovered family and closer to my newly discovered ex-fiancé.

Thinking back now, I don't really see the logic in my plan. How on earth I thought that moving to be near a man who wasn't even aware of me anymore would improve my wellbeing was beyond me. But him being where I had a chance to rebuild myself was fate. Maybe we were fated to meet? However, my other reasons were sound enough. I wondered if I wanted to tempt fate? Putting myself in the firing line for something. Like I wanted to jump into a fire just to see if I could survive. Maybe I just wanted to wake up out of my mundane slumber. Patrick was wrong: money didn't solve everything.

We'd moved during the end of the summer. Saltness is beautiful at that time of year. It breathes in some late summer glow, melting into a kaleidoscope of colours. We bought a house near the bay. Our house practically touching the beach. We'd wake in the morning and the sun would fight its way through our east facing shutters. The house was still an old ramshackle of an old faded grand Victorian holiday home. But it had charm. And I finally felt free of all the ridiculous trappings that Patrick had enforced on me.

We'd all wake early to the sound of the sea and race to get dressed. We'd put Toby in a sling and race Oli onto the sands, paddling before breakfast and for once feeling like a proper family. It was everything I'd dreamed of.

The agreement had been that Patrick would take some time off over the move. I told him I needed him to help me settle before he jetted off again. I was surprised when he agreed – although I suspected that Diane had a hand in it (she was always good with her boys). With a relaxed husband, the sea air and our two sons finding the new harmony, I felt it suited us all. I'd almost forgotten part of my reason for moving.

On the second week, after some prompting from Oli, who kept trying to chase other peoples on the beach, Patrick came home with a baby Jack Russell. I remember being a bit cross about him not asking. After all, I was here to look after the boys and restart my career. Not to train a puppy who required two walks a day. But Freddie won me round with his deep chocolate eyes and I was now outnumbered four to one in a man's world.

Sadly, the honeymoon period lasted about a month. Patrick was needed up in Scotland to help redevelop some old crumbling country estate. I knew it would happen sooner rather than later, so I bit down my jealousy and bitterness and threw myself into my own projects.

The hotel and children consumed me. Living by the sea and having to manage my own life again gave me a new sense of purpose. I wanted to wake up in the morning and I was desperate to get the day going. I experienced a hunger that I hadn't done in years. I finally felt some peace from all the madness. I also began to get myself back into some sort of shape. The old fire that made me successful before the boys, began to smoulder and I started to believe in myself again. However, when I remembered my confinement, my reconnection with my family, and subsequent Facebook stalking, I felt a sense of unease. A Pandora's box of emotions and lives had been connected; all of it needed carefully managing.

I kept in touch with Stace and the boys. I fed them a line or two about how busy I was in Adelaide. I kept lifting ideas from Kate's page and made sure that I was up to date with her news.

Moving to Saltness had been a bit of a master stroke – I was petrified I'd bump into someone in Leeds. After all, now were we talking again, I couldn't risk anyone seeing me. They now knew how I looked after all those years. I was less anonymous.

My stalking, my other reason for agreeing to Diane's plan, caused other issues. You see, as I started to feel better, I started to doubt my sanity in obsessing over him. What would it achieve? After all, we were both married. Two children each. Both out of reach but living so near. What was I thinking?

Well, I knew what I was thinking. Whether it was the correct thing to do was another matter altogether.

*****

The first time I saw him was whilst I was driving to work one morning in September. He was walking his dog – a chocolate Labrador puppy – towards the beach. I knew it was him as I drove up behind him. The way he carried himself, the way he walked like he was on the stage of life – like a front man. It was an overcast morning and he had on a navy parka with his jeans and converse. He looked fresh and young (in a rugged way), The complete antithesis of my husband who always looked polished and ready to meet someone for business at a moment's notice.

Anyway, I saw him, and I shook as I tried to keep driving. It was finally happening and without me checking out his life via Facebook. I felt sick and had to pull over. I watched him strut down that hill with his dog and felt this inexplicable need to chase after him. To stop him and tell him. *Tell him what?* That I didn't know.

I watched him until he reached the bottom of the hill. Where he turned left and out of sight. I quickly roused myself and followed him, turning left also, and catching up with him near the entrance to the North beach. Without thinking, I parked up, grabbed my Barbour and made my way to the beach.

I followed him so far, watching the way he kept throwing a ball to his lively chocolate lab, who played in and out of the incoming tide. The roar of the wind masked the noise, occasionally lulling, with Frank's laughter and calls to his dog filtering through. Each time I heard him, it felt like I was being blessed. *Finally*, the tide was saying. *Finally, you've found him.*

Then my phone rang and broke my reverie. I was needed at work. Reminding me of my responsibilities. He was a dream, a fantasy...

After that, I allowed myself to look at the Facebook account once a day. I'd also take long and elaborate drives to the supermarket, nursery school, home...I made excuses to Diane about minding the boys. I'd walk the route to the beach and look for him constantly. It took two weeks, and I was finally rewarded.

This time he was leaving the beach as I was driving past. I had to quickly do a U-turn at the bottom of the sea road and head back to where I'd seen him. He'd gone. So, I headed towards the hill I'd spotted him on earlier. As I turned up that road, off the promenade, I spotted him making his way back up. I parked up and watched. Again, I had no idea what I was going to do. I just watched. As soon as I began to lose sight I drove further up and parked not far behind him. As I did, I saw he was just reaching the crest of the hill, and then he stopped.

He stopped outside some weird looking Victorian folly. A bit of a cross between a big house and a doll's house. The size of a standard detached house, it was decorated with turrets and gargoyles – a bit of a beautiful monstrosity I decided. He let the dog off, who then shot through the gate and down the side of the house. Frank followed, he turned to look down the hill and I saw his face fully. For a split second, I felt like he caught my eye and warmth spread through me. That ability to make me feel like the only woman in the room had never left me. And just like that, he followed the dog out of sight.

DEJA VU

Jessica

Saltness
May 2010

"...and so, this evening wouldn't be possible without my daughter-in-law's hard work and determination. Her drive, talent and attention to detail has brought The White Cliff's into a new a modern era. I am forever grateful to my oldest son: Patrick, for marrying her. The day she became a Green, he gained a wife, and I gained the daughter I never had. I just wish her family would have survived to see how well she has done and achieved in her life."

Diane became misty eyed at this. I felt sick. Up until that last statement I was high on the praise. Now I felt ill with the deception.

"So, ladies and gentlemen, I would like you all to raise a glass to my project manager Jessica Green!"

Glasses were raised and cheers went up. The day had been a fabulous success. The journalists had been thrilled at the transformation. Local brides-to-be had come and made appointments the following week with my wedding team.

Two people had loved the set up in the ballroom – a cigarless, smoke free bar, redesigned with sleek glass and relaxing recliners. A cocktail menu was lit up on the bar and it was all in sumptuous colours of cool platinum and a deep rose pink. Very feminine, and a place a lady could sit back from the dancing. The theme continued into the main room, with mirrored walls, with platinum frames and large floral chandeliers hung from the newly painted ceiling. So much, had they loved it, that they booked a winter ball in aid of the hospice and a Christmas party for the head office of an advertising firm in York. Very lucrative clients and a great boost for the new business. The old buzz of success burst around my veins. I was wired and without the free champagne too!

I'd made my speech earlier when I launched our new look and plans. Now was the time to start to enjoy myself.

A pair of arms came at me and squeezed me tight "You've done well love. You've come so far" It was Moira. "I knew you could do it. Charles too. We have been rooting for you."

"I know. You've been great. So has Diane!"

"Who knew?" She laughed.

"I know! Last time we were partying in this ballroom, things were very different."

"And now is your time Jessica. You've come through to the other side and shown how amazing you are."

"Thank you, now stop or you'll make me cry" I hugged her again to distract her from my face. I felt sad as I didn't think Patrick felt the same way. In fact, I was suspicious about Patrick's 'joy'. I hadn't seen him for quite a while. I had sent him out networking the room with strict instructions that he was to stay quite sober.

Moira wanted to know if I'd managed to have a drink and I told her how high I was just from the day. She told me it was doctor's orders that we have a drink to celebrate my success and dragged me to the bar.

I could hear him before I saw him. That was never a good sign. As soon as I walked into the ballroom bar, he was braying loudly. Moira shot me an anxious look and I rolled my eyes. It looked like we had similar thoughts.

"Feck him" she whispered into my ear. "The Green boys aren't going to ruin your night."

We walked up to the bar and ordered a bottle of Bolly "My treat" Moira argued. I turned around and surveyed the room as the barman organised the bottle. There he was, my husband, surrounded by some of his hangers on and his brother Charles.

"He can't help himself you know. As much as he admits his brother can be a knob" She hesitated "Sorry, I know he's your husband but...Charles just loves him. He saved him you know?"

"Yes, I'm sure inheriting the lion's share didn't influence him at all"

"Jessica!"

"I've shocked you. I do know what he's like. Our marriage has to be worked at more and more these days. I think the scales have fallen off both our eyes as we've become older"

"But Charles is so grateful he didn't have to do his bit. It would have killed him you know? He might be tough, but he loves his career. It's like a priest with his calling."

We'd all made sacrifices.

"I know. I'm just mad at him. Holding court in the bar and I've done all the work. I bet he doesn't even know where the children are"

"Child minder?"

"Yes, but he never asked"

We sat down with our champagne and tried to relax. Patrick's loud voice competing with the band playing in the main room. Moira and I talked and couldn't help but compare the posh self-arrogance of Patrick's to the passionate tone of my guitarist-singer. He was so absorbed with telling his set about himself that he'd failed to spot us. Charles had though as he slipped away and joined us.

"Thought I'd come and congratulate you Jessica. Job well done I'd say! Certainly, gives Dad and Patrick a run for their money. You've reinvented the old place. And you've picked yourself up. We were worried weren't we M?"

"Eye, yes we were! But look at her, she's got a sparkle back in her eyes and it's lovely to see. Plus, the wee ones are growing beautifully. The sea air suits you all"

"Thanks Charles" I smiled honestly "Moira, that means a lot. It's good to know I've got some support."

They both shot each other a knowing look.

"My brother does not always see what he should. It's not that he doesn't care -"

There was loud laughter coming from Patrick's side of the room. Raucous, I'd call it, like from a wild animal.

"...seriously boys, she has been a good wife. Giving her a project to do has kept her busy and it stops the nagging!"

More laughter.

"But now this is all in hand, she'll be back with the boys and I'll be able to start my new project. I've bought three hunting lodges in Scotland. She's all about the boys now...Anyway, these lodges will be pure luxury. You should come up and write a piece Thomas. What do you think?"

He was addressing the travel reporter from The Telegraph.

Giving her a project? Stops the nagging? Back with the boys? Was that all I was, a wife?

I quickly stood up, knocking the low table with my knees.

Charles was straight to his defence. "Jessica, he didn't..."

I put my hand out to stop him. "No Charles, please don't"

Bitter tears were stinging my eyes. I wouldn't give anyone the opportunity to see them. I apologised to them and raced out of the bar and out into the ballroom.

The band were playing an old song. That one from Pretty Woman, where he is in his limo on the way to the airport, and realises he loves Julia Roberts. He turns around and rescues her from the fire escape.

It must have been love, but it's over now...

Oh, the irony! Patrick was labelling me as The Wife and The Little Woman. No passion. No pride. And there was Frank, singing with such longing in his voice. I couldn't take it anymore. I looked at him and he smiled at me as he sang. Hastily, I turned and headed for the main bar then the garden. I needed some alcohol and some space. I needed to think.

ONLY FOOLS
FALL IN LOVE.

Jessica

Saltness
May 2010

The warm and golden May sun was melting into the distant horizon. Losing its way behind the hotel, painting flashes of purple, orange, indigo, violet, across a Jackson Pollock of a canvas. Vivid brush strokes streaked like jolts of electricity. Reminding me that I was alive.

I found a bench hidden from the main part of the hotel. A bench which I'd often sit on to watch the early sun rise. All winter I'd come out here and take my morning coffee, whilst I'd make lists and mull over the plans. It was my thinking place with an inspiring view. Not for the first time, I thought about Corfu and how connected I always felt to the sea and the sky. This felt no different and calmed me.

The Thinking Bench sat near the edge of the cliff face. Hidden by two large oaks and a willow tree, it looked out into the vastness of the sea.

Black, the sea was calm. The indigo sky sat on top of the inky water. I steadied my breathing and took a large drink of champagne from the bottle, which I'd just swiped from the main bar. Diane would kill me. She'd call me a hypocrite. The amount of times...but I didn't care. I felt so deceived by her son, hurt and embarrassed about the way he was talking about me in front of all those important contacts I'd made. I felt sick. I took another drink. To numb the pain.

When I was trying to recover from the depression, I had to do some work on my self-worth. It was all about me putting myself first. Not because I was to be selfish, but to make sure I was mentally equipped to be a good mum. Happy mum. Happy children. That was the theory anyway. Moira had put me onto this particular train of thought, and it worked. I started by writing lists and with Moira and Diane's guidance, I put together a plan. Self-respect, building self-esteem, looking good, quality of life...that sort of thing. And sitting there on that bench, I thought about how far I'd come – with or without my husband's help.

Anyway, one of the reasons we moved here, apart from the purposeful work, was because I liked the idea of being at the edge of the sea. I liked to feel like I was teetering on the edge of the world. That little lost Leeds council estate girl fighting her way out of the concrete jungle and looking for something real and beautiful. I'd found that here. The peace I needed. Only, I couldn't control everything else; human emotion and nature. And that was the problem.

The tears fell silently. I could hear the music still playing and could guess from the amount of songs and the change in the genre of music, that the band had either finished or were taking a break. I have to say, at that moment, in all that wild beauty, with the eerily calm sea quietly beating against the rocks, I felt so trapped. I thought back to the romantic visions of my teens. The Mr Darcy scenario. Life wasn't fair.

"Jessie?"

My name was being called and it could only have been one person. My body stiffened. I didn't want him to see me like this. I was the damsel in distress, but I knew it was all wrong.

"Jessie?" He softly called. I wanted to call back but something was stopping me. Fear? All that weird stalking I did, it had all become too real. My worlds had begun to merge, and I'd allowed it. But I felt drawn to him; I knew from the tone of his voice that it was full of warmth and concern.

"Oh, you're there." He laughed "Oh, Christ! What's wrong Jessie?"

He was just coming towards the cover of the trees. He made quick strides to get by my side. He instinctively put his arms around me, his kindness filling me with love and safety. My dam of tears fell and wouldn't stop. I so wanted to explain but I didn't want to be disloyal.

Guiltily I pulled away "I'm sorry. You don't want to drag you into all this…"

"What this? What's happened. I've never liked seeing you upset. Has some eejit upset you?"

"Yes, but it doesn't matter. I can deal with it"

"Really?" He sighed "Jessie, don't keep trying to carry the whole world on your shoulders"

"I don't!" I argued.

"You do. I've watched you. A one-woman powerhouse. You cope so well on your own"

I laughed and shook my head. So right. It was like he was inside my marriage.

His tone softened "You see, I do know you." He looked into my eyes Jessie, I've always known you."

I can remember that look in his eyes. It was all that I needed at that moment "Me too. Forever"

And that was how it started.

BUT?

Aimee

Saltness
November 2016

"So, you stalked him and got what you wanted! My god Jessica, it is no wonder you two got on so well!"

"What do you mean by that?"

"You were both mad!" And then I started to laugh. The whole thing was ridiculous. I knew I was upsetting Jessica, as she started to cry.

"You have no idea" She spat at me. "He was there, and my bastard of a husband never was. He listened. He helped me. He made me feel less alone"

Patrick was a shit husband. Frank was also a shit husband. Something I could relate to. I understood more than she knew.

"I get that. He was a fantastic man when he was on form. However, just like your Paddy – "

She laughed through her tears. "Paddy! He lets you call him that!"

"Yes. And like your Paddy, he could also leave me feeling very lonely for vast amounts of time."

We both fell silent. I was thinking about what she had said. How she'd had to step back from her goals so she could support her husband, her boys, Diane...How we'd both been thwarted in our talents by marrying in haste and putting everyone first.

A colony of seagulls screeched overhead us, breaking our separate reveries.

"I admit that I was a little obsessive about Frank. But I really never intended anything to happen. In my dreams maybe, but never in real life."

REWIND PART TWO
Jessica's Secret Journey

After I'd found out where he lived, I began to drive that way to work most days. I'd catch him walking his dog. Always alone, never with his wife and children. I'd secretly follow him and try and work out how happy he was. He'd walk the beach like a man on a mission. All winter, all weathers, he'd be out, moving forward.

It had to happen eventually. We would have to come face to face. I'd been engineering a meeting for weeks. Thinking up ways I could get his attention on the beach. Always chickening out when I thought I could. Freddie was getting over walked and he was tired of my constant wanderings. However, physically I looked so much fitter. My skin glowed and mentally I felt stronger and more optimistic. If I'm honest, I think the reason I didn't force a meeting was because I was scared by life.

How would he react?

Turns out, I didn't need to over think things after all…

I'd been away for a week with the boys in Scotland. Patrick had insisted saying he '*needed me by his side*'. He was doing lots of business with hard up Scottish lairds and needed my '*skills*'. What he actually needed me to do was play the part in his 'perfect family man' fantasy to gain their respect and trust. Nothing that I needed to use my First in economics for.

Wanker.

Anyway, we'd just got back, and I was harassed and tired from taking the journey home with two small children and a dog (Patrick had stayed behind as he now had *important things to do*. I nearly pointed out that I also had lots of pressing things at the hotel, but I didn't bother. I was fed up of the arguments). Diane had rung and said they were up against it. She needed me to oversee the hotel as she was unwell with a virus, and the manager was away. It wasn't really my role, but I'd filled in like this before. I called the childminder and was there before the evening guests arrived.

I needed to assess the situation, so I went straight to reception and looked over what the bookings looked like. Rooms were at 70% capacity. There was a full restaurant and the ballroom was booked for a winter ball for the local sixth form college. It was a fundraiser for the Teenage Cancer Trust. I'd seen an article in the local newspaper about a pupil who was fighting testicular cancer. His school friends had wanted to do something positive for him. I felt warmed by their benevolence and this story of support and made a note to make sure we'd donated a raffle prize and to donate some money myself. I decided I needed to do a walkthrough of the room.

All business-like, I made my way through to the ballroom. The staff had done a wonderful job of setting it up. The band were banging about at the back of the dancefloor. I daren't look in case he was there. Those days every time I heard a band setting up, I ran the other way. Instead, I concentrated on the highly polished table settings, blue cloths and white flowers, which topped with the Teenage Cancer Trust balloons. All around the perimeter of the room stood easels holding pictures of the boy. He was in various poses with a mass of friends, family and what looked like him taking part in a plethora of sports: abseiling, canoeing, running, rugby, football...I spotted a programme and picked it up. There was a short biography about him:

Ralph Shore.
Ralph is an outgoing and well-loved member of our sixth form community at North Sea College. Last year he was our sportsman of the year, and at the beginning of this one he was offered a scholarship in Atlanta

**Georgia. He is one to watch in the future, with his talent and prospects pointing towards London 2012.
Unfortunately, and devastatingly, Ralph was diagnosed with Testicular cancer back in October.
Ralph has vowed never to give up and we, at his college, are here to help him on his journey.
Tonight, is about raising awareness and raising money for the hospital unit in York, where he is being treated. Please enjoy, donate and help us give Ralph the boost he needs.
#TeamRalph**

Unexpected tears threatened to spill over. Damn the tiredness from the drive; life was so cruel to the innocent. The awfulness of Ralph's story made me think about our precious boys and all our hopes and dreams for them. The was the one thing we were at least united on. I put myself in Ralph's parents' shoes. I hoped they would be here to see this wonderful event his friends had organised. He had his whole life ahead of him and yet again the cruelty of cancer was spreading its desultory poison onto the lives of the young. I thought about my own life. How my chance of freedom had been snatched from me by Mam's illness – although not cancer - it was just another unlucky throw of the dice of fate. I prayed to God for Ralph. For him to gain his freedom and to be given the chance to live the life he deserved.

And then I sensed someone coming up behind me:

"Jessie?"

My heart stilled. I knew it then. I knew the moment that I turned around from that Irish lilt, that my whole world would turn on its axis. It didn't matter what happened next, I just knew I'd never feel the same again. I put the programme down and turned.

"My lord, it is you!"

WHAT IS WORSE?

Aimee
Saltness
November 2016
What is Worse?

"And that's where it started. Nothing serious. No kissing, not even a lingering hug. To put it simply Aimee, I needed a friend. We started a purely platonic affair. Platonic because we rebuilt some of our friendship. Affair because as innocent as it was, we didn't want to tell you and Patrick. It just felt wrong. It was an unsaid agreement."

Before she finished her story, I knew it. It was what he did – cultivated friendships, liaisons, away from the family unit. He couldn't bear to be boxed in. He needed freedom, whilst I managed the background to his life. It was the deal I'd made.

"So, nothing happened?"

She hesitated, "I've never told anyone any of this – Patrick yes, but not everything, it's too difficult – a lifetime of secrets and hurt… Strange how the first person I'm telling is you. I guess no one else would understand, would they?"

"Most people try therapy" I replied waspishly. I wasn't about to be kind. *Yeah, she'd been dealt some shite, but hadn't we all? I didn't go around stealing people's husbands…had I? Friends, lovers, what's the difference?* I was no better than her.

"Believe it or not, we are. This, talking to you is part of it. Our therapist said that we needed to unravel everything before we could start again. We are starting with the infidelity – the result, I suppose, of all the other deep-rooted problems we have hidden away with the rest of The Greens' dirty secrets."

I laughed at the irony: I was her free therapist. I was meant to be absolving her of her sins just so she could repair her marriage. She really had no idea.

She must have sensed my unease as she hesitated. "Look, I'm sorry. You're right, it isn't right to unburden myself on you of all people. It's just…"

"What? It's just what?"

"I need to tell you the truth."

ROSE TINTED SPECTACLES

Jessie

Saltness
November 2016

"I remember the day it all changed. When all our worlds fell apart. It was one of those early spring days of optimism – a brief dalliance of warm weather promising something good for the year. After months of the dark days, there was light on the horizon. The days were getting longer. Finally, winter was letting in the harsh and fickle February sunlight. The sea gales cutting through the new warmth; chilling me to the bones.

I was out jogging. I'd pushed on, against the headwind, running along the promenade, harder and faster I pushed, moving to the beats in my ears. The previous week it had been dusk when I had run the route, now the sun was just starting to sink below the horizon. I felt life was opening up again. I took a right and ran up the hill, the direction of wind changing and easing off the pressure. Although I was now pushing against the incline, I felt energised and positive about the year ahead. Deeper and deeper I pushed myself into the steep hill, sweating out any tension from the day.

Running had been doing me good. Patrick was calling it my new obsession. I'd finished the project at the hotel, and apart from working on some of the online business and profile, my workload wasn't what it was. We were successful, and my job was to just maintain some balance. Diane told my 'dear husband' that I 'being cooped up would kill me'.

He'd laugh at me preparing for a long run. Asking me if I ever stopped for a cocktail. *Do they have champagne at those drinks' stations?* He'd tease, and which he'd once asked unhelpfully when I was competing in my first 10K. It was like he didn't really know me at all.

However, the joke was on him, as I got fitter and more toned, his lavish lifestyle and love for indulgence was starting to show. Diane told me I was glowing and that doing what made me happy had helped her enormously. She was ready for a new chapter too.

They both had no idea. They thought me finding running had saved me. And although it was important to me, for my physical and mental health, it wasn't my obsession or real reason for my glow: Frank was.

After that first meeting, he'd been stunned at meeting me again. Unlike me, who had stalked him for months, my existence in Saltness came as a complete surprise to him. However, like me, I sensed that he also still felt that instant connection and wanted to rekindle it. But it wasn't about the romance. It was more about our lost youths and our shared history. Like I said though, it was all platonic. Frank was from another part of my life and it felt good to revisit there.

We'd meet on a quiet part of the beach and walk the dogs. *Funny how the dogs found each other again isn't it?* We'd text daily and swap silly stories. We'd chat about stuff – you and the children. *He adored you all you know?"*

Aimee nodded. Her eyes were full of something of warmth and understanding. I thought she must have hated me though.

"I was jealous. But I promise that was not what triggered what happened next. I might have spent time hating you since. But after Jenna, then Patrick, and the therapist...I've begun to realise that my hatred has nothing to do with you. It was just a channel for my grief."

She was quiet. I could see the tears brimming in her eyes

now. I felt like I was killing something inside of her – maybe the tenderness only a true wife can feel for her husband? The father of her children. I was taking away her precious memories of Frank. The unfaithful husband who she clearly still loved. I knew how she felt.

I paused.

"Go on – "

I sensed she needed this over with. I decided to edit this last bit. Not denying her the truth but enough to understand.

We went along with this platonic – but flirtatious relationship, for a number of months. All until that night of the launch. May Day 2010 was the day it all changed.

HEADING INTO THE LIGHT

Jessica

Saltness
May 2010
After the Launch:

After Frank found me, picked me up and dried my tears, we held hands. He stroked his thumb across my hand, and it felt so nice. So relaxing and reassuring. My husband had never been tactile and the touch of another human being, who wasn't one of my children, felt incredibly beautiful.

He told me he hated the way I was treated. He told me that if I was his wife that he'd be showing me off to the whole room: *I'd be so proud of you.*

I cried more and he kissed me.

Instantly I was transported back to that summer of 96. I was that girl again who wanted rescuing. I was in his arms again and nothing had ever felt so right for the past 14 years.

And so it began...

It was so difficult in those early days. I thought everyone would see it written all over my face – the new glow, no matter the amount of running I was doing, no one would truly believe it could make me that happy. I had a new lightness to the way I behaved, as I nursed our precious secret like the box of memories which were hidden away at the back of my walk-in wardrobe.

The logistics became difficult. We'd meet further afield. We would both fabricate excuses to go to places. If Diane thought I was having a lot of shopping days she never said anything – I guessed she was happy I was doing something and not slipping back into some sort of depression. And, she was still upset with Patrick's insensitivity and behaviour towards me, especially when the Telegraph article came out praising Patrick for his well-managed project at White Cliff's Hotel.

The Millennial's Mogul's Midas Touch

Patrick Green does it again! This Svengali of the leisure industry has taken his old childhood home and pulled it into the 21st century. Creating an exquisite venue rivalling any of the top hotels North of the Midlands.

Assisted by his wife and mother, they have created a hotel for the future.

And so it went on.

Diane was furious of course and Patrick denied that he had any part in the report, stating that some reporters just '*get the wrong idea*'. She accused him of turning into his father.

Anyway, regardless of Diane's support and solidarity, it was difficult to meet up. I'd started running and that helped me cover absences – I'd go hill running and meet him somewhere on the moors. I'd never been so fit! Frank very much appreciated it though. The upshot being that both gave me a focus and a flush in my cheeks. But as autumn closed in, I needed to find a better way to meet.

Frank was addictive. I realise now, that I'd spent my whole life striving for one thing or another. It was like I couldn't breathe without a challenge. I treated our relationship like a drug; I couldn't manage a day without him. But he was different, I'd found he'd be full on one minute and the next he'd be quiet and aloof. For fear of pushing him away, and knowing how obsessive I could become, I chose not to pry, guessing those were the times he was keeping busy with you and the band. I contained the terror inside and used it to fuel my runs. I now realise how desperate I must have felt, but at the time, I was petrified of losing him. After all, it was an affair; I wasn't stupid. I knew the consequences.

Then I saw the cottage. I was out running one morning. I'd run up your hill to see if I could see him. Thinking back now it was all crazy behaviour – the stalking, the subterfuge, the planning my life around a man who I couldn't be with, a man who clearly loved his family – no doubt...as I said, there was a cottage. Just up the hill from the folly, and to the right. It stood on a massive field and looked out over the sea. The view was breath-taking. The cottage was derelict and needed pulling down. There was a for sale sign.

Patrick liked me having 'little projects' and this would be it. I'd let him think I had a new obsession.

It was easy. I told him I was going to build us a family home there. Something breath-taking and sumptuous. I said that it was an investment. That it would be another feather in his cap – something else to show the world how far he'd come. So, whilst I manipulated and puffed up his ever-growing ego, he agreed, but reminding me that I wouldn't be able to start straight away as I needed planning permission. All that stuff... like I cared!

It was perfect. I could wait. It was only for the time being. Until we'd organised what we were going to do. I now had somewhere to meet Frank and some breathing space. Also, it was a great project and would give me something to do – it wouldn't hurt getting the planning, an architect on board etc. The challenge of juggling it all gave me a renewed sense of purpose. I'd always been driven and yet again it was paying off for me.

Frank was hesitant at first. I'd rarely seen him rattled and I think I spooked him. It made me realise that I needed to be more careful. He said it was too close to home and that we really must think about what we had to lose. This panicked me I felt firmly in my place – I was the mistress. But, as a parent, I knew we both had children to consider. I told myself that was why he was reticent. Anyway, much to my sheer relief, I managed to convince him different and as of the end of October, I owned the cottage.

We'd meet most weeks. Sometimes twice. I couldn't get enough of him. I don't feel great telling you this, but you have to understand, my husband isn't a warm person. He was never very affectionate. For him, it's just sex. He likes things to be straight forward. He doesn't like mess or interference. Laying in Frank's arms I felt warmth for the first time in 14 years. I know I keep saying it, but he was my great love. My first love. 14 years previously, we'd been engaged to be married.

On those cold winter days, we'd talk about our time in Corfu. Romanticising it and going back to what happened the day I'd left. Discussing the what ifs...but always realising that we would have our beautiful children if things would have been different.

Frank explained that he had been elusive as he was lining up a deal to go to Australia. An agent had seen them perform and wanted them to go and launch out there for his label. He hadn't wanted to tell me until it was confirmed – that was what that note was about. *The reason he never contacted me?* Maria had told him she didn't know my forwarding address and never gave him my letter.

I was furious with her. We'd remained in contact for all those years and she had lied to me for every one of them. 14 years had been wasted because of missed messages and interference. The fury took my obsession to another level. I began to believe that fate had brought us together again for a reason. We were surely meant to be together? My one true happy ever after. *So much time wasted.* That's when the panic took hold and I didn't want to waste any more time. Very soon I started pressuring him to leave you. He said nothing either way; he said he needed time.

There was something else bothering me too. Something

which I kept choosing to ignore – like I said before - he'd blow hot and cold. I never knew what was going on with him. Of course, I blamed you, keeping him from me. At particularly low moments I would imagine you manipulating him and finding reasons to trap him. Ludicrous I know now, but I wanted to hate you. You were the one thing holding him back. What did you have that I didn't? Ridiculously, I believed you had no right to monopolise him – after all, I immaturely felt he was mine, as I found him first. I'd make comments to him about you. Say I'd seen you looking rough or tired. I'm ashamed to say I wasn't very kind. I'd ask him bitchy and leading questions. To his credit, I couldn't draw him in, and he'd shoot me down. Made me feel like shit. I wanted to be held in the same loyalty.

The longest time I went without seeing him was Christmas and New year. I was beside myself and had to mask my longing with overloading on work with the hotel, the family, and the building project. You'd all gone to Ireland and had stayed well into January. He said his Ma had been ill and you had to look after her. Patrick never noticed of course, but I noticed Diane and Moira whispering conspiratorially about me on Boxing Day. I batted away their worries and lied again to the two people who had dragged me through the past few years of hell. I felt wretched – what could I do?

When we finally caught up at the end of the month, he was full of it. It was glorious. All the tension that had been building up had gone and he was back to my Frank. Those last two weeks were glorious. I felt like I'd gained a brighter and bigger Frank. And just like the optimistic February sun, I felt there was change in the air.

That February evening, I ran up the hill to our cottage so full of hope. He was waiting for me when I got there and dragged me straight into his arms. So passionate and so tender. I'm sorry I have to say that, because I have to remember that at least. I want to remember that once I loved and was loved passionately.

Afterwards we laid in each other's arms and I asked him when we could meet again. He took in a deep breath and I sensed a shift in his breathing. His body tensed.

He told me that he'd told you he wanted to leave you. He said he hadn't mentioned me. He told me you'd threatened that he wouldn't see the children again if he did. He said I didn't understand what you were like. How dependent you were on him. He said you had mental health issues and he was scared what would happen if he left. He said he could never forgive himself if anything happened to you and the children.

His words felt like my world was crashing down around me. I'd been pinning my hopes on us running away together. The plans and sacrifices I'd made: I'd saved money for years – not just a few pounds but enough to start again. The penniless little girl inside of me whispering that I should never go back there: the poverty of my childhood. I'd seen how Jonny and Diane had ripped each other apart during the divorce; the fact she never really got what she was due. How I'd wince about the lies I'd told to her and Moira, and how they'd hate me. Meanwhile, Patrick had no idea. It seemed that the minute he'd been handed that bloody business that he'd stepped away from me and lost all respect. He had no idea what I was up to. And the children? We'd work that out. We had always had common ground there. I knew it was all going to be messy and destructive. But if I was willing to take those steps. Why wouldn't Frank?

I blamed you. You'd ruined all my plans. And as I needed to vent my aggression and anger, I took it out on the next best thing: Frank. He got the full force of everything. A lifetime of being let down, how he had no idea about my mental health – how much I needed him. How he had no idea what lengths I'd gone to find him again. How a world without him was a world without love and depth. I told him he was the key to my future and that he needed to choose. I thought he'd waver. I went from Hyde to Jekyll, saying that I could get you help, that I'd pay.

"The lengths you've gone to?" The usual cheeky glint in his eyes had clouded over. He looked at me in a way he never had done before. He said he'd *better leave before he said something.*

If you remember, it was a dark stormy night.

I don't know why I'm saying that, of course you do. You'll have it imprinted on your brain like I do.

I ran after him no longer caring. I hounded him to your road. He told me to stop. He said he needed time and space. I remember he was shaking. He did that sometimes, like he needed something.

I was hysterical and I remember begging. All the cool exterior I had held for so long had melted away. I was naked to my true vulnerable self. He must have sensed how I was coming undone and how dangerous it was to have his mistress rambling like a madwoman on the corner of his street.

He put his hands on my shoulders to calm me. He told me that of course he loved me. Always had, always would. He kissed my forehead and told me we'd speak soon. He tried to say all the right things. The last thing I remember was him smiling nervously as he turned away. He walked further away from me and turned towards his house.

Motionless, I stood. I had no idea if I'd lost him for a second time. Bile rose in my throat. My stomach moved into that rollercoaster of feeling when something monumental changes and you know there's no going back. It must have been a premonition as before I knew it there was a screeching of tyres, a heavy thud, followed by screaming.

"Frank!"

ABSOLUTION?

Aimee

Saltness
November 2016

Tears were streaming down her face. I should have felt angry, but I didn't. I was past all that and anyway, she really had no idea. Some might say I was too forgiving, maybe she felt like she was atoning herself – being honest, cleansing herself of all her sins – and there were a few, but...

"I can still hear it now. It wakes me up in the middle of the night. That screaming was Jenna. She saw it all happen."

She was sobbing. The Ice Queen was melting.

"Only, she hid so much from me" I thought about what Jenna would have struggled with in silence. "She only told me half the story. She had no choice"

"Jenna was protecting you?"

"Yes, she often did back then. It was her job. Sometimes it felt like there were three of us in that marriage."

Jessica looked shocked. "Do you think that's why he...and me?"

"No. It wasn't like that. WE both needed her..." I didn't know how to put it. "You two was something else. No, Jenna helped when things got tough"

She looked at me quizzically. I felt bad about what I was about to do. Fucking Frank. Full of bloody surprises, even from beyond the grave.

Here goes "We agreed to meet, so now we need to put these

ghosts to rest" I was gesturing to the bench and Frank's plaque. I smiled. She smiled back – warmly this time.

"I wonder what he'd do it he was here?"

"Probably hide knowing Frank"

"Not one to face the music, was he? I got that much from my crazed pressurising." She admitted.

"You did know something about him then! Below the front-man façade?"

"Only that he was all about the good times and that…"

"Yes, that was Frank. He was an incurable romantic and avoided anything dull or difficult emotionally."

I could sense a softening in her. The defences she'd held firm at first were beginning to show that she wasn't entirely stupid when it came to my husband.

"I thought you had him on a pedestal. And like I'd trapped him in the folly like some Victorian witch."

"I'm not stupid you know, I know he wasn't perfect, and I can see that you're not some possessive witch either. Patrick might be a prize dick sometimes, but he is quite discerning about the company he keeps. Or Paddy as he lets you call him!" She shook her head smiling.

Then she looked out to sea sadly, as if she had suddenly re-membered why she was there. "You talk like I didn't know him."

"Really?" This was going to hurt but she was being impos-sible and there was no easy way to say it: "You know you weren't the first, don't you?"

She went really still and deathly quiet. Her face went white and I felt sure she was going to faint. Clearly not.

"You didn't did you? Maybe I ought to tell you about him first. It might make it a bit easier"

PART SEVEN

THOU SHALL NOT COMMIT ADULTERY

IN SICKNESS AND
IN HEALTH

THEN
Aimee

Saltness
November 2016

"Frank bounded into my life a bit like he did yours. I think he was attracted to the power of breaking the strong will of an independent woman. Even though you say you wanted to be rescued, you don't strike me as someone weak or feeble. Maybe if I'd have met him when I was younger – before I'd been to uni, then I'd have been more susceptible to the romance. However, I was a hardened backpacker when he swaggered his way into my life."

I felt sick. Revisiting the past when I had been doing so well looking forward. I took a pause. This was difficult and not a story I was used to telling.

I wanted to say that *I longed to be that girl again, with my whole life in front of me. Not having to kickstart my art career at forty.*

"I guess though, he knew all the tricks. Like you, we met in a beautiful location and we were married in about eight weeks."

"We were engaged after three" She admitted.

"See, it's not normal is it? But older and wiser and all that..."

She nodded her head. She understood.

"Anyway, our whirlwind romance continued as we travelled around Asia: it was exciting as we flitted from one country to another. Beach to beach, immersing ourselves in another life. It was so hedonistic and romantic" I hesitated. "It wasn't real."

She looked down at her hands. I noticed that she was still wearing her ring. "Real or not, you had the life I wanted." She twisted the platinum band around her fingers.

"Maybe on the surface – it was a blast! But underneath, things were difficult."

I took a deep breath. Only Jenna really knew the story. She'd been my rock for so many years. I knew why she'd shielded me from that final truth.

"You see, it wasn't me with the mental health issues." I took a breath, like on the turn of the millennium, all those years ago. I was taking a leap of faith, this wasn't personal – even if she thought it was, "He lied to you." I couldn't read her face. "But, and I've no idea why I still stick up for him, he couldn't help it. He was ashamed."

Her stony expression barely moved, "Ashamed? We've all been there. Mental health shouldn't be something to hide away like a dirty secret...I've told you about me. And you must have guessed that my actions around your husband were slightly unhinged?" She blushed.

"Yes, and I won't say that word again." I was calmer now. She'd been very honest, and I understood. *So here goes;* "I think your mental health might have been the problem." I explained, "You see, he needed looking after. After what you told me about your outburst on that final night, well, he would have been afraid."

"Of me?" She shuddered. "I'd never..."

"No, I know, but Jessica, Frank was seriously ill. He was bipolar."

She looked shocked. "I never saw, I don't, mood swings? Oh..." she went quiet, thoughtful. I enforced the silence to allow her to process the information. "I suppose we only see what we want to see don't we?" Blinking back the tears, realisation flashed across her face "Poor Frank." She slumped down into the bench. The scales finally falling from her eyes.

Meanwhile, I was shaking. It was so difficult reciting it all, to say it all out loud. I'd buried it all away for so long – to protect everyone, that the release of the words was making me feel sick.

She took my hand and the instinct to push it away didn't come. I felt comforted instead. Maybe this was what I needed.

"Tell me" she quietly urged.

I steadied my breathing.

"I didn't notice it at first – his mania maybe, but he came across like that didn't he? So full of life and brimming with enthusiasm. Nothing was ever dull, and my life was spontaneous. He fitted into my new direction. I was desperate for excitement and running from my parents' ideal of trapping me here.

The irony! All roads lead to Rome, as the old saying goes. Well, all roads led to this little seaside town, didn't they? I never did get away in the end."

She nodded. I sensed she knew what I meant. She'd trapped herself here because of her husband too. Patrick had a great deal to answer for.

"We left Asia and the depression hit him as we came back to Europe. He was meant to be touring, but he was too ill. He told me he needed home, so we went to Galway and stayed with his family whilst he recuperated. He could get very black days, his mother explained to me. He'd always been the same. As the enormity of our situation dawned on me, I felt like I'd married into a lie."

She nodded knowingly, "I think we all did: you, me, Diane"

"You're right. One way or another, we all went into marriage with blinkers on. I think that deep down Frank needed looking after, and that's why he so desperately wanted to marry."

She looked deflated. The glossy beautiful veneer was peeling away revealing a troubled soul.

"You said I wasn't the only one?"

"Fiancé? I think you were. No, women – he had a few affairs. Frank loved the idea of feeling loved. The spontaneity of falling for someone. It wasn't real though, it never was."

"But how could you live like that?" She rolled her eyes at the irony of the question.

I felt like she slapped me, "Like you, you mean?"

"I'm sorry, I didn't mean it like that. I do get it...But you loved him. That's clear. How could you not? Patrick was/is a different story."

"Depends how you define love. Yes, I loved him at the beginning. But that Frank wasn't real. The Frank I grew to love was the one I helped through the black days. The one who would take me with him on his manic highs. The father of my children. It wasn't all bad you know? Once his ma explained what I'd walked into with romantic haste, I realised that I couldn't walk away even if I wanted to."

"You were trapped?"

"I prefer to think of it as putting him first – being the loyal wife. He was sick, Jessica. I gave up my dreams so I could support him. It wasn't exactly a hardship. But yes, I did give up my freedom."

"And the affairs?"

"It wasn't like I allowed it. They never lasted long, and I usually found out afterwards. They tended to end after a black period. He couldn't maintain the deceit. The mania gave him a mask to hide behind. I chose my husband. I stood by my vows: *In sickness and in health…*

I could see why he attracted them, "He could be so kind and charming." She sighed "I can't believe he would have deceived so many though." Fresh tears fell "Let me think I was special."

I wanted to reassure her. It wasn't her fault. As much as I wanted to hate her, I knew she was a victim like the rest of us. All of us were in our own ways. Victims of love, honouring, obeying, playing by the rules…

"He was kind Jessica. Loving too. And he could see the beauty inside another's heart. That was his problem. I think he had too much to give and it overwhelmed him. Love was like a drug to him. For some people it's drink, or cocaine; he was addicted to the high of love. I'm sorry, but that was him."

She sighed and smiled. "What a mess." She was quiet again.

"All the right pieces but in the wrong places." She smiled sadly.

I looked at her quizzically.

"The thing is Aimee, I know you owe me nothing but…do you think you can help me put all the pieces together - like they should be?".

HIS ROLE

JUST BEFORE NOW
Patrick

London
December 2016

I felt ridiculous. The deal was that I was to sit at the bar. Alone. Except not, I had props on and in hand: shirt and tie straight from Tom Ford, with a fresh manscape chiselling my jaw to perfection, all coated in her favourite – Chanel aftershave. An Old Fashioned sat in front of me, willing me to drink it: getting one in Don Draper style, before she arrived.

One large drink and it'd gone. I signalled for another. God I was nervous. I was never this nervous with the others.

I was such a cliché but then so were we. I knew she'd totter in, balancing in her red heeled wonders. A dress which hugged every curve. She wanted me to look. Not only that, everyone to look. That was her way these days - to make me beg. After all, she'd spent all those years struggling and alone. To make it work, she told me, I'd have to make her want her, want me again. I agreed. We'd spent fifteen years living separate journeys. We had a family and if we didn't give things a go then we'd never know.

I felt sure that we loved each other once.

I knew she'd order a gin and tonic in one of those great big goldfish glasses. All style and no substance...no originality.

'*Oh, for fuck's sake Patrick!*' I bollocked myself. I wasn't even trying. Even I was angering myself with my lack of effort.

Clean slate she said. Like we'd never met. A date. See what was there. We owed it to ourselves, our children. I needed to stop second guessing her and give her some respect. I had to curb the bitterness, after all, wasn't that what had got us into the mess in the first place? We'd been lying to each other all this time. Scratching the superficial surface and not delving into what goes on beneath?

Upping my game was what I needed to do.

"Bloody Mary please"

My wife's slightly polished northern accent pierced my thoughts.

"I'll get that" I signalled to the bartender. "That's an interesting drink…"

I turned to her and we locked eyes

"I wanted something filling, fiery." She smiled "Don't you think that sometimes you just need to try something different, new? Thank you…"

"Patrick" I smiled back as warmly as I could. I held out my hand and took hers.

"Jess" and I kissed it slowly. I looked into her eyes. I didn't look at her dress, heels, bag, all the superficial wrappings, I wanted to look at her. I needed to see her soul. Who was she - my wife of fifteen years?

The enormity of that question made me redden, feel sick, fumbling around for words. I floundered and began to babble about food

Would she like to eat?

What food would she like?

Would she like to eat here or that little Italian around the corner?

Banal questions I knew the answers to before I asked them. She'd want food. She'd want the Italian. She'd order antipasti, fillet steak and a bottle of champagne.

I was being so incredibly boring. Aimee would be taking the piss now, reminding me to laugh and to sort myself out. I knew I needed to try harder, much harder. I wasn't going to reignite my flailing marriage with my schoolboy nerves toppling the whole thing.

"Yeah, I'm hungry. Actually, I'd prefer some Lebanese food from the restaurant here."

"Lebanese? But you..." I wanted to laugh. She'd always gone for French, Spanish, or Italian. She never ventured far off the menu. Always happy for me to order for her. My wife had always been predictable.

"Yes, Lebanese, it's got an excellent review on TripAdvisor"

I began to raise my eyebrows, and quickly stopped myself. I knew that part of the problem was that I'd just made her fit into my ideal for most of our relationship. As she'd pointed out during our weekly counselling sessions, she needed to unpeel the layers so I could find the real her. Not just the identi-kit wife. *How can I not know her after fifteen years?*

My nerves were crippling me. I wasn't sure whether it was because I wanted it to work so much, or because I didn't. I was drastically rushing things. I'd already taken things too fast going from the drink to dinner with no preamble of the 'chat up'. I was failing miserably.

I looked at her, all glossy, groomed and gorgeous - I did have a glamorous wife and judging by the looks of some of the men in the room, I wasn't alone in my thoughts. I needed to make more of an effort. She was incredible and I was very lucky. Did I feel it though? That was what I had to decide.

I took the bait and went with her game.

"Well, how can I refuse such a beautiful woman?" I answered.

HER ROLE

Jess

London
December 2016

I knew he was nervous. I'd been spying from the lobby. He was on his second drink and he was anxiously checking his phone. Funny really, my husband of fifteen years, why was he so scared to spend time with me? Not so funny was the revelation that I felt the same.

As I sashayed into the bar, in my ridiculously high red soled heels, I tried to front it out. Slinking in wearing a dress held in by some ingenious underwear, I could feel all eyes on me. I'd still got it. I knew I looked good - you don't go to a yoga retreat for a month and come back lardy, do you? But it was more than that, it was the anticipation that maybe 'this', 'this blind date', could actually tell us if something was still living in this stagnant and murky marriage of ours.

If nothing else this was to be our final hurrah.

I quietly slinked up to him and as elegantly as I could, seamlessly perching myself onto the vertiginous bar stool and caught the bartender's eye with a slight nod and a smile.

I hesitated. What was I going to order? I needed something different. I needed to be a different version of myself...

"Bloody Mary please"

Why the fuck did I say that?

Patrick turned and looked at me. His surprised face made me want to laugh, it was as if he wanted to say something - be in on the joke too. '*That's good*' I thought. I made some stupid reply to his enquiry (about filling and spice?) and we made introductions (which was quite sweet and endearing if I didn't know what a bastard he could be).

With these thoughts in mind, when he asked about the food (too quick, no chat, no attempt to reel me in), I decided to be awkward. Of course, I wanted an Italian of antipasti and steak - I'd seen the restaurant as I'd walked from the tube earlier. However, I wanted to rattle him. Piss him off. Lebanese it was then.

A NEW DAWN

NOW
Patrick

London
New Year's Eve 2016

As a smoky dawn breaks, just like my soul's understanding, the bold and iconic skyline casts its shadows onto this vulgar tableau. Power mimicking power.

And I think, up until a few weeks ago, I felt like the prize cock (how ironic that simile is) strutting arrogantly - untouchable.

To my right; her soft contours sleep softly. Resting, after a night of surprises and lost love. I marvel at the magnificence of her. I devour the memory of her in the pink dress which she appeared to have been poured into, which I can't believe was only ten hours ago, it feels like a lifetime has passed since that first moment.

Lust stirs and I smile. I promise myself not to wake her; after all, when she opens her eyes, a lifetime of regrets will flicker between us. Too many times, and memories to remind me...I want to drink this feeling of what once was in. The bittersweet feeling of this will be the last time releasing from my soul. As history goes, I've never been good at keeping promises. But I want more than anything, for this new beginning to work.

Check out isn't until 12pm – it feels like we have all the time in the world before the new chapter dawns. Then, my promise is, I'm going to change.

Why do I want to change from being a person I despise? Stupid question, but then again, to change is harder than you think. After all, I have lived with him – this persona - so long, that he is deep within me; like a drug I can't live without. I am an addict. However, all addicts get to that point where they must make a choice. You can see what path you're on and you must be strong to make the right choice. Well, I'm at that crossroads. All the wealth and trappings...well guess what? I am far from happy. Don't get me wrong, like all addicts, I have tried before. I have made knowingly empty promises to myself and others. Shallow and hollow lies, which I have subconsciously built my, what should be, my most important relationships on. All a façade like the view from my expensive suite. Deep down I wasn't ready, but something new has brought us here: me and her.

As I reflect back to my teenage self, I decide that it is not too late to be the man I vowed to be all those years ago. I will find the inner strength to change. I know I've said it before, but this time I mean it.

And then I look again at my wife; Jessica. She is beautiful. Always has been and always will be to me. Stunningly attractive and perfect to a fault, I have always known why I married her. I have no regrets there. But that was then...

Before I saw myself for what I was. Before I was held accountable for what an utter arrogant twat I could be. When meeting Aimee 'bloody' O'Donnell – she was my undoing. She made me look at myself in the mirror and really look underneath – and see what people truly saw when they looked at me. I never knew what I was really missing.

I'd majorly fucked up.

I'd believed my own hype. If I really peeled back the layers, I'd admit to the competitive jealousy I secretly held for my wife. Not at the beginning, but as time went on. I knew she was a bright shining star and I was afraid she'd grow out of me and overshadow me. My dad's slight; my parents mess of a marriage; having Oli, then Toby; her depression...it all kept her busy.

What a shite way to think! To expect her to live a half-life of anxiety and dealing with my family's issues.

Mum was right, I should be ashamed of myself.

She'd said as much last week when we told her about all our problems – the affairs.

Jessica was desperate about how Mum would react. They'd become very close over the years and she felt terrible about betraying her. I sensed she had more guilt towards my mother than me. We decided to tell her whilst she was visiting for Christmas. It had been a quiet affair as Charles and Moira were forced to be on-call over the holidays. Their lack of a much-wanted child, meaning they were expected to take the anti-social shifts. We'd spoken to them both individually - before mum anyway. We had to, there were to be no secrets any more. Charles said I'd been stupid and that he'd seen it coming. I have no idea what Moira had said to Jessica, but when I found them both together, they were unusually holding hands and crying. Two tough bitches broken.

When we finally told Mum, she left the room and went off to make a pot of tea. We sat in waiting room silence. Both shaking. It was then I realised how important my mother had been to both of us. Holding our marriage together. If it hadn't had been for Mum, I don't think we'd have made it this far.

"Patrick, you've always been like your father. More than you'd care to admit. Too similar."

"That was always my fear as a child. I vowed…"

She stopped me. "Never mind that, you can't help genetics *darling*. He was like you when I first met him. We married for similar reasons – we made a good team and we were very attracted to each other in those days. But he could never settle. His ambition and determination held no bounds. Unfortunately, it was too late for me."

"Too late?" Jessica asked. "Diane, you have reinvented yourself. We: Patrick, Charles, Moira and I, all admire the way you've come through the past few years."

"Thank you darling." She poured the tea. Jessica was flustered. I could tell how scared she was.

"Jessica, I'm disappointed, however, I do understand. *Darling*, you were lonely. You were left to fight so many battles on your own whilst my son swanned around the world dealing with everyone else's' issues."

That hurt.

"I'll get over it. You're family. No matter what happens. You know how I feel about you don't you?"

"I hope so" Jessica croaked, tears threatening. *To be honest I wasn't far off.*

"Well then, I will say no more darling. Never forget" She was eyeballing me with that look only a mother can give, "That I lived a half-life too. But my philandering husband set me free. It was the best thing he ever did."

"I didn't chase women for all of our marriage mother!"

"That may be so. I can see that you were both lonely. But the question is, what do you do now?"

And so here we were. Trying our marriage out for size. And as much as I enjoyed her company, her body, and love making, she wasn't who I thought about every morning when I woke up. She wasn't the one I searched for every morning on the beach whilst I walked Freddie. We just didn't seem to fit. The fact was; they'd always been a missing piece and I had no idea how to fill it.

Looking at her here, in this bed, I feel like I am cheating, betraying someone else.

I close my eyes and pray for the strength of my convictions. I know I need to tell her. I feel she will understand. I just can't be with her anymore.

When I wake up a few hours later, she's gone. And there's a letter on her pillow.

DEARLY DEPARTED

Jess

London
December 2016

Moira was waiting for me in Starbucks. Bleary eyed after a long night-shift.

"I don't know how you do it M"

"You say? Och, it's part of the training. No sleeping and hard drinking. Only Charles and I have less time and inclination for the latter than we did."

My heart leapt for her, "Meaning?"

"Oh, I'm not. I wish. It's just that we are getting older. But I don't want to talk about that. Did ye' tell him?"

I wanted to talk to her. She was forever helping me. But I knew she'd tell me when she was ready. "I tried but I couldn't. I'm ashamed to say that I just couldn't talk any more. I was wrung out – as you might say"

"All out of words?"

"Yes. So, I wrote it down. Filled in the blanks."

"I am a guessing by the overnight bag and vanity set down there, that you've made a decision?" She nodded towards my designer luggage with a smirk.

"Laugh if you like, but I was never going to leave with my things in a bin bag, was I?"

"No lassie, you've come too far!" She laughed. "Anyway, you've more than that, don't forget I've seen the size of your walk-in wardrobe. In fact, everyone has since you put that bloody double page spread in the magazine!"

"What can I say? It was the businesswoman in me. When we come to sell, it will hold its value. Trust me, I know what I'm doing"

"The boys' legacy and your insurance." She nodded sympathetically.

"Do you blame me?"

"Never, we've come too far haven't we?"

She was right. Being a Green should come with a medal for bravery. "Through too much." For someone who never cried in public, I was making up for it just lately.

"Hell don't start. Nothing will change you know. We will always be sisters-in-law. I refuse to sob like you." She handed me a napkin, and then bucking her normal bedside manner, she changed her mind. *Bloody hell, things must be bad.* "Come here."

Moira was holding her arms out. I fell into them and felt her warmth and support surround me. I might have married the wrong man, but I'd chosen the right family for my own.

DEAR JOHN...

Patrick

London: The Southbank
December 2016

The winter grey sky sat like iron on the winding Thames. I knew how it felt.

If anyone had ever told me that I, the mighty Patrick Green, would receive a 'Dear John' letter I'd have laughed at them six months ago. But after all the loves, lies and deceit began to twist and unravel, I was glad than something had happened to release the suffocating stalemate.

You see I'd had enough. Last night had proved that we needed to part. Only, she'd beaten me to it. The old Patrick would have loathed her for it. The new one understood and didn't care. I was learning to let stuff go. To release my controlling nature.

I sat on a bench and pulled my coat and scarf around me. People were rushing about their business. London was a hive of activity – it was New Year's Eve. New beginnings. I took this as my sign to read, so I could think about my own new beginnings in 2017.

Dear Patrick,

Before I start, I need to explain why I am writing this letter, instead of telling you face to face, everything I have to say.

You might think it cowardly of me that I have chosen to run away and leave you this letter after such a lovely night. But that's one reason I have done as such. The last image I have of us to-

gether was of the perfect couple, enjoying each other's company and being attracted to one another. Last night we shared stories about the boys, and I remembered fondly, some of our happier times in our marriage. Anyone watching us would have thought everything seemed good on the surface, but I know, as you do that it is not. Deep down there is so much more going on. Therefore, before we delve deeper than we have already done at therapy, I needed to have a good lasting memory of us together. To remind myself that it wasn't all bad and that we have done some things brilliantly.

Our therapist told us to be honest with each other. We've spent the past few weeks going over the infidelity: the causes, the triggers. We have come so far and the fact that we can now 'get on' after years of hostility, means that 'our family', whatever that means anymore, will now be more solid and secure. However, there is a lot more I need to say. Therefore, as our therapist suggested, I've been writing everything down. All the hurt, all the depressive episodes, all the denial…and I've found it very cathartic. But, there's so much more inside of me that you don't know. Things I have hidden.

There's so much to say and I'm writing everything down for you so I won't miss anything, and so you can go over and digest my words. We've never been good at talking, have we? You see, I have so much to tell you. Things that you should know about me, conversations we should have had, and advice, had I have been honest for the past fifteen years, that I should have given. Please read and think about what I say. I need to put all my ghosts to rest so we can build something positive for our precious boys (Our greatest work).

I'm going in with the big thing first. You know how we'd go into a meeting and tackle things head on first? Well, this letter will be written in our business style (we were the best team in the boardroom, weren't we?).

From the beginning I lied. I am not an orphan. Well, not in the sense that I have no family, just in the sense that I had to run away from what was left of them. As you know I grew up on an estate in Leeds. You also know that I lost my beautiful Mam at the age of eighteen. That much is true. However, the rest of them are still alive and kicking. I know I told you I was an only child, but *that's wrong; there are four of us. I've older twin brothers: James and Mark. Plus, a little sister called Stacey. I also had, and still do, a dad called Davey. Davey was easy to kill off. He was and still is a rambling drunk living in his own urine-soaked high-rise in the city centre. He's still there, living in the depths of self-pity and claiming some sort of disability, to support his disgusting lifestyle. I have no sympathy. He has done nothing to help my siblings and he did nothing to support Mam when she was alive.*

Anyway, I refuse to waste any more paper on the man. My siblings however, I have so much to tell you.

After I ran away, I was mad with them all. James was heading for prison and Mark had run off to the army. I was furious with them as they left me to care for Mam and live with Dad. After she died, I had to exist with a man I despised. Also, Stacey was going down a path of teen pregnancies (she had two), drugs and unsuitable boyfriends. All I could see was me being sucked into a life of depression. I reached rock bottom and James saved me and packed me off to university. When you met me, I hadn't seen any of them for about three years. I had already wiped them out. And I was so focused on my future, that it was easy – you remember what I was like! That was that. No going back.

When I was confined with my pregnancy with Toby, I was lonely and started wondering about them. I tracked down Stacey first. She was scathing at first, but after some bridge building, I was devastated that I'd let her slip away. She had done so well Patrick! Four children, a steady home and a business of her own. I was so proud. She'd done it all on her own. And she'd never disowned any of us. Even Dad. I felt ashamed.

Then I spoke to Mark. He was living in Cyprus. He'd done tours in Iraq and Afghanistan. He had won medals for bravery and was now a sergeant. I was so overwhelmed. I'd been so selfish Patrick. How could I have pushed away my brave and strong brother? He'd done what I'd done. He'd run away. But he'd done something worthwhile and for his country. What had I done?

And James. My fairy-godfather, (as Stacey called him). He had gone to Thailand. He'd also run away as he was in trouble (that's three out of four runners – maybe it's genetic?) Anyway, he'd gone to Thailand to lay low. But he found he loved it there. He started again and now owns a hotel and retreat.

It seems we all had it in us. I think back now to that young and naïve girl grieving for her mum, and I see someone who thought she was special, different. What I've since learnt is that we all were. Stace thinks it's because I went to Grammar school and that they drilled it into us there that we were different. Only someone with an academic education could succeed. Maybe she's right? But, I'm not ashamed to say that it all has made me rethink my perceptions and prejudices.

At first, I didn't see them. I hid away in a fictional world in Adelaide Australia. (it was easier than hiding you all). But, as in all lies eventually, things catch up with you. That and the fact that I couldn't cope after Frank died.

I used to drive over to Leeds to talk to Mam at her grave. I had no idea what to do and where to turn. How do you hide such grief from your family? I wasn't allowed to show it. So, I'd still run, walk, drive, shop, anything so I didn't stop. I'd only allow myself to cry at the cemetery. It was my release. And then one day I was found, sobbing on the bench. It was my sister who found me when I needed her the most.

As you know, I've always been very guarded, but after everything that had happened, and because what did I have to lose telling my sister everything? After all, she's known me longer than anyone. I let all my defences down and told her the lot. And that is where another of my second lives began.

Ever wondered why I was suddenly having all those treatments? It was Stace. I'd go to the salon and let her do things – I'd be her guinea pig. Spending time in her business, I saw what she needed to do to expand and improve. Before long, I was helping her with plans, and I began to invest my own money. As we built her business up, our relationship grew. I can't imagine a life without her in it now. What was I thinking Patrick? What kind of person walks away from her own flesh and blood?

As you know, in October, I went to a retreat in Thailand for a month. If you haven't already guessed, it was James's. Stace and I went to see him and look at how we could move our beauty business into the holistic market. We are sick of all the Botox and fillers. We see the future in mental health and spiritual well-being. It was lovely all three of us being together. And Mark flew out for a fortnight whilst we were there too. We all felt that it had been too long. Too many wasted years. We made a pact to look at what we wanted in our future – to be true to ourselves and each other.

And that's what brings me here, to this letter. When I returned last October, I wanted to tell you so much. But the minute I came back and saw the mess that was unravelling around me, I found all my lies closing in on me again. That first morning when I saw Aimee with the children, it was my worst nightmare. Why was she with my boys? And then the state of you. I knew you only drink like that when jealousy and ego are involved. I guessed that there had been something going on very quickly as the boys wouldn't stop telling me about all the fun you'd all had. I was so jealous and blamed her yet again for ruining my destiny. It wasn't until Jenna broke the whole façade of my deceit with Frank, that I knew I was on a road to it all coming out.

I most feared what your mum and Moira would say. Diane taught me so much and once I'd allowed her in as we became equals in love and war, I found I had another mum. Don't get me wrong, no one could ever replace Mam, but Diane has come a close second. I love her Patrick and she has saved us both more than once. Don't ever mistreat that love, it is too precious to our family. Because, what I have learnt is that family is not just that unit you create from attraction and blood ties, it's about how you all show each other kindness, love and respect - no matter what.

I shouldn't have worried though. Moira, who is the best friend and ally I could ever have the fortune to find on that awful sixtieth bloodbath all those years ago, didn't really care. She told me that my lies had started out to protect myself and then others. She said that I needed to think about myself, and how my duplicitous life was probably to do with the disappointment and trauma I experienced at such a young age. She also said that because I am so driven and clever, that my obsessive behaviour had been a way of coping. Moira is no psychologist, but she said that if she was to guess, Frank was my way of trying to go back to a life of freedom.

And your mother? She already knew about my family. It turns out that Jonny had investigated my background before we married. 'He couldn't let just any girl marry his heir, could he?' He decided, with Diane's prompting, that I was a good bet for a wife, even though I'd lied about my family. Ever the snobs, they both had said that they'd have done the same and admired me for being such a determined young 'gel' and hard worker. Jonny liked my drive. However, not enough to give me equal share of the company. My un-orphan status was a step too far.

So, there you go. Why did I tell your mother and Moira my story before you? I guess because I could. I have always been able to talk to them with as much honesty and respect as my dual life allowed. You? Well I think we'll both agree that talking about our feelings isn't something we've ever been good at.

What next? Well, as you're reading this, I'm heading to meet Diane and the boys at Heathrow. That's right, I'm running away again, and with your mother! Jokes aside, don't worry, I'd never take the boys away from you, like I say, whatever our futures hold, we will always be a family. Instead, I'm taking them on a break to see my friends in Corfu. I'm looking at a property for sale over there, possibly turning it into a retreat. I wanted to start the new year as I mean to go on, proactive and positively: being my own boss. I think it's important that I become more open and happier, I've hidden away too long haven't I? That's why I'm going to see Maria and Spiros; they knew the girl I wanted to be before it all went out of my control. They also tried to protect me all those years ago... We will be back in a couple of weeks and we can sort out our future plans then.

Lastly, I said I have some advice for you. Patrick, I want you to be happy. I know you've been an absolute bastard at times, but I do think I am not blameless in your fall from being a good husband. When I look back and think about it, I know that you did plenty to make me happy for a very long time. But as I unravelled mentally, I think I pushed you further away and made it easy for you to stray. I also know your ambition and ego got in the way, and needed feeding – so neither of us are really to blame, are we? But I do know that I never gave you enough love. Maybe it was all enough once, but not now is it? I think we've both learnt that we deserve to be happy and no amount of money or success is going to give us that happiness is it?

But I think you have found it. With Aimee, you have finally met your match. When I finally stood back (objectively) and listened to her and thought about what she said, I realised what it was that made you two become friends so quickly. Patrick, she's stunning, talented and fiercely loyal. She takes no shit and is so honest that it must be refreshing in your world of lies and ego. Plus, and as much as it pains me to admit it – she is beautiful. Her soul shines from her inside out, making you want to be a better person. My advice is to take the step to becoming that man you wanted to be all those years ago. Drop the ego and be humble. If she comes to you like I think she will, she will give you the love and balance you have always needed and truly deserve in your life.

Patrick, my husband, my lover, the father of our beautiful children, I love you. I'm just not in love with you.

Yours,
Jessica
XXX

FINDING HER FEET

JESS

New Year's Eve 2016
Heathrow Airport

"Mumeeeeeee!!" Oli was hurtling towards me, arms windmilling as he halted to a stop at my feet. Toby speeding up behind him on his blue Trunkie.

"I'm here boys!" I said with my arms out and hugging them tightly.

Diane came panting behind them.

"Boys, you'll knock your mother over!" She laughed.

"Darling" she drawled after I'd prised the boys off me. "You look – well better than I thought actually" She laughed.

"Do you approve?"

"Oh yes darling! I do."

The facial I'd had yesterday and the new trouser suit I'd chosen for the flight had worked then. I might have been living a past life of lies, but no one wanted to look truly rough, did they?

"No tears sweetie?"

"There were, but..."

"Him?"

"I'm sorry to say that I left the letter and ran." I admitted.

"Was that wise? Darling, do you think..."

Beep Beep. My phone had received an incoming text:

Patrick: Thank you for the letter, honesty
and advice.   I love you too but I'm not in love
with you either. XXX

Diane saw me looking. A single tear betraying me.
"Is that him?"
"Yes. All good"

Me: Always love XXX

It was the most loving and kindest we'd been to each other
in years.

Patrick: Are you with the boys?
Me: Facetime?

My phone burst into life.
I put my brightest voice on "Boys it's Daddy!"

Oli pushed his face onto the screen "Hi Daddy. Missed you!
We are going on holiday. You won't be lonely, *will you?*"
He laughed, it was good to see and hear. If nothing else,
my children had the best dad. "I'll be fine! Make sure you get
Mummy and Granny to get you lots of snacks and chocolate
for the flight! Look after them for me, won't you? What are
you doing now?"
"We are just about to check in. Mummy and Granny are talk-
ing in code and Mum is crying"
Oh bloody hell Oli!
"Is she now. Give her a big hug from me. And a kiss."
Toby snatched the phone from him as Oli dove in for another hug.
"It's me Daddy. Can you make sure Freddie facetimes me
later Daddy, as he really misses me, and I don't like leaving
him. Granny said I can't take him on the plane, but I had to
leave him on his own and he looked so sad."
"Will do. I'm going home now and I'm sure he's having the

time of his doggy life being spoilt at the hotel!"

"Okay doke. Love you Daddy." Toby chirped.

"Me too shouted Oli"

They both waved manically at the camera.

"Love you all too." He grinned, and I knew no matter what, he did.

"What now then Jessica?" Smiled Diane.

"Check in and a break in the winter sun." I smiled.

"Sounds just the ticket *darling*. I can't wait! Now tell me again about where we are going. And tell me more about the beautiful Maria and her father Spiros, who used to buy his wife flowers every day..."

I laughed as I realised that It felt so good to no longer have that awful weight on my chest. I thought about my family, the big messy sprawling one that had accepted me with all my imperfections and realised that I was lucky. I had a rich, deep life full of love.

FREEDOM

Aimee

Wakefield: The Hepworth Gallery
February 2017

Standing on the bank of the River Calder, I tried to gain some sort of calm from the water. My anxiety was racing. I'd not seriously exhibited in years and as much as my promising career would have meant that I'd be an old pro at this at one time, apart from the odd showing in the arts room at the local theatre in Saltness, I was not used to my work being critiqued in such detail.

I breathed in, sucking in a lungful of cool air. I steadied my breathing after days of a whirlwind finish to putting together my show. The pieces I'd chosen were all taken from a series of works that I'd done on the beach at Saltness. I'd juxtaposed them between some of my earlier work from when I was travelling. The blues and greys merging. Different states of water. Different subjects; people, animals, shells, driftwood and debris; all united by a sense of being alive and at one's own peace. Finding itself freed from the confines of expectation and duty.

Of course, my children and SDD littered the show. At various states and stages of their lives. And Frank too. A glorious portrait I sketched and then painted of him, running with his guitar in his hands, and singing. The children and dog chasing him across the sand. He looked like the pied piper. It showed him at his best: no depression, no mania. The way I wanted to believe he was living now in heaven.

Deep down, I've never known if the accident was real or intended. He'd been backed into a corner, and although I've not really admitted this to anyone, I do know that he wasn't in the best place that February. We'd had the worst Christmas and January we'd ever had. It took his whole family to help me. We spent days holed up at the Irish pile, trying to coax him back into life. The children were only young, and Harry especially can't remember much. For that I am grateful.

My poor Frank, he was so trapped. His double life gave him an outlet. What he realised too late was that it trapped him more. Frank was a free spirit, and if you were to ever listen to his lyrics and playing, you'd understand that he was only truly free when he lost himself in his music. That's why I was playing his music in my exhibition today. He was and always will be part of the story.

I thought about what he'd say today. He'd have been proud. He knew he'd held me back; the sacrifices I'd made to support him. '*Wasting my talent*' he'd called it with my sketching and painting for holidaymakers...he felt I was so much more. But then what could I do? My vows meant something. *In sickness and in health.*

I took one last steadying breath and walked towards the entrance, as I did so, my parents, Phoebe and Harry, were coming from the carpark.

"There she is!" Shouted Harry, all dressed up in a smart shirt and tie. Teamed, of course, with his jeans and trainers. Phoebe was dressed in a beautiful floral playsuit, which made her look older than her years and brought a tear to my eye - she was growing up.

"Mummy, we've missed you!" exclaimed Phoebs as she came up to hug me. "It's been so many days since we saw you! We never spend time apart" It had been two and I already felt guilty enough.

"Don't make your mother feel guilty Phoebe." My mother said primly, with a hint of moisture in her eyes, "Mummy has been doing something important"

"More than us"

"Nothing is more important than you two!" She laughed.

"Little devils" Dad coughed. "Your mother has made many sacrifices for you. Today is her day."

"Roger, they don't need to know all that. What's important is that we all show Mummy how proud we are and how much we love her today"

I swallowed down the emotion. Suffice to say that our relationship had moved forward in the past few weeks. Skype is a wonderful thing and it means that if the discussion gets too heavy; you can pretend it's a bad connection and try later on. They admit to their wrongs, and me mine. None of us are perfect. After all, I realise now that I enabled Frank to behave erratically. I too feel guilt that I should have done more to stabilise him. But as they say hindsight is a wonderful thing. What we have all since learnt is that time is a great healer.

Within an hour, the gallery is incredibly busy. I knew it had a great deal of publicity, but I never expected this. I should have known though. Once I'd finished the painting of Oli and Toby, I chose to present it to Jessica. Along with the money Patrick had already paid me. I said that it was my gift to her – a way for us to start again. It turned out that Frank really did have great taste in women and once we'd got over all the messy stuff, we began to talk and let the children hang out again. This caused lots of whooping and cheering from both sides. Also, hilariously, (if Frank was looking down, I've no idea...but I'd hope he was laughing) Jess helped enormously with childminding whilst I put together the show and my main piece. She was a real brick, along with Jenna and my parents who returned early – much to my surprise.

"Miss our daughter's professional debut at the Hepworth?"

The painting of Oli, Toby, and Freddie now hangs in the gallery – on loan of course. The money was donated, after much discussion and friendly arguing, to the charity MIND. We agreed that this was more fitting than anything else.

Anyway, due to the new family painting hanging and Jess's

new appreciation for my artwork, she'd contacted all the people she knew in the media and created quite a buzz. My god, that woman is a whirlwind! Frank would never have stood a chance.

Scanning the room, I could see all our children together. They were alternating playing some surreptitious game of hide and seek, and stealing the canapes, which were being handed out around the room. I spotted Jess and her mother-in-law, Diane. They strode over to me.

"This is wonderful Aimee." Beamed Jess.

"Yes darling! Such talent. When Jessica told me you were good, I never dreamt we had our own Tracey Emin living up here in the wilds of Yorkshire! You are very talented. And look at my boys!"

She was motioning over to the portrait of the children. She said 'My boys' very loudly, wanting the whole room to know it was her family depicted in the painting.

"I've got to say though Aimee, I love your main piece. It's so brave and exciting"

"Thank you, Diane." I smiled.

"It took my breath away Aimee. I had to study it for a very long time. I still keep going back and taking a look. It's addictive, like you're emanating what every woman wants to feel." Agreed Jess.

"You are a warrior darling!" stated Diane.

We all looked over to the centre of the room. A life-size papier Mache structure of me was looking out of the window and onto the River Calder. Dressed in a cape, my corkscrew hair blowing wildly behind me, I was emanating standing up on the Saltness cliffs; my whole form was exposed. Either side of me were my two precious children gripping my hands, but not holding me back, as if coming with me into the unknown. Facing life. All three facing the world and it's wonderous freedom. My cape flowing, with a decoupage collage of all our lives so far, all flying away: my childhood, uni, my travels, our lives, everything that was once there but no more – a feeling that nothing is permanent. And around my neck, open and flying from my open locket, a picture of Frank, flying towards our futures. All of us free and all of us together. A family which knew love and lived by it every day – no matter what its form.

And then I thought about Patrick and my future. I knew I'd been too stubborn, choosing to think of him as the bastard husband who was the catalyst for Jess's problems. Pushing him away. Ignoring my own feelings because I truly believed that he couldn't be different. But if he couldn't change for her, his wife, what chance did I have?

Still, I knew I shouldn't have been upset. But it didn't stop me feeling let-down. I thought he might have come, but then again, I only had myself to blame. After all, I'd pushed him away so many times in the past few months, that I knew he must have finally understood I wasn't interested. Any attraction, that I admitted now might have existed, must have fizzled out as quickly as it started for him. Part of me was pleased – I wasn't sure I had much room for a high maintenance male in my life again.

However, he wouldn't leave my subconscious. He lingered there, as much as I tried to forget him. But then again, he's not that type of character, is he? I'd constantly go to text or call him, as something would have made me laugh, or I wanted another opinion about something - and then I'd remember…Ultimately, that bloody man had gotten to me and now the exhibition was taking care of itself, I no longer had anything to hide behind. I felt alone.

Beep Beep. I checked my phone thinking that it must be nothing as everyone was here.

```
Paddy:  You look beautiful
Me:  You wouldn't know, you're not here
Paddy:  You do, and I want to ask everyone to
leave so I can tell you why
```

I scanned the room. I couldn't see him. I suspected he was in a corner with the free champagne.

Me: How much of that free champagne have you had?

Paddy: None. Sober. I'm not going to fuck this up again.

Me: Fuck what up again?

Paddy: Me, my feelings. I need you to take me seriously. Come outside?

Me: Well, it's my party and if you think I'm going to leave it for you Patrick Green, you can eff off.

Paddy: So, when am I going to be able to check then?

Me: Check what?

Paddy: If you're as magnificent in the flesh as you are in that bloody great big installation?

Bloody man! My stomach flipped and I could feel myself going red. *Sexist pig!* I couldn't help but laugh. Whatever his faults, he held his heart on his sleeve and he was always refreshingly honest with me.

"Find something funny?"

I spun around and he was there, his eyes twinkling and a big smile on his face.

"See, I came to you Aimee. I'm turning into a modern man."

"Well done Paddy. You're growing"

"So they all tell me."

"What else do they tell you?"

"That I'm so obviously in love with you that I need to be the man you deserve before any of them let me near you. My estranged wife included."

Love? "Are you sure you've not had any champagne?"

"None. I'm a new man. I've made those changes...What I have had though is a long look at my life. I want to tell you that I'm in the process of selling off bits of the company. I believe they call it downsizing. I'm also putting various managers in. I'm taking a back seat and I'm going to please myself for a change."

"Doing what?" I was intrigued.

"Studying, travel, love...they call it enrichment."

"Wow Paddy, good on you. You're never too old to learn."

"Or find someone you want to learn with."

I wasn't sure what he was suggesting. But my pulse was quickening, and I just didn't want to second guess him. He'd said love, but then again, he'd said many other things.

"To clarify Annie, I want to begin again."

"At forty?"

"Yes, so let me introduce myself" he held out his hand and I went to shake it. He held it firm.

"Hi, my name is Paddy and I am here today to admire your work. You are a very talented artist and I also see you have two very beautiful children who rival my own from a previous relationship. I hear that you have had many adventures in your life. I wondered if you'd like to take a chance and start a new one with me?"

He must have taken my laugh for a yes, and with my hand still in his, he pulled me in towards him, signalling the beginning of a new journey.

THE EPILOGUE

Much Later After Now

Aimee
Corfu
August 2018
The Last Supper

The smell of jasmine and bougainvillea filled the air as it cascaded down from the cliffside pergola. The house stood majestically, perched on the top of the bay, the garden next to it. The sun descending the mountainside after another baking day. It truly was a glorious place to live. Jess, the boys and Diane were so lucky.

I watched them all, smiling with a serenity, which I had only learned existed when your puzzle fits. Like Paddy said, we needed to start our own adventure. And without being tied to each other or anything, we all chose to follow our hearts and see where it took us.

A large table was laid with a white linen cloth under the pergola. Set for thirty, it was ready to host the wedding party. Jugs of iced water covered in muslin, were being brought out from the kitchen, placed in amongst the vases of fresh flowers. People were beginning to gather around it. Diane, Paddy, Jess, Charles, Moira, all our collective children. Maria, her husband and two daughters, and the man himself: Spiros, his other children and their families...were all chatting animatedly. Spiros was clapping and telling everyone to gather. Wine was being poured and Ouzo was given out as they all chorused *'yammas'* at the happy occasion. He looked over to me and I shook my head, I would soon but I wasn't ready yet.

Jess went into business mode and removed Spiros of the alcohol and announced that the bride and groom should now sit at the head of the table for the wedding breakfast. The group arranged themselves in order and I laughed as the children were all fighting with who to sit next to. Spiros and Diane taking their places as the new heads of our wonderful sprawling dysfunctional family. I quickly began to sketch as the mezze was delivered to the table.

Out of everyone, the two of us who deserved love the most were Spiros and Diane. Spiros had been lonely 'forever' until the formidable Diane stepped into his life with her glamourous granny status and endless amounts of energy. Both without any worthy tender love, somehow, they managed to help each other heal. All very uncomplicated and ridiculous when you see the way they look at each other. Paddy, although finding it embarrassing that his mother has a new-found sex life, which she liked to tell him that she'd discovered that 'Greeks are the best lovers in the world', he feels blessed in the fact there is finally someone loving and looking after his mum the way she deserves. After all, after all her false starts, and mistakes, she always put her family first.

I furiously commit their glowing faces onto paper. Charles laughing at something Spiros has said to the children. Moira kissing her baby on the head as she passes her to Jess for a cuddle – that's now more girls than boys, as Phoebe likes to tell me. We are a family expanding with feminism. And there's Paddy: the man who two years ago, now admits, when he first met me, wanted to run away from me as fast as he could. But apparently my tenacious spirit won. He tells me he knew that night after the hospital. He said it was like coming home.

Just five more minutes and I'll join them.

Patrick
Corfu
August 2018
Life Begins

I'm watching Aimee draw. She is concentrating so intently, she doesn't know I can't take my eyes off her. Focusing on her work, endeavouring to capture the atmosphere of this celebration.

The painting was her idea. We wanted to give Mum and Spiros – her bloody Greek lover! Something really special for their wedding. After all, she has been our rock and she deserves all the happiness and more. She has stood by her family without fail and been the parent I want to be for our ever-growing menagerie of children.

I sit waiting, watching, an unnatural space next to me (She will paint herself in later). I've become quite the obsessive boyfriend these days. Jess laughs at me knowingly. She was right about finding true love.

We took it slowly. We dated and got to know each other before we even slept together. It's not that I didn't want to (I went a bit crazy for a while), it was just that we were on a new journey and we both wanted it to be perfect. I joke that she turned me into a romantic. Charles thinks it is hilarious and often asks me where my balls are. I tell him *'very happy and content thank you.'*

It turns out I can be that man I wanted to be at the age of fourteen. That man loves his ridiculously unconventional family, his life, and the arms of his girlfriend. She is what I call home.

ABOUT THE AUTHOR

Lucy Swan

 'It took her a long time to get here...'
Would be the main response, of my exasperated family and friends, about the birth of my debut novel. Not because I've talked about it for so long, (well I have but anyway...) but because I've been right around the houses and lived many different lives to get here: a published author.

And whilst I may be older than I hoped, I have only recently had the confidence and tenacity to actually complete one of my many musings.

Shallow Lives, is a book about people. About life. About our best bits and our worst. Taken from one of my many rambling notebooks, I felt it was the time for my three characters' voices to be heard.

At just a nudge over forty, my greatest work to date has been my beautiful family. As well as writing, I am a teacher, wife, mother and (baby faced) grandmother. Living on the Lincolnshire east coast, my favourite thing ever is walking my beloved best friend and GSP: RosieDog, on the beach.

However, just like with my characters, this is only one side of my story. To find out more, feel free to follow me on

Instagram: @swannie_ramblings and read my blog: madramblings.blog
Both of each will keep you up to date with my next project.

I am currently writing my second novel 'The Golden Figure', which will be out sometime this year.

ACKNOWLEDGEMENT

Dear Reader (see what I did there), I would like to say a huge thank you for reading my debut novel 'Shallow Lives'. I hope you enjoyed reading it as much as I enjoyed writing it . The process has been a real labour of love (just like the lives of my characters) and has been quite a lengthy journey.

'Shallow Lives' has been a lifetime ambition. I have always wanted to write a book and decided it was on my 'bucket list' at the age of eighteen. However, unless you are Mary Shelley, I am not convinced you can 'really nail what life is about', until you have (ahem) a few years under your belt (at this point I would like to point out that there are many young and talented authors who are far more talented than me!). Therefore, my path to get here has been long, winding, and full of twists and turns; leaving a scattering of scribbled notebooks in my wake, plus many unfinished stories.

The main theme of the novel: living behind a mask, started off from a germ of an idea regarding our perceptions of others. It was something that resonated with me, at a time when I was dipping in and out of the dreaded world of social media (I am only an Instagram faithful now). A place where (and I know I am not alone) that many people feel uneasy with the false-hoods it enables. However, it wasn't until somebody encouraged me, that it was a must for 'My Goals for 2020' list, that I really got to grips with it. And I am thrilled that I did!

Telling Aimee, Patrick and Jessica's stories, turned out to be a cathartic process, which I felt would encourage people to think about themselves and the way they perceive others. When I read a book, I like this to happen to me - to be able to empathise with characters. Furthermore, I also like to laugh a lot as I believe life is much better when you are laughing. And although they are completely fictional, I do think we can see shadows of ourselves within them all.

They say write about what you know. That is why the book is set in Yorkshire and Corfu. These are both places I know very well. However, Saltness is purely fictional - a ubiquitous North Sea resort on the east coast. I am sure you could come across if you travelled this coastline. Although, I have never been to Thailand (I promised myself I would visit and then Covid happened...), but I have had a lifetime of wanting to go. This meant I had to get it right...as well as all my online research, I reread 'The Beach' by Alex Garland (I seriously forgot how good it was). And the true story 'The Backpacker' by John Harris, which is an intriguing tale of life on a backtracker trail. The disclaimer being, that any mistakes are compltely my own and not the fault of others.

And speaking of others, to get here...well I have many acknowledgements to make.

My first three readers: Ali, Mariola, and Loretta (in order of getting to the finish line). Thank you all for the ongoing support and putting up with my questions. You have no idea how you kept me going when times were tough.

My mum - who I just knew would love Part Five and the character of Diane! My Dad, who always tells me that I get my literary creativity from him - I beat you to it though Dad! All my in-laws, who might be crazy and outrageous (at times) but far more dignified and supportive than Jonny, and Jess's father, were to their children. To my girls: Ella, Lois, and Erin. I wrote this for you. I always tell you to be strong and independent. I hope this shows you that anything is possible in this mad world! Carter, who is my favourite little person and biggest noisy distraction. My Rosie Dog - who has spent many hours, walking, and wearing her little paws out, whilst I mulled over the development of the plot and characters.

To all my cheerleaders, who have read my musings and put up with me on my incredible journey of becoming a writer - beacuse that is what I am now! Especially Kate - champoin of the squad - for always being there and telling me I can do it.

And last but not least - and because he likes to make it all about him (in-joke) my husband Ricky. Who despite not being a reader, has helped me immensely with all his support. Without him, I am not sure I would be writing this now.

Printed in Great Britain
by Amazon

65393380R00183